Twisted Fish

An Aquatic Anthology

Edited by
Anthony Giangregorio

OTHER LIVING DEAD PRESS BOOKS

TWISTED FISH: AN AQUATIC ANTHOLOGY

Table of Contents

FOREWORD BY ANTHONY GIANGREGORIO 1

BLOW HOLE BY NELIA THOMPSON 3

REVENGE IS BEST SERVED WET BY DANE T. HATCHELL 15

THE OTHER FOOT BY ANTHONY GIANGREGORIO 29

SCHOOL'S IN BY ROB ROSEN 37

SMARTEST IDIOT ON THE LAKE BY JESSY M. ROBERTS ...45

FISH FUCKER BY ANTHONY GIANGREGORIO 52

MILLIE'S EYES BY KELLY M. HUDSON 59

MAN'S BEST FRIEND BY ANTHONY GIANGREGORIO.........73

TIME AND TIDE WAIT NOT BY DANE T. HATCHELL.......... 85

LITTLE MURMUR BY RICK MOORE 103

CAREFUL WHAT YOU WISH FOR BY TONIA BROWN 109

THE CAVE BY MARC SHEMMANS 123

THE ONE THAT DIDN'T GET AWAY BY MATT NORD......... 137

ONE LAST SWIM BY KELLY M. HUDSON 147

INNOCENT BLOOD BY REBECCA BESSER...................... 155

FISHECSTASY BY ANTHONY GIANGREGORIO 167

HOOKED BY ALAN SPENCER 175

BLOODSTREAM BY V. M. VITO................................185

AIN'T NOTHIN' LIKE LIVE BAIT BY DANE T. HATCHELL 196

ABOUT THE WRITERS................................215

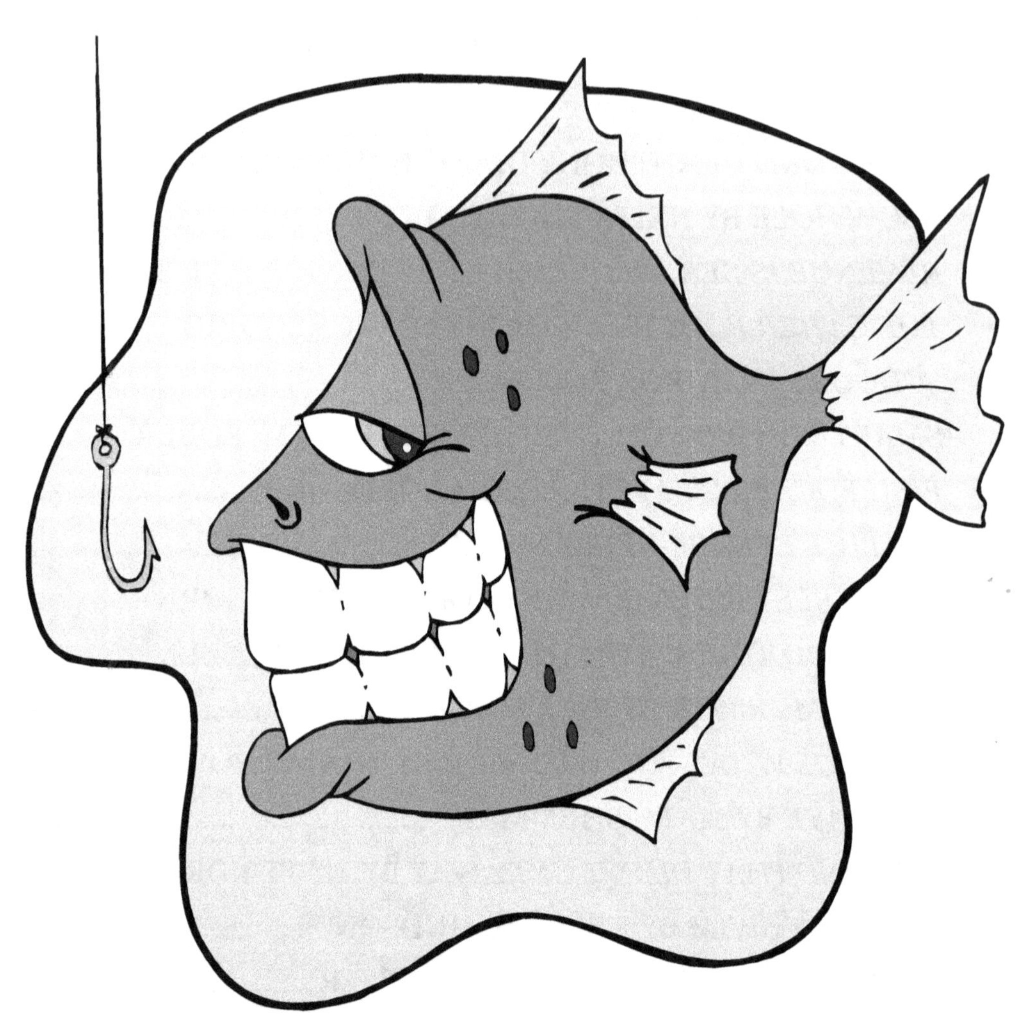

FOREWORD

If you have ever wondered how some anthologies come about, then here's your answer for this one.

The origin of this anthology was a simple one. I wrote a story about a guy screwing fish. Now, I wanted to have some fun and so went all out, I didn't hold back at all.

But what I soon found out, however, was that the story was a little too far out, too risqué, so to speak. So I was stuck with a story I thought was hilarious and over the top with nothing to do with it.

So I could either shelve the story or make an anthology of my own about fish.

But not just any old anthology about guys fishing or talking fish or lame stuff like that.

Oh, no, I wanted to make something fun, something wild, that people would read and say, "Oh, shit, did they really write that?"

So the book you hold in your hands isn't for the squeamish, or the sexually reserved.

In other words, if you have a stick up your ass, either pull it out now or stop reading! Because you're not gonna like what you read.

The stories in this book are about as wild as they come. No, not every one is about sex with fish, but a bunch are.

Why?

Because sex with fish is fucking hilarious, that's why!

So if you're like me, have a sense of humor, and like to express yourself the way you see fit—as long as no one else gets hurt—then this book should make you laugh, cringe, get nauseous and chuckle. And for all I know, it might even get you a little turned on.

So strap yourself in and get ready for the most fucked up, twisted tales about fish ever made.

Welcome to Twisted Fish.

When you're through with this book, you will never look at sea life the same way again.

Anthony Giangregorio

BLOW HOLE

NELIA THOMPSON

Charlie Greek and Bob Newman stood at the far end of the maintenance hall. The haze of smoke lingering in the air obscured their faces from the customers that were leaving as the facility closed.

"Pass it back," Bob grumbled, elbowing Charlie in the ribs.

Charlie coughed and passed the joint he was sucking on to Bob.

The two hadn't worked at the aquarium long. As a matter of fact, they never held any job long. They got hired, messed up, and usually got fired within two weeks. They had fallen into this job. Bob's cousin Ann was in charge of hiring. She had warned them not to screw up. It was an easy job and she didn't see why they couldn't handle it.

Both of them were nineteen. They had been out of high school for less than a year, and all they wanted to do was get wasted and go to parties, not necessarily in that order. This attitude, and the fact they didn't have a job, led to neither of them having a girlfriend. They had jumped at the chance at 'easy' work, thinking they would have money and not really have to do anything.

For a month they had been able to keep their heads down, staying under the radar of their supervisor. Their main duties were to feed the sea creatures and clean the holding tanks once a week. Since it didn't take too much brain work, they got fried before each shift.

After Charlie stopped coughing, he walked down the hall and peeked around the corner. He saw the security guard locking the doors and knew they wouldn't be disturbed for the rest of the night.

"Locked up tight," Charlie announced, as he walked back to join Bob who handed the joint back to Charlie and grinned.

"Great, I have a fun game we can play tonight," Bob said.

"Oh, yeah? What might that be?" Charlie asked as he exhaled.

Bob laughed deviously and winked. "We flip a coin when we go to each tank and the loser of the toss has to rub a fish all over his dick and try to get whatever animal we're feeding to blow him."

Charlie chuckled. "Sounds like fun. What about Wally? We gonna play with him, too? He could do some damage."

Bob shrugged. "Sure, why not. Makes it more interesting that way. Besides, have you seen how big his tongue is?"

Charlie thought about it for a moment and shrugged. "All right, let's get started."

* * *

They arrived at the penguin section with a couple of buckets of fish. Bob pulled a quarter out of his pocket and set it on his finger and thumb. "Call it!"

"Tails," Charlie said, his eyes intent on the silver coin.

Bob snatched it out of the air and slapped it on the top of his opposite hand. "It's heads."

Charlie sighed. "I was hoping you would have to go first, besides, have you seen the beaks on these things?" He gestured to the penguins.

"Hey, you agreed to play," Bob said with a chuckle. "Besides, they're gentle."

Charlie rolled his eyes as he undid his pants. They both knew that the penguins could be violent if they were really hungry. Both of them had sustained minor pinches and cuts on their hands from the little creature's darting beaks. After he exposed himself, Charlie grabbed a handful of fish and vigorously rubbed his genitals with them. Bob laughed as Charlie got a bit excited from the friction. "Been a while, has it?"

"Shut up!" Charlie snapped and they went through the door into the penguin hold. He was still holding the fish in one hand—while he held up his pants so he could walk—in the other. Pausing inside the door, he picked his victim.

Walking over to a medium-sized female penguin, he fed her a couple of the fish he was holding.

Bob hurriedly dumped the two buckets of fish, attracting all of the other penguins, then went over to watch the show. "Come on, Charlie, get on with it, will ya."

4

Charlie gave Bob a dirty look and held the next fish along the side of his dick. The penguin pecked at it a couple of times, and when it wouldn't come loose, she tried to grip it with her beak and tug it.

"Ow!" Charlie yelped. "She's pinching the tip!"

Bob started laughing hysterically. "Try harder!"

Charlie growled, and dragged the fish from the tip of his dick to the base, trying to get her to come closer. It worked. The penguin stepped forward, took his erection in her mouth, and tried to swallow it, her throat muscles squeezing hard around him.

Charlie groaned with pleasure, and in moments, climaxed, his face scrunching up, and his legs shaking slightly as he curled his toes inside his sneakers. "Holy shit, that was awesome!"

Bob was still laughing his ass off so couldn't speak.

Charlie fed the penguin the rest of the fish he was holding as a reward, grinning like an idiot.

They left to get more fish and go to the next area.

Charlie was still grinning.

"You should have seen your eyes bug out when she tried to swallow you!" Bob all but yelled, before bending over laughing. "I think you have a new girlfriend. Don't forget to call her tomorrow or you might hurt her feelings!"

"Shut up, you idiot," Charlie snapped, blushing.

* * *

Next they arrived at the seal hold, toting more buckets of fish.

"I'll flip this time," Charlie said, grabbing the quarter from Bob. "Call it!"

"Heads," Bob said, as he watched the coin.

Charlie looked down at the coin. "It's heads."

Bob grinned. "You're awfully horny tonight, aren't ya?"

Charlie frowned, wondering if he could perform again so soon. But then he thought about the sensational feel of the penguin's throat and felt a tingle of excitement in his crotch.

He followed Bob through the door, shutting it tightly behind him. After setting down the bucket he was carrying, he undid his pants, and proceeded to rub a couple of fish on his genitals again.

Charlie didn't get to pick his 'friend' this time. Before he knew what was going on, a large male seal flopped its way over and watched the fish in Charlie's hand with interest. It was Bubba, the seal trainer's favorite. He was used to being hand fed.

Bob dumped the buckets quickly and came to watch the show. He had enjoyed the first one—not as much as Charlie—but it had been worthy of a good laugh. Bubba wasn't as hard to convince as the penguin had been, he latched on right away. He nibbled, yanked, and thrashed his head back and forth.

Charlie yelped, moaned, and shuddered. "He's a rough bastard."

"Yeah, he is," Bob said, grinning as Bubba shook his head from side to side with Charlie's manhood in his mouth.

Before long, Charlie was gasping excitedly and soon had another orgasm. Bubba wasn't as eager to swallow though. He threw back his head and sneezed, spraying semen all over Charlie.

"Fucker," Charlie growled, wiping the slime off his face.

Bob was laughing so hard he couldn't breathe, and was lying on the floor, rolling back and forth, holding his stomach.

Charlie kicked him. "Get the fuck up and let's go."

* * *

The dolphins were the next in line for a feeding. After collecting more fish, they headed down the hall to the door that led to their tank. Charlie could barely walk, sore from the rough treatment Bubba had given him.

"I don't want to play anymore," Charlie whined. "This is a bullshit game."

Bob shook his head. "Nope, can't quit now. We have three more to do. You'll live."

Charlie growled. "Fine. Flip the damn coin and let's get this over with."

Bob flipped the coin.

"Heads," Charlie mumbled without prompting.

"Shit," Bob said as he looked at the quarter. "It's tails."

Charlie grinned. "It's about damn time!"

Rolling his eyes, Bob went in as he started to undo his pants.

Charlie followed—carrying both the buckets—and watched Bob kicking off his shoes. "What the hell are you doing?"

Bob glanced up as he slid off his pants. "Well, I figure I'll have to get in the water. They can't come out to see me."

"True," Charlie said. "I didn't think of that."

Bob took a couple fish and tossed them into the clear water. They landed with a loud splash. Pretty soon, four dolphins swam up to the edge of the tank, looking for more food.

Bob sat down on the edge, his legs hanging in the water. Taking a hold of two more fish he held them on either side of his dick, rubbing them against it slowly. It wasn't long before he had an interested victim, a young female that was new to the aquarium.

At first she swam back and forth in front of Bob, rubbing up against his legs. When that didn't lead to the fish being dropped in, she stuck her head out of the water.

Bob gave her one of the fish, pulling it back to get her head closer to his crotch. She gobbled it down and came looking for more, and that's when she latched onto his penis.

Bob gasped as he was pulled into the water. "Holy shit!"

Charlie grinned widely; it was about time the tables turned.

Bob thrashed around in the water groaning and panting, trying to stay above the surface. Charlie couldn't help but laugh as a mixture of panic and pleasure crossed Bob's face every time he broke the surface. His amusement increased as Bob climaxed, swallowed a bunch of water, and started to choke.

After that, Bob got free of the dolphin and lay half-in, half-out of the water. "Fuck, that was intense," he said while panting.

Charlie grinned and helped Bob up and out of the pool. "You gonna call her tomorrow? Wanna double with me and the penguin?"

"Yeah," Bob said with a smug smile. "We'll go out for fish. Who knows, maybe we'll get lucky."

They both laughed.

* * *

They had the manatee and Wally left to feed. Both of them decided they needed another joint to make it through the rest of the night. Their buzz was starting to wear off, and they were sore.

Sitting on the bench in the visitor's section, they watched Mel the manatee swim in her tank.

"Wonder who will get to have fun with fatty there," Charlie said, motioning to the tank and passing Bob the joint. "Never was into fat chicks, but I bet she can really suck."

Bob laughed, and took a long, deep drag. "She's starting to look pretty hot. If you get her, I promise I won't tell the penguin about her."

Charlie grinned. "Same here. I won't tell the dolphin."

Bob laughed as he exhaled and choked slightly. "I won't tell the penguin about the seal either. She might not like you any more if she knows you're bi."

Charlie punched Bob in the arm. "Shut the fuck up. I hope you get Wally after that remark, you bastard! I hope he rips your dick off!"

Bob shook his head. "I'd be more worried about the tusks. That would be one hell of a penis piercing."

They both laughed and finished their weed in silence.

* * *

They weren't walking too well by the time they carried a bucket of fish into Mel's area. They stood, looking down into the water as she swam around. Her gray body was hidden in shadows, only to appear moments later where they least expected her.

"Let's flip," Bob said, handing Charlie the coin. "It's my turn to call."

"Okay," Charlie agreed, tossing the coin.

"Tails," Bob said.

Charlie slapped it on his hand and peeked at it, grinning broadly. "Heads. You're gonna get sucked again, water boy. I'm actually kind of relieved. I can't swim."

Bob sighed. "So I get to have fatty. Hopefully she doesn't rip it off or drown me."

Charlie just stood there grinning. "How does this compare to your fantasy of gettin' blown in a hot tub?"

Bob ignored the smart ass remark as he kicked off his shoes and removed his pants again. Sighing, he took a couple fish and rubbed them on his genitals, mentally preparing himself for his upcoming aquatic experience. Even the fish caused him pain. He was sore, but the thought of getting sucked again started to turn him on. He knew Mel could suck hard. She often pulled fish out of their hands with just her tongue.

"This is gonna be awesome," Bob said, slipping into the water and waving his erection and the fish at Mel.

She swam by twice, not paying much attention, before advancing slowly toward him. He groaned and closed his eyes as her tongue closed around him, sucking him hard. He let go of the fish, letting her have it.

She backed away, swallowing the fish, and then took him back into her mouth. Confused, she backed off and tried again, this time latching on and sucking for all she was worth, back peddling.

"Grab my arms!" Bob screamed between moans. "She's trying to pull me under!"

Charlie laughed, but took hold of Bob's arms, pulling back so he didn't get dragged under. Mel let go again, only to latch on a moment later. This time she didn't let go, but sucked extremely hard.

Bob moaned loudly as his body shuddered in a violent orgasm. "Fuck yes!"

Charlie dragged him out of the water. "How was it? Did the fatty please you?"

"Holy shit," Bob said panting. "I'm gonna start dating fat chicks from now on."

Charlie chuckled. "Really? We'll have to hit on those two we keep seeing at the bar. Might be a fun night."

They made eye contact with each other as Bob stood. They both burst out laughing, thinking of the chicks Charlie had mentioned. Once they started, they couldn't stop. Pretty soon, they were both holding their stomachs and were on their knees. They were both sore and exhausted. Being high, things were already funny. Being tired, they were even more so.

Charlie dumped the fish in the water while Bob dressed. It didn't matter that he'd taken off his pants before entering the water, both times. The water from his shirt, his hair, and his legs had soaked them. They clung to his body like a second skin.

"You look like a drowned rat," Charlie teased.

"I feel worse," Bob said. "Who knew getting blown could take so much out of you."

They staggered out, walking bowlegged because their crotches were so sore. Getting the last bucket of fish they would have to handle for the night, they headed to the last tank, to feed Wally.

* * *

Standing outside the door with the sign that had **WALLY** written in black script, they looked at each other and took a deep breath.

"You know," Bob said. "Tonight gives the term 'blow hole' an entirely new meaning. It's not just for whales any more."

Charlie doubled over laughing, grabbing Bob's shoulder to help support himself.

Bob started laughing, too. "Let's get this over with. I hope you get him, since you're the bi one and all. Besides, I don't know if I can get another erection after Mel, she was some girl."

Charlie winked. "Sounds like true love. I hope you got her number."

Bob grinned. "I think I'll dump the dolphin. She's not for me. I need a female with a stronger jaw, who likes to use her tongue the right way."

They both laughed again. Once they calmed down, they went through the door, each dreading who would get stuck with the walrus. Wally the walrus was big, with a stringy moustache and two long, ivory tusks. He was pleased to see the men that brought his food and jumped out of the water, flopped over to them, and sat back on his tail, clapping happily.

Bob looked at Charlie. "Ready?"

Charlie nodded.

Bob flipped the coin.

"Tails," Charlie said in a solemn voice.

Bob looked down at his hands and sighed. "It's heads."

"You have got to be shitting me!" Charlie yelled. "This is bullshit. I don't want my pecker ripped off!"

Bob grinned and held a large fish out to Charlie.

Mumbling, Charlie undid his pants and slapped the fish against his dick, rubbing it against himself almost violently, staring at Bob the entire time. The expression on his face said, *I'm gonna kill you for this, fucker.*

Bob winked. "Don't worry, I won't tell your other boyfriend."

Charlie waddled over to Wally and presented himself, the fish in his hand still on his genitals.

Wally eagerly grabbed the fish, swallowing it whole, and bent back down, sniffing Charlie's penis. Sticking out his tongue, Wally licked it. Since it tasted like fish, he sucked it into his mouth. When it didn't easily slide down his throat, he released and sniffed again. Sucking it back into his mouth, Wally lifted his head, shaking it back and forth.

Charlie screamed, now standing on his tip toes, prancing back and forth to try and avoid the walrus' tusks.

"He's gonna rip it off!" Charlie screamed. "Get him off me!"

Bob didn't make any move to help. He stood laughing, mimicking his friend by standing on his toes and dancing back and forth with a scared expression on his face.

Wally got more vigorous after that, and tried to drag Charlie toward the water. But Charlie pulled back and wiggled, trying to get this over with as fast as possible. Closing his eyes, he started thinking about women.

And breasts.

He envisioned big, bouncing breasts and soon he came in the walrus' mouth.

Wally didn't like that. He let go of Charlie's dick, snorted, and darted back into the water of his tank.

Charlie fell to his knees, panting. His penis was so sore it was throbbing. He doubted that he would be able to walk at all tomorrow. Glancing down at his crotch, he saw that he was turning black and blue.

"You're a fucking jerk," Charlie growled at Bob. "I'm gonna have to pack ice in my shorts for a month to get the swelling to go down."

Bob saw what Charlie was talking about. "Damn, and I thought blue balls were bad. So, uhm, did his moustache tickle you off?"

Charlie scowled at Bob. "If I could stand right now, I'd kick you in the dick until you bleed. You're an asshole."

Bob bit back a laugh. "Come on, let's go get you some ice."

After dumping the rest of the fish, they left and went to the employee lounge. For the rest of their shift they lay on the couches with bags of ice on their bruised dicks.

* * *

At eleven o'clock they punched out and waddled toward the door. Once they were outside, they slowly made their way to Bob's truck, leaning against each other for support.

Neither of them noticed the little red car parked off to the side until a young woman spoke.

"Hey," she said, rushing over to them. "Are you guys okay?"

They instantly straightened up, despite the pain. Standing in front of them was the cute blonde they had been talking to at the bar for a long time. Her brunette friend, who was just as hot, came walking up behind her, a big smile on her face.

"Hey," Bob said. "What are you two doing here at this time of night?"

The blonde bit her bottom lip and tucked her hair behind her ear. "Well, we were at the bar, and got a little drunk. Now we're horny and remembered that you guys would be getting off work about now."

Charlie cringed as she said, 'getting off work'. She had no idea how true that had been tonight.

Bob inwardly groaned. These hot chicks were horny and looking to get lucky, and their dicks felt like they were going to fall off any second. The game really had been stupid. How could they possibly turn them down without offending them? This could be their only chance at getting with these two, totally hot women.

Bob caught Charlie's eye and shrugged. The message was clear. It was a 'why not'.

Charlie's eyes grew huge, and he inwardly groaned. He could barely stand and Bob wanted him to perform!

"So, what do you guys say?" the brunette asked, walking up to Bob and pressing her hand to his chest. "I've been thinking about you and that leather seat in your truck."

Bob plastered a grin on his face. "Sounds great to me." Slapping Charlie on the back, he took the brunette's hand and away they went to his truck.

Charlie gulped as he looked the blonde over.

She giggled. "Don't look so scared. I won't hurt you." Stepping forward, she kissed him and gripped his belt buckle as she drew him over to her car.

* * *

A couple of hours later, Charlie and Bob kissed the girls goodnight and sat in the truck, watching them leave.

"You're a fucking asshole," Charlie growled. "It's a damn good thing my dick was so swollen that she thought I had an erection, or I would be fucking strangling you right now."

"It wasn't a picnic for me either, jackass," Bob said. "That was the only way I could perform, too. Don't get so damn pissed, I got us a double date next weekend. We should be fine by then."

"I'm never playing any of your games again, you prick," Charlie growled.

"Aren't you happy about the date?"

"Yeah," Charlie said grudgingly.

"How was I supposed to know they were going to show up tonight," Bob reasoned as they drove home to the apartment they shared. "I wouldn't have insisted on the game if I'd known. I'm sorry, I was horny and the idea seemed fun. You can't say you didn't enjoy it just a little bit."

Charlie looked out the window and tried not to grin. "I'll never be able to look at those animals the same way again. I'll probably get a chub every time I smell fish for at least a year!"

"So, you're now addicted to 'blow hole'?" Bob asked, and then laughed when Charlie punched him. "Don't worry. I won't tell the blonde."

"Asshole," Charlie said.

They laughed.

They'd had the most adventurously sexual night of their young lives, and they could still walk.

What more could a guy ask for?

REVENGE IS BEST SERVED WET

DANE T. HATCHELL

"**L**ook, I don't see what the big deal is. We've been married for ten years and you still haven't given me a blow job," Randy said, now lying on his side with his back to Evelyn.

"Randy, we just made love for almost an hour and all you can think about is me sucking your dick?" Evelyn asked incredulously.

"I just don't see what the big deal is. Before we were married, the other girls I went with didn't have a problem with it."

"Well, I guess you should have married one of those girls, asshole." Evelyn jerked the sheet over to her side of the bed and put her back to Randy.

Great, he thought. *Two weeks in a return trip to the Bahamas to celebrate our ten year wedding anniversary and I've gone and pissed her off.*

He felt like a cad for spoiling the evening. "I'm sorry, honey. I guess my feelings are hurt. It's sort of like having a Corvette and not being able to drive over sixty miles an hour. I feel like you're rejecting me."

"Unfortunately," Evelyn sighed, "I actually understand your feelings. I've come to realize that men never mature in their sexual thinking past the age of seventeen. So you pout like a child when you don't get everything you want."

"I've never denied you you're pleasure in any way," Randy interjected defensively. "I've had my tongue on and in every part of your body, and I mean *every* part."

"Yeah, well, in the heat of passion I let you do just about anything you want to me, whether I like it or not, just so we don't end up like *this* after making love."

Randy knew he was digging a deeper hole for himself. He needed to fix this thing now before it blew up any further. In a softer voice he said, "I'm sorry, honey, I shouldn't have acted that way. Will you forgive me?"

"Let's just go to sleep. I forgive you...*again*," she said.

She heard Randy snoring in less than a minute. Their entire relationship seemed like the same recycled garbage. Evelyn was hoping two weeks of time together without the distractions of work and home would change that—hoping to reset their relationship. But it was the same old crap, different day.

Randy and Evelyn were in line at the Iguana Beach Club's dive shack to sign up for the next outing. Guests had to arrive thirty minutes before departure to sign the roster and check out a snorkel, mask, life vest, and fins.

"The Garretts, room 2031, please," Randy said when it was his turn, holding up his left arm and displaying the turquoise-colored plastic band that identified him as a current resident of the resort. The attendant, Hazel, a beautiful young girl of Hawaiian descent, handed them their equipment. Randy especially appreciated Hazel's swim suit bottom; two tiny triangles that covered just enough not to be offensive to other women. His eyes lingered on Hazel longer than they should have and he hoped Evelyn hadn't noticed.

The two climbed on the forty foot snorkel boat that was unimaginatively named, ***Miss Iguana***. There were six other couples on board, as The Iguana Beach Club was a couples-only resort. The captain and the dive master helped each one aboard and set out on the daily aquatic adventure.

Evelyn had been in a chipper mood all morning, seeming to have forgotten the conflict from the previous night. Randy was glad of it, he didn't want to start the day off rehashing any of it, and pledged to himself he would watch his words and be as nice to her as possible.

As the boat headed for the snorkel point, Randy looked at the shore line and was amazed at the amount of development that had sprung up over the last ten years. Back then, The Iguana Beach Club was the only resort on the pristine sands for more than a twenty mile stretch. Now, there wasn't a vacant section of land as far as the eye could see.

Other resorts and high-rises dotted the beach in a hodgepodge of architectural designs. Each offered some type of water sports, gaudily displayed just feet from the ocean shore.

Sail boats of different sizes tore through the waters haphazardly, dodging windsurfers and kayakers in their path. Large colored parasails dotted the sky; one being bright yellow and marked with a 'have a nice day' happy face. Randy was told that one of the parasailing operations allowed you to do so in the nude. The idea intrigued him.

Despite all the modern amenities, he still felt grief that the quaintness and solitude of the paradise he remembered was gone. Before, you could walk the beach for an hour in one direction and never see another soul. Now, the beach looked like someone had kicked an ant pile over with people scurrying everywhere.

The roar of the boat engine prevented any meaningful conversation between the two. But he made sure to smile at Evelyn from time to time and give her hand a loving squeeze to let her know he loved her.

Fifteen minutes from departure, the boat slowed as it approached the anchor point's bright orange float. The dive master hooked the float with a special pole, and tied the boat to the permanent anchor resting on the Caribbean's ocean floor.

There were five more minutes of instruction before the snorkelers were allowed in the water. The instructions always included, "This is a national preserve. Do not feed the fish or touch anything. You can be fined up to fifty thousand dollars and or spend five years in our prison."

Yeah, right, Randy thought, knowing how well the laws were enforced.

Randy and Evelyn walked cautiously in their flippers to the ladder leading to the ocean. They were the first in the water, and swam towards the reef in hopes of spotting exotic fish before the rest of the group caught up and spooked them away.

The water wasn't nearly as clear as he remembered it. It was a calm day and the water was smooth as glass, so he knew it wasn't this murky due to the weather. The water clarity was fifty feet on their previous trip. But now, he couldn't make any distinction of objects until he was within ten feet of them.

Randy recognized many of the marine plants; the Venus sea fans, the salt water ferns, and the sea lilies. But everything looked like it was withering and dying. The vibrant greens, blues, yellows, and reds were faded or gone.

A certain coral reef the locals had given the name of 'The Christmas Tree', because of the variety of colors; looked more like an algae-covered brown rock. The plants of the ocean all had a dull, greenish-brown, sick and pale yellow look to them.

The tropical fish they came upon were few and far between. Instead of teams of Sergeant Majors, Durgons, and Parrot fish playing and feeding among the reef; only a few scraggly Squirrel fish and Wrasse came out to scrounge for what little food the ocean now provided.

The sea creature they most wanted to see was the spotted eagle stingray. Evelyn had seen one on the first trip ten years ago, and it was by far the most magnificent thing she had ever seen in the water. Its black skin was peppered with small white spots, and seemed to 'fly' gracefully in the water, moving its pectoral fins up and down.

Evelyn pulled on Randy's shoulder and made a hand signal that she wanted to talk. The two popped their heads above water and removed their snorkel and mask.

"What's the matter, honey?" he asked, blowing his nose in his hand.

"I'm starting to cramp a little. I'm going back to the boat. There's nothing much to see here anyway," she said.

"What do you mean? I've seen three tennis shoes, two pairs of sunglasses, beer cans, a hamburger wrapper, and a chair," Randy said, sarcastically.

"I'm going back. Are you coming?" she asked.

"No, we've got about fifteen minutes left before they blow the whistle. I'm going to look around some more and see if I can spot something different."

"Okay, see you on the boat. Evelyn returned the mask and snorkel to her face and mouth, then started her swim back.

Randy continued against the current, so it would be with him when it was time to swim back to the boat. As the next reef came into focus, he saw a fish unlike any he had seen before. At first he didn't think it was a fish at all, its shape made it look more like a piece of pipe. But it had eyes and gills, so it certainly was a fish.

It was about a foot long and four inches wide. Its skin was bright yellow with tiny neon blue specks that glistened as the rays of the sun reflected off them. The mouth on it was its most unique feature. Unusually big, and remained perpetually open, never once did he see it close.

Randy swam closer to it and stopped when he was just a few feet away, fearing of getting too close and scaring it. But the strange fish seemed to be as curious about Randy as he was about it.

The bright colored fish flapped its thin pectoral fins and moved closer to him, just inches away from his mask. It looked at him eye to eye.

Randy wished he had an underwater camera and that Evelyn had been there to see this amazing fish. She was more the snorkeling fan than he was, and this might be a once in a life time event.

Man and fish stared at one another, and Randy felt himself being drawn through its eyes into its consciousness. It was nothing that overwhelmed him, but a connection, *soft* and comfortable, filled in his mind. The sun's rays cascading in the water and the rhythm of the ocean made him feel one with it, and one with the fish.

Three shrill reports from the dive master's whistle broke Randy from his captive trance. He snapped back to reality again; the fish was still there looking at him. Once again he regretted not having a camera, but it was time to go. He gave the fish a wave goodbye, turned, and swam back to the boat.

Randy had not been swimming long when he felt something slither up the left leg of his swimming trunks. He immediately stopped kicking his fins and looked down to see the tail of the strange fish sticking out from underneath. Before he could reach down and grab it, he felt the mouth of the fish slide over his penis until it came to rest at the base of his man-shaft.

An electric charge shot through him, disabling the muscle control of his arms and legs. His head stayed supported above the water only by his life vest, but he could do nothing about the fish that had now curled up in his trunks.

Numbness came over his entire body and quenched any panic he thought he should be feeling. Then, a warm feeling of pleasure engulfed his penis, and the muscle control slowly returned to his limbs.

The whistle blew three more times, and Randy was able to return to his swim to the boat.

What the hell just happened? he wondered. *A fish just swallowed my dick! It's still there! What am I going to do?* The total absurdity of the situation made him feel extremely embarrassed. What next? Pull down his swim trunks and ask the dive master to pull the fish off his dick? He could hear them all laughing now, "Hey, man, you shouldn't use your dick for bait!"

But there was something more than just the embarrassment he felt. The hypnotic oneness with the fish still lurked just below the surface of his consciousness, and he didn't want to do anything to betray the feeling he felt.

Randy made it to the boat's ladder, removed his flippers, and handed them to the dive master waiting above. He decided he would keep the event to himself until he reached shore, then have the resort's nurse look at him if he couldn't get the fish off himself.

Evelyn was waiting next to the dive master with a towel.

"See anything?" she asked, as he climbed up.

"No...nothing really. Civilization has come to paradise and destroyed it." He quickly grabbed the towel and wrapped it around his waist, as he and Evelyn sat down for the ride back.

Randy felt the lump in his swimsuit grow smaller and smaller as the boat bounced off the water, making good time back to the resort. When he thought no one was looking, he would reach his hand down the towel and feel inside his trunks. The fish itself felt like it kept getting thinner, until it felt like it was no thicker than a condom.

The boat slowed as it made its approach to the dock, and came to rest against the vinyl bumpers. The captain and dive master secured the bow and stern with thick ropes, then helped everyone disembark, making sure to shake each person's hand in hopes of palming a tip.

When Evelyn stood to leave, Randy noticed a reddish puddle of water where she sat.

"Evelyn," Randy said and nodded towards the puddle.

"Darn it, I've started my period," she said.

That's just fucking great, he thought.

But then again, it was much the same story every time the two made a beach trip.

Randy turned the bed covers down on the antique, four post bed while Evelyn finished in the bathroom. The bed was one of the special amenities that added to the fond memories they made on their honeymoon. He especially remembered the night she had tied his arms and legs to the bed posts, and had her *way* with him.

Evelyn climbed into the left side of the bed and immediately laid on her right side with her back to him. "I'm tired, goodnight," she said.

Randy immediately flipped on his right side and supported himself on his elbow, hovering over her.

Evelyn felt his hot breath on her neck, "What?" she asked in a weary voice.

He paused a moment, then said, "Well...you know, second honeymoon and all."

"I've got my period and the back door's closed tonight. Go to bed, Randy."

He heaved a big sigh, then caught himself; he didn't want his disappointment to sound like he was pouting again.

"I know, I know," he said. "It's just...it's just that I don't know how we're going to have kids if we don't 'do it', he said in a leading way, then stretched out on his back.

Evelyn thought a moment and sat straight up in bed. "Kids? Did you say kids?" she asked as if she didn't hear him right. She had always wanted children, but that had been a hot subject with him. She knew when they married that he wasn't in favor of having children, but she thought she could change him. But that never happened. After a huge fight over it three years ago, she hadn't brought it up since.

"Well, yeah, it's been ten years since we got married. It'll be like we're starting over again with this second honeymoon. Let's start a new life with children," he said.

Overwhelming joy surged through Evelyn. She could hardly believe her ears. "Oh, Randy, are you serious?" she giggled, her tiredness now giving way to new energy.

"I couldn't be more serious," he said calmly, his voice now drifting off as if he was tired.

"Oh, that's so wonderful," she said, and started giving him multiple kisses on his face.

"Hey, hold on there," he laughed. "I thought you wanted to go to sleep?"

Evelyn pressed her lips firmly against his, and started kissing him deeply and passionately. His hand flowed down her back to her hip as she partially lay on top of him.

Her hand wandered down his chest, to his penis...and found it.

He was glad that by the time he reached the room, the fish was nowhere to be found. He didn't know exactly what or how it happened; if he had absorbed it into his body or if the fish had simply evaporated or fallen off. It was gone now, and that's all that really mattered.

He still had that different feeling he first felt when the fish latched on to him. That was the only thing remaining from his encounter. He had examined his penis for a full ten minutes when he returned to his room. But there was nothing unusual, no strange cuts or marks; it looked like the same penis he had been entertaining for the last thirty years.

Randy settled back in the bed, thinking he was going to get an unexpected hand job. Instead, he felt Evelyn's lips brush past his chin, travel down his stomach, and then felt her take him in her mouth.

His body jolted with surprise and he let out a gasp of delight.

She was slow and methodical in her pleasuring. Randy moaned softly so she wouldn't have to wonder how much he was enjoying it. And when he came, it was the most incredible orgasm he had ever felt. Evelyn didn't stop until he let out a final sigh of completeness.

"Oh, wow, that was fantastic," he said, grabbing the tissue box on the night stand and handing it to her.

"What are these for? Do you need me to dry you off?" she asked.

"No...I thought you might...you know, spit it out."

"I don't need to do that," she said.

"Okay...you swallowed it?" he asked, astonished.

"Not really, it just kind of hit the back of my throat and slid down. I don't taste it in my mouth or anything," she said, lying back down and snuggling next to him. "I'm really tired now." She smacked her lips together, making a kissing sound as she leaned forward with her lips puckered.

"What? You just had my dick in your mouth and you want me to kiss you now? Gross," he said, turning over so his back was to her. He was snoring before she could think of an adequate reply.

That night, as dreams came and went, only one remained in his memory the next day.

He found himself ten thousand feet in the sky on a cloudless day, behind the cockpit of a 1944 Mitsubishi Zero Japanese fighter. His was one of ten planes in formation over the Pacific Ocean heading for a speck on the horizon. A black and white photo of him with the rising sun of the Japanese flag as a back drop was taped to the instrument panel. The hum of the Sakae engine gave him a feeling of oneness with the other planes, the same feeling he had shared with the fish in real life.

The speck on the horizon grew larger, until it was easily identified as a U.S. Destroyer, their primary target.

The lead plane pointed the nose of his Zero towards the destroyer and Randy and the rest followed suit. He awoke abruptly before his plane made contact.

"Honey, thank you so much for last night. You'll never know how much that meant to me," Randy said, kissing Evelyn on the cheek while pouring her orange juice from the mini-fridge.

"I'm glad you liked it. It wasn't as bad as I thought it would be. But I swear, there must be something hallucinogenic in your cum," she said.

"Oh, really?" he asked confused.

"I dreamed all night long about beautiful flowers; thirty or forty different kinds of them. First I would see a bud, then the flower would open, make seeds, and then wither and die. Then I would see another bud, and a different kind of flower would open, make seeds, then die. It was beautiful and strange all at the same time," she said, trying to recreate the dream in her mind. "I feel...different inside; a feeling of belonging. I don't know how to put it into words."

Randy knew just what she meant; he couldn't put his feelings into words either.

* * *

Randy and Evelyn had been home from their trip for a few days, and over a week from the 'event'. They were sitting by their pool with some eighties music playing in the background. The two of them had never felt closer. He knew it had something to do with his fish encounter, and something to do with the oral sex that night in their room.

Evelyn was reading *The Complete Book of Baby Names*, and sipping on some lemonade. Spots started appearing in her vision as she tried to read and suddenly she felt as if she were falling.

"Randy, I feel sick," she said, feeling a wave of vertigo pass over her as she dropped the book.

Randy had been dozing while working a crossword puzzle. Her words woke him, "Huh, sick? Can I get you something?"

She stood up from her chair. A chill came over her, then goose bumps popped up on her arms. "I'm going to go in and lie down." But before she could take two steps, she fell to her knees in front of the pool, vomiting into the deep end.

"Evelyn! Are you okay? Oh great, did you have to puke in the pool?" he yelled as he sprang from his chair and went to her side.

"'I'm sick, damn it, just throw some more chlorine in the water," she said, spitting.

A jelly like mass floated just above the water's surface, by the edge of the pool.

"Randy, what is that?" she asked.

He looked to see what 'that' was. He expected to see the remains of her turkey sandwich from lunch, but instead he saw small, tiny white sacks, with little things inside. "I'm...I'm not sure. It sort of looks like fish eggs," he said.

"Fish eggs? I haven't eaten any fish eggs." Evelyn had recovered enough to stand and was rinsing her mouth out with lemonade.

The two stood and watched the mass of eggs sink deeper in the water, towards the middle of the pool.

"Turn off the pump," she said.

"Why?"

"They'll be sucked up in the drain. I don't know why, but I feel we must protect those eggs."

Strangely, Randy felt that way, too.

* * *

Having a pool makes you popular in the summertime. Randy and Evelyn had four couples over to celebrate the fourth of July. It had been a tradition of sorts for the past three years.

A large ice chest was full of domestic and imported beers, and a plastic table was set up to be a makeshift bar with rum, vodka, gin, and whiskey to help the guests get their drink on. And hopefully to get the women looped enough to go skinny dipping later.

The pool was set up with a net across it for volleyball; the men at the five foot level and the woman in the three foot side just to keep things fair. Randy had a reputation for taking the game a little too seriously; his aggressiveness tended to increase proportionally to his alcohol intake.

Today, though, he didn't go overboard. Everyone was having fun, playing game after game, and downing drink after drink. Randy served the ball harder than usual and it landed outside of the pool on the patio area. Evelyn climbed out of the water and picked it up, then gave Randy a questioning look.

He nodded his head slightly in return.

Now was the time.

"Hey, Cindy, Tricia, Lori, and Tracy, let's go inside and get dinner started. Most everything's made, we just have to take it out of the fridge and cook up the meat on the grill," Evelyn called out to the girls.

"I'll help," Bob—Cindy's husband—volunteered.

Randy moved over to Bob and whispered to him, "No, Bob, stay here. I've got something special for just us guys."

Bob gave Randy a sneaky wink of affirmation. "Never mind," Bob hollered. None of the girls cared that he wasn't helping; all he wanted to do was look at their asses anyway.

The women were all in the kitchen and the sliding glass door closed when Bob felt clear to ask, "Okay, Randy, what's the secret?"

"Secret? What secret?" Jim asked, with Blake and Duane looking at Bob curiously.

Randy flashed them a big smile. "Guys, you're not going to believe what I have to show you." And before anyone could ask, he dove down to the deep end of the pool.

On the bottom of the pool, under a blue tarp, lay a rectangular shape. Randy removed the tarp to reveal a three by six foot cage. He opened the door on the side.

He came up for air and swam back to where his buddies were all eagerly waiting to learn what was behind this mystery. The men were standing chest high in the water as Randy joined them, wearing an evil grin on his face.

"What the fuck, Randy?" Jim asked. "What were you doing down there?"

"You'll see," Randy chuckled.

Blake was the first to notice that there was something in the water. "Hey, something just swam past my ankles! There's fish in here!"

Bob was the first to feel it. "Hey! A damn fish just went up my shorts! What the hell!"

Jim, Blake, and Duane cried out in surprise as their swim trunks were invaded by the determined, large mouthed fish.

"Guys, take it easy. There's nothing to be afraid of. Trust me," Randy said with his hands raised in the air.

The tension on the three men's faces started to relax as the fish had their penises secured firmly in their mouths, then began secreting their mind and body altering chemicals.

Looks of pleasure now replaced the last signs of anxiety, the men feeling orgasmic warmth to their core. Their arms and legs felt rubbery and they struggled to remain standing with their head above water.

Soon, the hypnotic spell broke, and the men turned their attention back to Randy, all of them now sharing the same sense of oneness.

"The fish'll disappear in less than an hour. Act like nothing's happened. You'll know what moves to make and when to make them when the time comes. You'll just have to trust me on this," Randy said with a knowing smile.

The four understood without full comprehension. By the time the food was ready, it was as Randy said—the fish were gone. The party continued late into the night, until tiredness took over. The four couples said their goodbyes and left for home.

"Did you have much trouble?" Evelyn asked when they were alone.

"No, no trouble at all. It happened quicker this time, smoother, too. I guess those things are still evolving," he said. "It's late. Why don't you go to bed? The foods all put away and I can help you with the cleaning in the morning."

"That's a really good idea," she said.

"I'm going to check my email, I'll go to bed later," Randy yawned.

Evelyn kissed him on the cheek, took a shower, and went to bed. She died five minutes later as she slept.

Randy finished reading his email and was surfing some of his favorite porn sights.

One of the thumbnails immediately captured his attention. A slutty looking blonde was in the middle of two naked men, on her knees, with her hands on each of their enormous dicks.

Randy clicked on 'play', and the blonde went to work, stroking and licking each one.

Randy was totally mesmerized at the sight of the low hanging penises. His eyes glazed and his jaw dropped, his mouth forming a large 'O' shape. Unknowingly, his lips opened and closed in rhythm to each stroke.

Taunting him like a squirming worm dangling on a hook, Randy wanted to strike as the penises became further engorged. He was consumed with a craving to seize a penis with his teeth. And there was nothing sexual about his insatiable new hunger.

THE OTHER FOOT

ANTHONY GIANGREGORIO

The water splashed against the hull of the small fishing boat as Martin hauled in the last catch of the day.

There weren't many fish in the net and he frowned deeply.

Swinging the net onto the weathered deck, he began pulling the fish out and tossing them into a bin near the aft end. Next to the bin was a wooden table, its top scarred from years of blades being used on it. The table stank of fish guts and seawater, the latter used to clean the former.

When all the fish were pulled from the net and tossed into the bin, Martin pulled the first one out and slapped it down on the table. Pulling his favorite carving knife, he jammed it into the stomach of the fish and began sawing from top to bottom.

The eyes of the fish grew three sizes bigger as it was gutted while still alive. Sometimes Martin could swear he heard them scream, a high-pitched one, so high only a dog could hear it.

He liked to think that was true anyway; he liked to cause pain.

When Martin was a boy, he used to sit for hours on end in his backyard, using a magnifying glass to burn ants. He loved the way they sizzled under the thin ray of burning fire, like a tiny laser beam. As the smoke curled up from the small carapaces, he always felt a rush fill him, like when a skydiver jumped out of a plane for the first time.

Soon he graduated from ants to larger bugs, such as grasshoppers and beetles. He would use pins and tack them to a piece of corkboard, then one at a time, he would pull off their legs, watching as they squirmed in what he dreamed was unimaginable agony.

But soon that became boring so he moved on to small rodents, such as mice and rats. Field mice were prevalent in the large field near his house and he had more than enough specimens to torture. Frogs were another fun creature to play with and he loved pinning them down and slicing them open, then slowly taking out their organs, thrilling at the sight of the small heart in his hands. Then he would squeeze the tiny heart between his fingers, loving the feel of the blood and fluid coating his skin.

Years later, Martin graduated to small dogs and cats. What he did to those animals would make the most hardened serial killer wince and grow nauseous.

It was very possible that Martin would have graduated to serial killer status very soon if not for his father taking him on as one of the crew on the fishing boat he worked on.

On the boat, Martin excelled as an expert gutter. Shark, tuna or squid, Martin sliced and diced them with skill that made the most experienced crewman jealous.

As for Martin, he was able to keep his bloodlust in check, slaughtering the sea life day after day, reveling in the fish guts that became so much a part of him it was all he smelled no matter how many times he bathed.

Now he was middle-aged and was the captain of his own fishing boat. He didn't work with anyone, wanting to do it all himself and thus earning the greatest reward.

Besides, he didn't want to share the killing with anyone, either, enjoying being alone as he worked.

He pulled the next fish out of the bin and began carving it. The mouth opened and closed, as if the fish were screaming, and Martin felt himself grow hard as he reached inside it and pulled out the guts. Then, with the fish dead, he cut off its head and tossed the leftovers into the water. He never chopped the head off first for that would be too quick a death for the fish. Instead, he gutted them first, loving every second of the pain he believed he was dishing out.

Hours went by and he gutted fish after fish, his mind lost in the carnage. This was the best of both worlds. He needed to clean the fish and he got to feed his lust for blood and death. No one would ever criticize a fisherman for cleaning his catch—no one.

Hell, most people never even bothered to consider where their food came from, how it had once been a living creature until it was slaughtered, sometimes without mercy. All the customer saw was the nice clean, sterile packages in the frozen or fresh meat section of their local grocery store—that piece of fish or meat wrapped in cellophane and ready to be breaded and fried.

Martin reached into the bin and pulled out one of the last fish. It was a big one, twice as large as the rest, and its scales gleamed silver, looking like precious metal.

As he slapped it down on the table and prepared to slice into its stomach, anxiously looking forward to when the innards would squirt out and splash onto the table, the fish did something that none before had ever done.

It talked.

"Wait, please don't kill me," its garbled voice said.

Martin blinked and held the blade an inch from the fish's gullet.

Surely he had imagined the voice he just heard. It was hot out, the sun bright, baking anything not protected from its harmful rays, and surly he must be suffering from heatstroke.

The fish looked up at him with wide eyes and Martin stared at it for another five seconds before he prepared to slice it open.

His arm flexed.

"No, please, I beg you. Don't kill me."

Martin looked around the boat, as if he expected to see someone standing near him—perhaps a ventriloquist throwing his voice. Ha, ha, a big joke, and all at his expense.

Of course there was no one there. And there would never be as Martin was a loner.

"Please, I beg you, show me mercy," the fish pleaded.

Martin looked down at the fish and this time he saw the fish's mouth move in rhythm to the words spoken.

"You can talk," he said. A statement, not a question.

"Of course I can talk, I'm a fish," the fish said matter-of-factly.

"Well, either I'm crazy or you can really talk, which is it? I have no idea."

"No, Martin, it's true, I can talk. Many of us can, we just choose not to."

"Uh-huh. Well, good for you." He raised the blade to slice into the fish and continue filleting it when the fish cried out once more.

"No! Please, Martin, don't kill me, show me mercy."

"You know my name. How is that possible?"

The fish seemed to nod as it lay on the table. "Most of us know of you. You are the Great Killer. You slaughter our kind and after vivisecting us, you toss our insides into the ocean."

"Yup, that sounds like me. I'm a fisherman, it's my job."

"Perhaps, Martin, but the way you kill my kind is so barbaric. You don't cut off the heads first like other fishermen do. You gut us alive. *Alive,* Martin."

"So, what's it to ya?"

"Martin, we are living creatures. And most like me, are sentient. I have feelings, I think, I dream. Don't you have any empathy for me?"

Martin paused as he stared at the fish. He looked at the knife in his hand, considering the fish's sage words. Then he shrugged and said, "Nope, I gotta eat," and he plunged the knife into the fish's belly, slicing it up and then down, its insides squirting out to slide across the table.

The fish's mouth went wide and its eyes practically bulged from its head as it looked up at Martin. With its dying breath it said, "Martin, you are evil and you will get what you deserve. You will know how it feels to be a fish on your carving table."

"Uh-huh, sure I will," Martin said and he raised the blade and hacked off the fish's head, then scraped the offal into the ocean.

As he carved the fish into strips and scraped the silver scales off its sides, he shook his head as he thought about what the fish said and the reality that it had actually talked.

"Huh, so fish talk. Imagine that. You learn something new everyday."

He reached in to pull out another fish but as he placed it on the table, this one didn't talk. It just glared up at him with its eye, the other facing the table.

"So, go 'head and talk. Beg me to spare you," he said to the fish.

The fish did nothing but open and close its mouth as it struggled to breathe.

"That's what I thought," he said and he gutted it, pulling out its insides like he had done a hundred, no, a thousand times before.

By the time he was finished with his entire catch, and had put away a six pack of hard ale and was working on the second pack, he had totally forgotten about the talking fish.

Now, as he thought about it, he decided it was nothing but a weird daydream, brought on by the hot sun.

"Fish don't talk," he slurred as he cracked open another beer. He was good and drunk and on his way to being completely plastered. He wasn't the only one who liked to get good and drunk after a hard day at sea. He knew many fishermen that drank till they puked, most of them lonely men without families.

He steered the boat back to shore, but halfway home the motor began to sputter and then died completely. Cursing his foul luck, he went to the aft end to inspect the motor, which was in the lower deck under a hatch.

As Martin pulled on the hatch to open it, he cursed repeatedly. The hatch swelled from the moistness of the sea air and he always had to tug on it until it finally popped free.

But as drunk as he was, he wasn't standing correctly, and when he yanked on the hatch, it popped open, sending him falling backwards and over the railing.

He went under, turned in the water and swam back to the surface. He found he was immediately covered in seaweed and kelp.

Spitting water, he saw red leave his mouth.

A sudden pain in his mouth told him he had bitten off the tip of his tongue. He yelled out and his voice was garbled, the entire tip now gone, causing him to mumble unintelligibly. He splashed in the water and tried to swim to his boat, but as he turned around, he saw that the boat was a hundred yards away and still moving. Caught in the current, it was already too far away to catch by swimming alone.

He treaded water, not knowing what to do. He stayed calm, knowing that was the only way to survive. He was in the main shipping lane. Cargo and other fishing ships used this route all the time. If he could hold out long enough, he might get lucky and be saved.

And so the day moved on as Martin floated in the water. The seaweed was wrapped around him tight and he couldn't pull it off or risk sinking in the process. He floated on his back, blending in with the ocean, looking like a small manatee to the casual eye.

Two hours after he had fallen in, he found himself surrounded by a school of fish. They did nothing but jump around, some over him and some swam under him.

He ignored them, though a few times he yelled at them out of anger but his words were nothing but guttural grunts. The blood in his mouth had slowed but his tongue was still bleeding. He would need stitches and he imagined his stomach must be full of blood by now.

Hours later, his lips cracked, his face beet red from exposure, another fishing vessel came upon him and the school of fish surrounding him.

He called out but his voice was lost in the engine noise and the churning of the water, as the boat cut through the waves. There was a man on the port deck and as Martin watched, the man dropped a net right over him, catching the school of fish and Martin, too.

Oh what luck. He thought as the net was hauled in and he was dropped onto the deck amidst the jumping fish and pounds and pounds of seaweed. Martin looked like a sea monster, wrapped in so much dark green.

The man stumbled over to the net and began opening it. Martin tried to say something but all that came out were weird noises. He tried to lift his arms, to wave to the man, but they were lead weights from all the hours of treading water. He could barely move his limbs, and when he tried, all he did was roll around on the deck a little, in more than one way mimicking the fish flopping around him.

The fisherman wobbled on his feet and Martin could see the man was stone cold drunk. The fisherman's eyes were glazed over and his mouth hung slack, the look of a man who liked his liquor hard, such as vodka or scotch.

The man was old, well in his seventies, with a balding pate, liver spots covering his arms and head, and thin lips. An aquiline nose rounded out the picture, giving the man a hawk-like appearance. The man wore rubber boots and overalls, his chest bare and dark from the sun. He sang a tune to himself as he drank from a clear bottle of liquor.

Martin called out again but all that came forth were more garbles. He heard his voice and thought he sounded like a walrus. The old man began picking up the fish and tossing them into a bin, one very similar to the one on Martin's lost boat.

As the man worked, he downed more than half the bottle, and by the time all the fish were in the bin, he was so drunk he couldn't see straight.

Martin called out again, but once more his voice was nothing but grunts and groans. The fisherman dropped the bottle, burped loudly, and walked over to a small cabinet, where he opened it and pulled out a long serrated knife.

The old man looked down at the seaweed-covered body of Martin and licked his lips greedily.

"My, you're a big one. I'll have to gut you right here on the deck. These old bones can't pick you up, as big as you are." He began walking towards Martin whose eyes were now wide with fright.

"Damn if you ain't the biggest tuna I ever caught. Your meat's gonna fry up good tonight on my grill, yessiree, you just wait and see," the old man said as he knelt down next to Martin and prepared to get to work.

Martin tried to raise his arms and push the man away, but the seaweed and the net were constricting his movements so all he could do was flap his hands a little. To a stinking drunk of a fisherman, Martin looked just like a big tuna flapping its fins.

"This is gonna be fun," the old man said. "I like to have some sport before I kills ya," he said as he slid the carving knife into Martin's abdomen and began sawing upwards.

Entrails spilled onto the deck, offal sliding into the seaweed to mix with it. As the old fisherman sawed away, Martin screamed in absolute agony. His eyes popped out of his head and his tongue, missing the tip, splashed blood everywhere.

The old man never stopped carving, and soon was slicing into Martin's throat, severing his jugular and then cutting back down. As Martin twitched in his own gore, the man began pulling out Martin's insides, tossing the offal to the side to be used as chum later. Martin's screams went higher in pitch as each of his organs was pulled out, much in the same manner as he had done to countless fish. As of yet, the old fisherman hadn't touched Martin's heart and thus, he was still alive, though in abject pain.

As Martin let out yet another blood-piercing cry that reverberated out over the water, the old man cackled and said, "Well, I'll be, fishy, you almost sounded like a real man there for a second."

Then he went back to work, gutting his catch and preparing it for the grill waiting for him back on shore.

Later, as the old man washed the deck clean, and bits of Martin's now-cooled organs sluiced off the boat and into the water, the waiting fish began dining, knowing in this one particular moment, revenge really was best served cold.

SCHOOL'S IN

ROB ROSEN

The remains drifted in to shore, piece by grisly piece: a finger, then two, bloodied severed limbs, marred flesh—nasty stuff, to be sure. It was enough to make a grown man sick. Well, three grown men, in fact: the three who were unfortunate enough to discover the gruesome remains.

"Shark," the first one said, wiping the upchucked breakfast from off his chin.

"Definitely," agreed the second. "Shark."

The third man wasn't so sure, his head swaying back and forth. "Odd bite wounds for a shark," he couldn't help but notice, mopping the sweat off his brow, the pounding overhead sun sending his pores into overdrive. "Must not have been a very big shark. In fact, I'd say it couldn't have been more than a baby."

"Nah," said the second man. "The babies don't attack. They let their mamas do that for them. Maybe it's a weird kind of shark that's far from its home waters. A pigmy shark or something, brought in by a storm. Lord knows we get enough of them around these parts."

"Or a piranha," said the first man, with a snap of his fingers, the proverbial light bulb, however dim, lighting up above his head.

"Off the coast of Florida?" asked the third man. "How would a piranha make it all the way out here, and in open seas?"

The light bulb, naturally, flickered out after that one.

"Shark," said the first man, yet again. "Definitely a shark. There ain't no other fish around these parts that could've done something like this. Born killers, they are."

Which, of course, was strictly a matter of opinion. After all, killing can be learned. Or so Captain Stucky thought, the man called in by the local authorities shortly after the disembodied pieces washed ashore.

He surveyed the scene, asked questions of the only three witnesses, took the appropriate measurements of the bite wounds, and came up with his conclusion. "Beats the hell out of me, fellas," he said, with a shrug and a tilt of his head.

"What?" they all said, in unison, the first one quickly adding, "But aren't you the expert?"

The captain pushed out his chest, stood an extra few centimeters more erect, and replied, "That's what it says on my business card." Which he then promptly handed out to the three of them.

"Captain Luis Stucky, Shark Expert," the second man read aloud, looking down as he read before turning to his friends. "Yep, he's the expert, all right."

To which the third man added, "Then what did this, Captain? The only man-eaters around here are sharks. No whales, least no Orcas, no octopi, least none big enough to tear a man apart, and no piranhas, which we done already worked out amongst ourselves."

The dim-bulbed one blushed, the red barely making its way through his dark fisherman's tan.

"Good points," Stucky agreed with a nod. "In fact, there have been reports of shark attacks in these waters over the years; numerous ones, for that matter. But the bite marks, so strange." He paused, playing with the whiskers on his chin. "Must be a new species. If so, gentlemen, we're in for a heap of trouble. Big, bloody, trouble." The three words were emphasized with a finger point to each of the men's chests, sending chills down each of their spines.

The trio looked at each other, then over to their ramshackle houses so close to the shore, and then back to the captain. "Then tell us how we can help," offered the first, speaking for all three of them. "After all, that ocean out there is like our very own backyard."

The captain smiled. "Good men," he said. "My own crew was waylaid off the coast of Bermuda—bad tropical storm. It'll take them days to catch up to me here." He grimaced and shook his head from side to side. "And, by the looks of things, we can't afford to wait."

That, of course, was a gross understatement if there ever was one. And so, they set sail the very next morning.

The captain's boat was sleek, long, expensive, equipped with the latest gadgets; enough to locate a school of man-eating sharks.

Though, naturally, they prayed there was but one killer that needed to be found.

Sadly, it seemed, it was just that very one they came across almost immediately. It was 'sadly' because the remnants of another victim were already floating about, the shark nibbling at an exposed thigh, its ubiquitous school of pilot fish downing the fleshy cast-offs, until quickly enough there was nothing left, save for a loan serrated pinky finger bobbing in the water.

The captain raced across the deck, leaping for the spear gun as the shark breached the water, its bloody, jagged teeth glinting in the harsh morning sunlight. Fortune, however, wasn't smiling on them that day; the gun locked, the spear holding in place, the sleek, gray shark speeding away, nearly out of sight.

"Grab the flare gun!" shouted Stucky, his spit and sweat flinging to and fro. "If we can't capture it, we'll have to kill it!"

One of the men lunged for the flare gun and let it rip, sending the smoking trajectory into the churning ocean. Miraculously, it hit its target, the shark exploding upon impact, its charred flesh dousing the men in a bloody downpour to land in a hundred dull thuds on the deck all around them.

"Yuck," spat the first man.

"Least we got him," said the second.

"A tad too late," moaned the third, retrieving the finger from the water below. "And it's not the same victim from yesterday. Look." He held the brown lone digit up for all of them to see. "This was from a black person; the other one was definitely white. That makes two poor souls in two days."

They all stood in place, dripping in shark carcass, their heads bowed in silent prayer. And then, "But we did get him," repeated the second man as he pointed to what was left, the finger, ironically, pointing right on back.

"Yep," the captain agreed. "That we did. Strange, though that the shark we shot was an oceanic whitetip."

"Not a man-eater?" asked the third man, with an obvious frown.

The captain couldn't help but smile, despite the dire situation at hand. "Oh no, they're killers, all right; eaten their fair share of sinking ship survivors over the centuries, too. Only, they're not often found this close to shore. Plus, the bite marks on the first victim, not to mention this finger we have here, doesn't seem to match." The finger in question was gladly handed over. The captain turned it around and around, staring intently at the wound, and, with a shrug, said, "But we caught the bloody beast red, er, handed, as it were. Maybe that's some sort of mutant shark we hit: big body, small, sharp teeth. Or just some genus I've yet to encounter, however unlikely that may be."

"In any case," said the first man, breathing normally for the first time since the encounter began, "it's dead, and there won't be any more victims."

"Amen," agreed the third man."

"Amen," echoed the other two.

"Let's get back to shore, the first rounds on me," Stucky said as he swung the ship around and headed back to shore.

Unfortunately, they were a tad too quick in counting their blessings. There was another chicken soon to hatch, so to speak.

The third victim washed ashore a mere day later. It was a fresh kill, the flesh ripped from the body within the hour, or so it appeared to the captain, who once again had been called while the Coast Guard now slashed through the waters, searching for yet another rampaging murderer.

"I don't get it," Stucky said as his ragtag crew of three once more boarded his ship, all looking fairly miserable.

"Yeah," said one of the men. "We killed the shark yesterday."

"No," Stucky said. "I mean, the odds of two killer sharks being found in these waters is astronomically high. Plus, I saw the remains from today's victim. Different prey, same bite marks. If there is a new species, they must hunt alone, because we only saw the one whitetip yesterday." He started the engine and sped off, adding between gritted teeth, "Not good, gentlemen, not good at all."

The boat zipped out to sea, leaving a shimmering spray of white in its wake. It didn't take them long to find another shark, another victim, another scene of death and disarray. The whitetip was ripping apart flesh from bone, its pod of pilot fish racing about, plucking off the gruesome remnants, with the sea churning all around them, red and blue mixing in a deep, dark black.

The three men heaved their lunches overboard as the captain circled closer. This time, the spear gun worked properly, shooting its metal-tipped arsenal into the shark, sending the predator thrashing, the ensuing waves rocking the boat. Unfortunately, though hit squarely behind its eyes, the shark wrenched away at the last second and snapped the tether in two before swimming deep beneath the surface.

"Damn!" the captain howled, fists punching the air above his head.

"It could happen to anyone," offered one of the men with a pat to the captain's back. "Cheaply made wire, and all."

"No," Stucky grumbled, turning away from the water as he scratched his mop of hair. "I meant, damn, this doesn't make a lick of sense. Two killers, perhaps three, in just as many days? It's unprecedented. Something must be making them mad. Either that or this new species of ours just naturally devours everything and anything that gets in their way."

The three men gulped, clearly ready to be finished with their volunteer duty.

"So now what do we do?" one of them dared to ask.

"Now?" the captain replied, duly prepared for the only option that remained. "Now we get in there with them."

"Huh?" said the first man, with a hardy gulp and a squint of his eyes.

"Um, yeah, huh?" echoed the third with the same exact gulp, same exact squint.

Not wanting to be left out, the second man tried, "Um, are you friggin' nuts?"

"No," Stucky said. "We have to get in the water—in a shark cage. We need to observe their behavior, see if this is an instinctual thing. Because if it is, we have to warn the entire eastern seaboard that these waters, I fear, won't be safe for anyone."

"Then, um, just to be clear here, why would it be safe for, uh, us. In there, I mean," asked the first man, a trembling finger pointing to the swirling ocean.

The captain grinned. "Fear not, good man. You've seen these sharks. Big suckers, they are. The size of a fully grown lion, and just as lethal. Still, the cage is made of steel, the bars only a couple of inches apart. The best these sharks can do is go for a bite and get a mouthful of metal. Trust me; we'll be safe and sound."

"Sound being the least optimal word," mumbled the third man.

"What's that?" the captain asked.

"Oh, nothing, I just said that I'm up for it, if my friends are."

The friends in question looked at their buddy like he recently escaped from a mental ward, but nodded just the same. After all, if he wasn't afraid, then neither were they.

Of course, such wasn't the case, not by a long shot. Not even, it appeared, for the captain. The boat was taken further out to sea, where, it was assumed, the whitetip could be found in greater numbers.

"To better our odds," Stucky informed the men.

"Oh, goody," moaned one of the men, staring out to sea as the distant shore disappeared from sight. "Just what we needed, a whole group of man-eating sharks for a group of stupid shark-hunting men."

The captain, however, didn't hear the gripe; he just powered further and further out, the water now turning a murky, choppy midnight blue.

When he figured they were out far enough, he cut the engines and dug out four sets of scuba gear, which the men reluctantly donned, save for the one who would monitor the equipment and lower and raise the cage. He, of course, breathed a heavy sigh of relief.

The cage was lowered, quickly disappearing beneath the surface. The men inhaled the tank air and jumped in after it, diving below as they entered the metal confines, quickly locking the cage door behind them, their eyes scanning in all directions. A light flicked on, casting the surrounding waters in a dismal, dim, murky glow.

The captain turned on his communication device, as did the others.

THE SMARTEST IDIOT ON THE LAKE

JESSY MARIE ROBERTS

Callie leaned back in the water, raised her legs in the air, and wiggled her pink toes.

"As you can see, Greg, I'm not a mermaid."

Greg scowled and leaned over the edge of the small fishing boat, a toothpick dangling from the corner of his mouth. His lips were chapped, his face sunburned, and she could hear his stomach rumbling from where she treaded water in the middle of the lake. "I know what I know, Callie Jane. And I know you're a mermaid."

She rolled her blue eyes. "You're an idiot. Have you ever heard of a mermaid living in a lake? I mean, aren't they a saltwater kind of species?"

Greg flushed, color seeping up from beneath his sweat-soaked tank top. "You're trying to trick me, mermaid. You're not as smart as you think you are."

Callie laughed and dunked her head under the water, then surfaced quickly, her long red hair wet and sparkling in the mid-afternoon sun. "Maybe not, but you're as dumb as I think you are. I'm getting back on the boat, Greg. This experiment in stupidity has to end sometime, and I'm getting tired. I've been in the lake for over an hour now."

With expert precision, Callie sluiced her arms through the water and kicked behind her, crossing the distance to the boat with ease. Her hands reached up to grasp the edge of the boat and were promptly smacked with the round edge of a fishing net. She cursed under her breath and slid back into the lake. "Did you just hit me with a fishing net? Feel good about yourself when you hit girls?" she asked as she swam away from the boat.

"You ain't a girl, Callie Jane. *You're a mermaid.* And I don't feel bad about slapping around a fish. You'd better hurry up and do like I told you and show me your fins, or I'm gonna leave you out here," he threatened with a leer.

Callie shook her head in disgust. "Let's talk about your logic here, Greg. If I really was a mermaid—you know, could transform into a finned creature of the sea and breathe under water—why would I care if you were to leave me out here in the middle of the lake? Wouldn't I just swim to shore and exact a supernatural sort of revenge? Drown you in the bathtub or by some other equally ridiculous method of murder?"

Greg shuddered despite the heat. "You're a cold fish, Callie Jane. Are you telling me that mermaids have special powers? I mean, other than all the being half fish stuff?"

"Yes, moron, that's exactly what I'm saying," she mocked, her voice oozing sarcasm. "Thinking back on what I just told you, I can't believe I let it slip about all of my awesome mermaid powers. Aquaman is going to be pretty pissed off that I let the cat out of the bag. And King Triton? He'll never forgive me. I'll be scrubbing the shells on his throne for a year!"

"You're a mean mermaid, Callie Jane. Always acting like you're better than everybody else. But you're just a cold-blooded fish-girl, and I know the truth about you."

Callie twisted her body in the water until she was lying on her back, floating on top of the rippling surface of the lake. She weighed her options: she could either approach the boat again and hurl herself over the railing while Greg pelted her with the fish net still clutched in his meaty grip, or she could stay in the lake indefinitely. She glanced over her shoulder at the sun starting to slide down the horizon. There were still a couple of hours of daylight left, but she intended to be on dry ground long before dark.

"That's it, Greg," she threatened, swimming full speed toward the boat a second time. She swam around the boat and yanked herself out of the water while Greg tried to shift his weight to get to her without overturning the vessel.

She was just inside the boat when she felt the fishing net wrap around her head, the thin, nylon thread digging into her face.

"Get that thing off me!" she screamed.

"Back in the water, fish!" he shouted as he jerked her head backward. Scrambling for footing, she tripped and fell back over the edge of the boat with a splash, the net still wrapped around her skull.

Frustrated, she gripped the net by the handle and freed herself. With a grunt, she turned away from the boat and threw the net as far as she could, smirking as it landed twenty feet from the boat.

Greg stomped his foot against the wooden floorboard of the fishing boat and grimaced. "That's my dad's favorite fishing net, Callie Jane."

"Not my problem, you ass," Callie retorted from her position in the water. "Maybe you shouldn't assault people with your dad's favorite fishing equipment."

He barked out a laugh. "I don't assault people. You're not human. You don't count!"

"Are we really going to go through this again? You said I would grow fins if you threw me in the lake water. I still have legs and feet, which you can clearly see. I'm obviously human, and you're obviously delusional. Just take me back to shore and I won't tell anyone that you tried to drown me."

"Maybe you can control changing into your true form, Callie Jane. Did you ever think about that?"

"*Did I ever think about that?* This isn't even a conversation! Listen, I'll make you a trade. Your dad's fishing net is still floating on the water. If I swim over and get it, I'll give it to you after you pull me onto the boat and take me to shore. Do we have a deal?"

Greg squinted his eyes in concentration, his forehead crinkling with thought. "Show me your legs again," he commanded, leaning over the edge of the boat to get a better look.

With a sigh, Callie did as requested and raised her legs out of the water. "There. Satisfied?"

He shrugged. "I guess so. Hurry up and get the net before it sinks."

Smiling, Callie dove beneath the surface of the water and swam out to grab the net. Upon obtaining her bargaining chip, she returned to the boat. When she reached it, she held one hand out of the water and gripped the net with the other.

"Pull me up," she demanded.

Greg's eyes darted from her outstretched hand to the fishing net. "Give it to me first."

"No. A deal's a deal. I'll give you the damn net when we get to shore."

He shook his head. "No way. I don't trust the word of no mer..."

Callie pulled her hand back and swam away from the boat. "Were you going to say 'mermaid?'"

He looked away.

"Greg? Do you still think I'm a mermaid?"

He clenched his fists. "I know what I know, Callie Jane! Just give me my damn net and I'll take you back to land. I promise."

She saw the cruel glint in his light brown eyes, the crinkle of a malicious smile curling up the corner of one lip in a mean-spirited sneer. She slowly swam toward the boat and lifted out the net, keeping a firm grip on the pole.

As soon as his fingers curled around the outer rim of the net, Callie jerked it toward her, offsetting Greg's balance. Within a second, he toppled out of the boat and belly flopped into the lake. His head shot out of the water, spitting liquid out of his mouth, anger distorting his plain features into an ugly visage.

"You're gonna pay for that," he threatened. He reached out and grabbed Callie's red hair, twisting it in his palm until he had a firm grip. With his face inches from hers, he whispered, "Want to call me an idiot now?"

Around their legs and feet, Callie felt scaly bodies swim by. Greg shrieked and let go of her hair, looking into the water in fear. "What was that?" he squealed.

"Those are called fish, *idiot*," she retorted. She refused to be frightened by the overgrown oaf.

His eyes met hers and narrowed into rage-infused slits. "I warned you about calling me names, Callie Jane. I guess I'm going to prove, once and for all, that you're a mermaid."

"And how are you going to do that?" she asked, though she half-feared she already knew the answer.

He smiled, the expression never quite reaching his simple eyes. "I'm going to drown you." He reached out with both hands, and submerged her head beneath the water. She struggled for a couple of minutes, scratching at his wrists and arms, then went limp.

Greg pulled her out of the water, staring at the body. "Holy shit! Callie! Callie Jane, are you okay?" he cried, incredulous. "Oh my God, oh my God," he whimpered, holding her against his chest.

He pressed the palm of his hand against her stomach and pushed, trying to expel some of the water from her lungs. Nothing happened. He pressed against her chest, hoping that would work.

"I'm so sorry, Callie Jane," he cried as he lowered his lips to her and breathed into her mouth.

Her eyes shot open. "Are you trying to kiss me after you tried to kill me?"

"That there is called CPR, Miss Smarty Pants. And you should be grateful that I saved your life."

Callie laughed. "You tried to *kill* me, jackass. I don't think attempting to save my life after you tried to end it deserves a thank you card. Besides, I wasn't in any danger."

He frowned. "What're you talking about?"

Then he gasped and looked down into the water, cloudy with dozens of fish encircling their legs, hips and torsos. "Where did all these fish come from?"

"They're here to help me," she answered, a slow grin stretching across her pretty face.

"Help you? Why would...oh, shit," he exclaimed. "You *are* a mermaid, aren't you?"

Callie nodded. "I'm afraid so, Greg. And now that you know my secret..." she let her words trail off. Even with only a half-finished statement, her meaning was implicit.

"You're going to kill me, aren't you? You won't get away with this. I told everyone I know that I was taking Callie Jane Fitzgibbons fishing today out on the lake. They'll figure it out."

"That I killed you to cover up the fact that I'm a friggin' mermaid? Give me a break, Greg! Nobody except a blithering idiot like you, would ever come to the conclusion that I'm a mermaid. They'll just think you fell overboard and drowned in the lake. By the time they find your body, my cousins will have picked your bones clean, leaving nothing but a skeleton for your mama to cry over at your funeral. But don't worry, I'll be sure to give your dad back his beloved fishing net."

Fat tears rained down Greg's cheeks to splash in the water. "I knew you fish couldn't be trusted. I just knew it!"

"One thing, Greg. How did you figure it out? I've been living on the land for years with my adopted family, and nobody has ever guessed my secret."

"I saw you. In the bathtub. I saw the fins."

"How could you? Wait a second...were you in the tree outside my bathroom window? Jesus, Greg, you're a moron *and* you're a pervert! It's a really good thing I'm doing here today, saving humanity from your depravity. Good riddance!"

She grabbed his shoulders and applied pressure, pushing him beneath the water. Hundreds of fish circled them, their movement causing the water to swirl into a small whirlpool, helping to suck him into the depths of the lake.

He tilted back his head, his lips sucking in breath as the water lapped around his cheeks. "Why didn't you change when I tossed you in the water? Why didn't you grow fins?" he gasped, gurgling and spitting water as it invaded his mouth.

"Because I can control my shifting...at least during the day. If I get wet at night, my legs become fins. Now, let's get this over with quickly. I need to be out of the water and on dry land before nightfall."

Callie dipped below the water, gripped Greg by the ankles, and swam toward the bottom of the lake. A shimmering light sparkled as her legs stretched into a single, scaly purple fin. Her fish brethren continued their death spiral, spinning Greg to his watery demise.

Greg was dead before Callie laid him against the rocky bottom.

The rhythmic thrusts of her fin had her head above the water within minutes, leaving Greg with the hungry fish. She changed back to human form as she hauled her exhausted body into the boat. She lay on her back, gasping for breath. Changing was tiring.

As she recovered, she practiced her story to the police and rescue units. They would believe her. They weren't dumb enough to believe she was a mermaid.

FISH FUCKER

ANTHONY GIANGREGORIO

In the small village of Squire's Junction, lived a man with a peculiar fetish.

He loved to fuck fish.

Johnson Mahoney knew it was wrong, that it was unnatural, but he couldn't help himself. There was just something about a fish. From the sleek scales, the slickness, the lipless mouth devoid of teeth, that got him hard every time.

The palms of his hands were cut up from grasping the scales as the fish would try to escape him, but he accepted it as part of the fun.

Others in town knew of his predilection to fish and they would comment to one another as he passed them on the street.

"There he goes, the damn fishfucker," they would say.

"He's sick, is what he is," others would say. "What kind of a man fucks a fish?"

"Oh, I don't know," one man said to another one time at the local pub. "Maybe it feels good, you know, all slick and wet."

The man was looked at with astonishment by the other men in the pub and he quickly changed his tone. "I was only joking, fellas. Ha, got you, you thought I was serious."

A few more looks were tossed the man's way but then something of interest was brought up and the man's outburst was forgotten. Johnson didn't care what any of them said. He loved fish and that's all that mattered.

Every Sunday morning he would go out to the shore at the edge of town and he would row out to sea more than half a mile. There he would drop his fishing line and patiently wait for a fish to take the bait on his hook. As he waited, he rubbed himself gently, his mind already on the pleasure to come, wondering what sort of fish would be his lover this day.

A Grouper would be nice as the mouth was nice and tight, or perhaps an eel. A Trigger fish would be exciting or better yet, if he was really lucky, he might catch a Sweetlips. He had almost tried a

Bluefish once, attracted to the small scales and the bluish green coloring, but the teeth had been too scary and he had let the fish go, not wanting to take a chance he would hurt himself.

Still, the Bluefish had been so sexy. The one he caught had weighed a little more than three pounds, with a sexy mouth and dainty scales. And the way it had looked at him, as if it had been begging him to do it. But in the end, the teeth were too risky and he had let it go free.

He sighed, thinking of the last time he was out here. Last week he had caught a flounder. The Fluke had been almost two pounds and its small, tight mouth had done the job well. He wasn't that big himself, a little over five inches, and he wasn't that thick, which made fish fucking all the more easy for him.

He closed his eyes and remembered the sensation as he held onto the fish and it sucked on him, filling with an ecstasy he had never been able to find in a normal woman.

He sometimes wondered why he was attracted to fish, and why he could only seek pleasure in his aquatic brethren, but he would usually not think on it too hard.

He was who he was and had learned if he wanted to live with himself, it was easier just to accept it.

Besides, he wasn't hurting any of them. After he had his way with them, he would set them free, though a few had their mouths stretched a little bit more. But if he hurt them he never gave it much thought, always thinking of himself.

Sometimes he wondered if another fisherman had caught one of the fish he fucked. Did they take it home, clean it and fry it up, eating his love juice as they dined on the meat?

He didn't know how he felt about that and tried not to give it much thought.

The line began to move and he sat up, excited he had his first bite of the day. His pants were tighter now in expectation of what would soon be happening. Breathing hard and fast, he began to reel the line in. At first it was easy, but soon the line grew taut. He found himself struggling to stay in the boat and the fish tugged and pulled harder.

The sun beat down on his head, causing him to sweat profusely, and he battled the fish for all he was worth. He would let the line play out, then take it in, only to do the same again and again. Slowly, ever so slowly, he drew the line in.

He still didn't know what fish he'd caught but his imagination was running rampant with imagery. He even imagined a mermaid and wondered how that would be. But he quickly pushed the thought down. First they weren't real and second, if a woman was attached to the fish body in any way, it wouldn't be the same. It had to be all fish, that's what made him feel whole...like a man.

The battle continued for hours and though he tried to reel it in, the fish more often than not got the better of him. There were times when he had to let loose the reel, the line playing out once more.

But he never gave up, for this would be the fuck of his life. He didn't know what he'd caught, but a fish this size would be incredible. Hell, maybe he could screw it from behind, like a person. That was something he had never done as the fish were never that big. With the idea of an entirely new position in his future, he redoubled his efforts to pull in his catch.

The hours crawled by with still no luck and he began to grow tired. Johnson waited for a chance when the fish wasn't fighting him and he reached down for the canteen of water he had taken with him. Slurping it down, he let some overflow his mouth and wet his chest.

Closing his eyes, he sucked in a breath of cool sea air. The fish was a fighter, there was no doubt about it, and though he was tired, he knew it would be worth it when he finally had the fish in the boat.

The tug of war continued, with neither winning until, an hour later, he finally had the upper hand. He assumed the fish was tiring and took the advantage, quickly reeling the line in. And then, finally, Johnson peered over the side of the boat to see a glorious catch, one that would have him remembering the experience for years to come. This would be his greatest exploit, the one that would have him laying in bed and touching himself, imagining the large form beneath him. Though it was so big he didn't think he could get it into the boat.

It was as he was leaning over the side, his mind lost in fascination, that his catch jerked back, catching him totally off guard.

Before he knew what was happening, he was falling into the water, the air in his lungs replaced by the frigid liquid that caused him to cough and choke.

Spinning around under water, he swam back to the surface. Reaching up, he grabbed the edge of the boat and hung on, spitting sea water out of his mouth.

He needed to catch his breath, and when he did, he would pull himself back into the boat.

His catch was forgotten now as he thought only for his life. He was alone in the ocean, no one around for miles, and if he died, no one would know it until they found his derelict boat when it drifted back to shore.

It was as he was gathering the strength to climb into the boat that he realized there was something behind him.

Turning around, he saw his catch floating there, the same one that had been on his line. His heart stopped in his chest as he stared at the massive teeth, the beady eyes, and he knew he was about to die. But his catch didn't attack, instead it looked at him, the eyes seeming to say, "Hi, what brings you out here on a Sunday morning? Are you single?"

For some reason it hadn't left and it wasn't attacking, and though he thanked his savior for this, he still wondered why it was still here...with him.

And then he found out why.

Murray was a great white shark.

Though the lower forms of sea life feared him as a predator, around others of his kind he was teased and sometimes shunned.

The other sharks would talk about him behind his back, saying things like, "There goes that human fucker."

"There's the shark that likes two legs, the sick mammal."

Murray tried to ignore their comments but still it hurt.

He didn't know why he was different. He didn't know why he liked to fuck humans. All he knew was their pink skin and warm orifices turned him on like no other shark ever could.

Murray was twenty years old and if he played his cards right, he would have another ten years of life. He was almost fifteen feet long and weighed more than three thousand pounds. He was a handsome specimen for a shark and he was proud of it.

He would swim in shallow water and close to shore, waiting for some ignorant fisherman to drop his lines, then he would take the bait, only instead of being pulled into the boat, he would pull the fisherman into the water. From there he would screw the human till he was exhausted.

Usually the human would survive and swim away, but there had been a few times when they had died.

He felt bad when that happened, but not bad enough to stop. After all, they had been trying to catch him to eat him.

So when he saw the line of yet another fisherman in the water about a half mile from shore, both his penises began to twitch in expectation of what was to come next.

He had taken the bait and the fisherman had tried to pull him in, but Murray had stayed well below the waterline and the man had no idea what he had caught. The tug of war went on for hours as Murray slowly chipped away at the strength of the fisherman.

Then, when the time was right, he showed himself, pulling on the line at just the right time and toppling the man into the water.

As the man struggled to climb back into the boat, Murray went into action.

He rolled against the man, causing the man's pants to be pulled off, then he spun around, pulled the man deeper into the water, and mounted him.

Like many shark breeds, Murray had dual penises, both side by side, similar to how two fingers looked pressed together. Called claspers, these two members would unite inside the mate during copulation, forming a channel for sperm.

As the fisherman slid beneath the waves, Murray went to work, sliding both members inside the man, using his bulk to keep him in place.

If a shark could smile, Murray would have done so.

Johnson's eyes went wide as he slid beneath the waves and found himself penetrated by a great white shark. He opened his mouth to scream but nothing came out but gurgles.

His head filled with spots of light as the pressure grew inside him. He felt like his insides were about to explode and he realized he was getting a taste of what it must have been like for the fish he'd molested over the years.

His lungs filled with water and he knew he was going to drown, when as fast as it began, the pressure on his rear was released and the shark let him go. As he turned his head, in the wan light under the surface, he watched the rear fin swinging back and forth as the shark swam away.

With his oxygen fading fast, he made a last ditch effort to swim to the surface. It was as everything was going black that his head broke the surface, and as he coughed and spit sea water, he sucked in the best tasting air of his life.

He kicked off his pants that were around his ankles and swam back to his boat, which was a hundred feet away. Apparently, while he was underwater, the current had taken him.

As he reached the boat, he had to rest before climbing inside. But then he thought he saw a shadow beneath him, and he suddenly had the energy to climb over the side and tumble into the boat.

Lying on the deck with no pants, his ass pointed up at the sky and breathing heavily, he felt like he would never walk right again. He was sore at the waist level, and when he rolled over, he moaned loudly.

Though hard to believe it, he knew he had been raped by a shark!

The question was; what to do about it?

He couldn't tell anyone. No one would believe him, and even if they listened, after what they knew of him they would only say it was a just dessert for the sick things he did with fish.

Shaking terribly, he went back to shore, never wanting to go to the sea again.

He already planned on selling his boat to the first person who wanted it and he knew the trauma he'd suffered would haunt him for the rest of his life.

Just remembering what it felt like to be under the water, a massive shark behind him as it pumped in and out, in and out. Ugh, he felt like he was going to be sick.

When he arrived at the dock, he tied up his boat and went home, taking the next three days to recuperate. He was lucky and though in pain, by day three he was doing fine and his backside was okay. Evidently, the shark had been gentler than he had ever been with all the fish he'd taken as lovers over the years.

Just thinking of fish made him cringe and he knew he was finished fucking them forever.

But then, how to satisfy his sexual urges?

Going outside to get some air, he walked into town, ignoring the jibes and comments of the townspeople. He watched the women as they walked past him, but try as hard as he might, they still didn't turn him on.

Giving up after a few hours, he walked back home, taking the scenic route through the countryside.

It was as he passed a herd of sheep that he paused and admired the animals.

He watched them graze and stand around, doing nothing of any particular interest. He was about to leave when he spotted a stunning female at the far end of the herd, with a glowing white pelt and deep eyes that seemed to call to him.

"Well, hello there, beautiful," he said with a smile.

MILLIE'S EYES

KELLY M. HUDSON

It's funny how a simple thing like a slap can snap you out of an unreal moment and back to reality in a way no other thing could. When the fish-man struck my wife, Millie, so hard that two teeth flew from her mouth, and the thunder crack of the blow echoed around the wood-paneled walls of our basement like a pipe bomb, it was precisely like that for me.

Yes, I said 'fish man'.

I'll get to that.

At the moment, the fish-man gurgled and grabbed Millie by her throat, wrapping one of its webbed hands around her larynx and squeezing. I leapt at him, knowing full-well I wouldn't be able to do much. No one had, not when they first arrived and not even later, when we organized and fought back. These creatures were resistant to just about any bullets, drugs or gas, and our fists were useless. Still, it was my wife being choked and I had no choice but to attack the unstoppable.

It was horrid, the way the creature slouched and the briny stench dripped from its scales. It stunk of the Gulf it was birthed from, a combination of oil and dispersant chemicals, as well as sea salt and fish. It also had another, underlying smell, one of decay and rot. You could smell them up to twenty yards away, and even over time and frequent exposure, it was hard to keep from vomiting in their presence.

The creature was barely five feet tall but was solid muscle. It had the shape of a man with the skin of a fish. Gills slashed its neck and its large hands and feet ended in gnarled, webbed fingers. They had talons the length and width of a pencil for fingernails. The scales were dark green, but when the light hit them just right, they gave off a chromatic glow, so bright at times it could blind you. Its face was terrifying to look upon because of its round eyes, their size exaggerated because there were no eyelids. They were the color of the sea, and they roved around like those of a madman, independent of one another. Glands surrounding their eyes secreted a clear liquid to keep their eyes wet with moisture.

Even then, in that horrible moment when the creature was threatening to kill my wife, it looked as if it were crying, weeping most terribly over its actions. But those tears were a lie and a mockery. There wasn't one shred of morality or mercy in the fish-men. They were monsters spat out of the bowels of Hell itself.

Millie and I had met in college and it was one of those love at first sight kind of moments. We were at a fraternity mixer when her beautiful brown eyes batted in my direction and I felt the pull and swoon of their fantastic depths.

We fell in love and married right out of college and moved down to Mississippi shortly after Hurricane Katrina. We were young and idealistic, as college men and women often are. We wanted to make a change, an impact on the world around us. And Millie, with her marine biology degree, and me, with my pre-law background, thought we could do some good things. The devastation we witnessed, however, was nearly enough to cripple our idealism and turn us to cynics. We moved in as close to the Gulf of Mexico as we could and assimilated with the natives. They accepted us, even though we were Yankees; at that time, those people were so desperate for help they were willing to look past their natural distrust of strangers and invite us in.

What was supposed to be a year of volunteer work turned into two. And the two turned into three. And soon, an oil rig blew and the next thing we knew, we were knee-deep in another environmental disaster.

Oil was everywhere. Fish and birds were washing ashore, drenched. Not only was the oil poisoning everything, but the chemicals they used to try to disperse it may have been worse. I can't say what caused the birth of the fish-men, other than a few whispered rumors I heard, of fishermen caught out after the explosion, men who never came home, their bodies caught up in whatever was happening out there; their dead bodies, floating, sinking, mixing with the oil, chemicals and dead fish.

Yes, I know how preposterous it sounds. But you weren't the one standing in your basement, watching a fish-man choke the life from your wife. Explanations meant nothing at that point, only action.

I flew through the air, lowering my shoulder like I'd been taught in Pee-Wee football as a kid, and crashed into the creature with all my weight. I might as well have run headlong into a parked car. I bounced off it, my neck snapping violently to the right and my shoulder popping out of joint with a loud *pop*. I hit the floor and rolled until I smashed against a wall, the whole room spinning. I couldn't feel anything except the burning pain in my shoulder, and the scorching abrasions lacerating my arm where I rubbed against the monster. Its scales were like sharpened knives and sliced on touch.

The fish-man turned to look at me, tears flowing from its un-blinking eyes. They came together and held me, staring hard. It was one of the most unnerving things I'd ever experienced. There was nothing behind those eyes but a blank, cold glare of indiffer-ence.

I blinked through my haze and tears, the world slowing its spin, in time to see the fish-man's mouth open and a long, barbed tongue flick from between its fat lips.

Millie, still held firm by the creature, nevertheless whimpered between her clinched teeth as the fish-man ripped her shirt from her chest, exposing her pale, naked breasts to the cool air. The tongue slathered across her breasts, leaving behind a slimy trail of phlegm and tiny black bits. It licked her right nipple and her body cringed, going rigid and finally limp, as she passed out.

I thanked God for that small mercy. For what was to follow was something no human should ever have to go through.

The fish-man laid her down and ripped her pants off, its talons digging deep into the flesh of her thighs and tearing out long, red scratches of skin. I tried to sit up, tried to think of something I could do, but every time I attempted to move, indescribable pain would rifle through my body. I gasped, begging for breath, the agony was so intense.

Its tongue licked at Millie's nipples for a few moments before the creature positioned its head between her legs. Its gnarled hands pushed them open, revealing her womanhood. And then, without a moment's hesitation, the barbed tongue drilled inside of her, entering like a rattlesnake seeking warmth, worming deep into her womb.

Millie's eyes, those beautiful eyes, flew open for a moment, and she screamed, her throat so bruised and swollen that the shriek came out as a strangled whine. She passed out again.

The fish-man stayed where he was, his body shaking now, as if it were reaching some type of orgasm. It shuddered all over, the scales buzzing in the air like a swarm of bees. It tensed and collapsed, lying on the floor, wheezing.

I found enough strength to sit up. I wept furiously, crying for my lovely wife and her violation, for my own pain, and for the town, because I instinctively knew this same scene was playing out all over.

The fish-man roused from its stupor and its tongue slithered out of my wife, covered in blood and tiny clots of meat. It clambered to its feet and staggered, grabbing my bad shoulder and wrenching me into the air. I screamed from the pain as its taloned fingers pawed me, tearing off my shirt and pants. The creature slapped my face and I fell to the floor, the impact popping my shoulder back into the joint.

It settled between my legs and pushed them apart. I was too weak and stunned to resist. I felt its barbed tongue slather over my testicles, leaving behind a sticky trail of mucous. I wanted to vomit. I wanted to kick. I wanted to run! Sensing my panic, the fish-man punched my stomach and all my resistance left me as I slumped over.

That's when I felt the barbed tongue tickle the tip of my penis.

It whirred and I thought, *Oh, my God*, and then it burrowed into me, sliding up my urethra, the tongue burning a path through flesh and blood. I could take no more and passed out.

The pain brought me back.

The creature was retracting its tongue and this hurt more than the insertion. I could feel it, stripping clean the tubes running from my testicles to my penis. A white-hot pain stabbed through me, the agony indescribable. I screamed and screamed but it did no good; the pain would not go away and the fish-man was undaunted.

It pulled out with a plop, splattering semen, blood and bits of my insides on the floor between my legs. The fish-man stood, slightly hunched, and huffed for breath. It was in the same condition as it was after it had finished with Millie, its scales dull and its eyes not quite as intense. It stared at me for another moment, then slunk towards the stairs. The creature left behind a slimy trail of sea water and oil as it climbed the stairs, slow and sure. It disappeared through the open doorway and I heard it walk across the floor above me, the boards creaking. It paused for a moment and then it crashed onto the floor, landing so hard it shook the walls of the basement.

I sat in a pool of my own fluids, my groin throbbing from my rape, tears streaming down my face. I crawled over to Millie and held her unconscious form, cursing the day we came to this godforsaken place.

Later that day, I managed to get the two of us upstairs and to the medicine cabinet. We treated each other to dress our superficial wounds. Neither of us said a word, crying occasionally as the alcohol burned and the peroxide bubbled, and when we finished, we crept to the kitchen, our eyes hollow and empty.

The creature lay on the floor, dead. A pungent stench hung in the air as it leaked blood and oil from between its scales. The floor was awash with its detritus.

Millie fainted. I carried her to the couch in the living room before returning and wrapping the monster in trash bags. It was too heavy to move on my own, so I picked up the phone to call my neighbor, Carl, to ask for his help.

He didn't answer.

I called for an ambulance. Unfortunately, no one answered there, either.

I tried the sheriff and let the phone ring for twenty minutes before finally giving up.

My stomach sank. Deep in my heart, I knew what had happened. I knew now the reason no one had come to help us, despite our screams. I knew, as soon as I hung up the phone, that Millie and I weren't alone on that cold, cold day.

The fish-men had come for the entire town.

The following two weeks were a blur. We both eventually made it to a doctor and found out he wasn't in much better shape than we were. His hands trembled as he examined me, feeling my testicles and my prostate before applying an antibiotic ointment to my penis. His eyes never met mine.

"You're fine," he said. He smelled of cigarettes and whiskey.

"Thank you," I replied, sliding back into my pants.

"I'll give you a prescription for that ointment," he said. He popped a peppermint into his mouth. He was a nice man, in his late fifties, with bright white hair and a slight build. He had the presence of an old country doctor, but one who'd been through a terrible lot in life.

"What about everyone else?" I asked.

He sighed and shook his head slowly, his lips sucking on the mint.

"It's the same. What happened to you happened to..." he trailed off. His voice broke and his shoulders shook for a moment before he cleared his throat and regained his bearings.

"It happened to everyone," he continued. "And everyone, including the women, show no ill effects—besides the obvious, of course."

"I see," I said. I didn't know what else to say.

"Some people have infections, but that's from the physical nature of the assault. There are no long-term effects that I can determine," he said. His teeth crunched the mint, smashing it into tiny pieces.

"It's almost as if these creatures had one last act to perform before they died," he mused. "I think it was some kind of instinctual revenge. They wanted to punish us for what humanity has done to the oceans."

I nodded. I didn't really know what else to add to that.

"Of course, that's the religious man in me speaking," he said. "Not the man of science."

If only he'd been right. If only their assault had been just that, revenge for what had happened to the Gulf. But we learned soon after we weren't that lucky. Our rape, the violation of over one hundred people in that small, coastal town, was just the beginning.

Two weeks later, the first of the symptoms revealed themselves.

We kept it quiet, all of us. It was the town shame. Nearly every resident had been raped by one of the creature and there was no need for the outside world to know about it. We didn't need to worry much because the camera crews moved on to another story once they tired of oily fish and birds.

The media...

They have the attention span of three-year-olds.

The TV people went away and the town went back to how it was before the spill, when it was small and insular. People kept to themselves. None of us could look one another in the eye, knowing the shame we all felt. It made for unpleasant visits to the grocery store. Millie and I had some money saved, so we stayed in most days and nights, keeping to ourselves.

Eventually, the grant money we'd earned to study the effects of the oil spill on the environment would run out and we'd have some decisions to make. But that was for another time.

Millie and I drifted apart. I found it hard to speak to her, knowing what I'd seen and felt, and she returned that same neglect for similar reasons. We talked about little things, like our bills and what was on TV, but when it came to expressing our feelings, we buttoned-up. I hated this, I resented that our love for each other had been so profaned that there was nothing we could do. I hoped over time this would fade, and we would draw to each other like we always had.

The symptoms showed shortly afterwards.

It started as a small rash, just under the right side of Millie's jaw, a red patch that itched like the dickens and flared like fireworks on the Fourth of July. She scratched at it one day and I noticed but didn't think much of it. The next day, it spread down to her chest.

"Let me see," I said.

She batted my hand away like it carried the palsy.

"I'm all right," she said. "It's just an allergic reaction to something."

A day later her skin cleared and I thought she must have been right. I didn't know, however, that the rash had simply moved to her groin. I found out later that same week when I caught her itching furiously at the waist of her pants.

"What's wrong?" I asked.

"Nothing," she said. She dismissed me with a wave of her hand. But I knew, deep in the innermost core of my being, something was very, very wrong. I hadn't connected it with our assault yet, but I soon would.

That night, as she slept next to me, I lifted the covers and carefully slid her pajama pants down so I could get a look. The skin was like her neck had been, only worse. Large bumps flared, thick and heavy, less like pimples and more like boils. I ran my finger over one of the inflammations. It was hot to the touch and the skin felt weak, like it was ready to break open. I was gentle, feeling around it. There was something foreign about it, something unnatural.

Millie moaned in her sleep and her fingers found some of the sores and scratched at them. My heart ached for her, the numbness of the past few weeks falling away. I wanted to do anything I could to ease her pain.

Something moved in the bump I was touching.

I jerked my hand back and looked at the rash.

Had I really felt that?

I stared until I fell asleep, but nothing else happened.

The next day, I broke out in a rash of my own. It was on my neck, like Millie's, but it soon moved to my groin. Mine moved much quicker, and by the end of the day, it was already around my penis and running over my testicles. It burned and itched so badly I thought I might go mad. I tried all sorts of creams and ointments, but all they did was slow the itch down for a moment. Before bed, I stood in the bathroom, door closed, and looked at myself in the mirror. I looked like an abomination.

Millie knocked and burst in, worry stitching her face. Her eyes went to my infection.

"You screamed," she said.

"I did?" I wasn't consciously aware of doing so.

Millie pulled her pants down and revealed her rash. Our eyes met and I stared into those lovely pupils of hers, so dark brown and beautiful. We moved as one, embracing each other, and wept.

As the night passed, we confessed all our feelings, returning to the people we were before the oil spill, sharing our secrets, fears and love.

It was to be the last good moment of our lives.

The next day passed and things stayed as they were, not getting better or worse. We talked of seeing the doctor but he didn't answer his phone. Instead, we spent the day holding each other.

When we went to bed that night, I was overcome with a heat in my genitals the likes of which I hadn't felt since I was a teenager. I reached over and tentatively touched her left breast. Millie growled like an animal and rolled onto me. I tore her nightclothes off as she tore mine and within moments we were pressing our naked bodies tightly. The heat built between us as we rubbed our groins together, scratching our itches. We screamed and ground against each other. I could feel the bumps burst and release and our privates were washed in leaking pus.

I got on top and entered her, driving my rock-hard member as deep into her as I could. She screeched and wrapped her legs around my buttocks as we gyrated, overcome with an animal lust. I was out of my mind, driven by primitive instinct and there was nothing rational about our action, nothing logical or thought-out. We were caveman and cavewoman, grunting and humping against the night surrounding us.

My body seized up and I pumped her full of my semen. She pushed against me and I could almost feel her vagina gulp down my fluids. And then, at the last moment, when the final drops dripped from the tip of my manhood, something *moved* inside of her.

A tentacle circled my still-erect member and latched onto it. I screamed and pulled out, feeling the tentacle attach itself to my foreskin, latching on with tiny teeth. As I jerked my hips back, rolling off Millie, she shrieked and tried to come with me, attempting to keep our groins connected.

I grabbed her shoulders and shoved her away, desperate to get free. My knees found her inner thighs and I pushed her back as I yanked away. She shrieked so loud I thought my eardrums would burst. I looked down and my scream joined hers.

Lying on the bed between us was Millie's uterus, torn from inside her, and attached to the end of my penis.

Needless to say, I fainted.

I awoke later to find my wife dead. She had bled out, the sheets now a dark red. I cried, hoping to God she was spared any further pain. One look at her face, however, told me a different truth. It was a mask of terror; her mouth open and distended, the jaw broken and pulled out of joint, her skin pulled so tight and sunken she resembled a skull. And her eyes, those beautiful orbs of hers, popped out like boiled eggs, long streaks of torn blood vessels in the whites and the pupils as wide as the abyss to Hell. Her hair had turned white and the rest of her body was curled like a burnt spider.

I hardly had time to register my shock and grief before my own suffering began. Her uterus was still attached to me, and as I stared at her dead body, I felt it shift and move. I looked down and gasped as it folded itself, full of my semen and her juices, until it was the size of a dinner napkin. The uterus rolled itself up, tightening at every turn until it was the width of a pipe-cleaner and the length of a ruler. That's when it whirred and drilled inside my penis.

It was like when the fish-man stuck its tongue inside me, only much worse. It slid into me and I could feel it, every inch, every millimeter, as it moved deeper and deeper. My body screamed as it traveled the length of my urethra and into my groin, continuing on into my testicles. It curled there, expanding and contracting, filling my balls until they threatened to explode. Stars burst in my eyes and the pain was so intense I can't begin to describe it. But this passed, as the uterus again contracted and kept moving, further inside me, until it reached my prostate. Once it arrived there, it expanded again, drilling tiny holes from the inside out, until it bled through and blew up, covering both the outside and the inside of my prostate.

Something inside of my rectum popped, blinding pain filled me, and darkness engulfed me once more.

It was hours later when I woke again and I couldn't move. The uterus had grown to the size of a baseball inside me, filling my bowels. It hurt so bad all I could do was whimper.

I crawled over next to my dear, dead Millie. I knew I must follow her soon, that there was no way my body could endure what it had without eventually failing. I didn't want to face what was coming, what was going to happen next. I thought of the gun we kept in the hallway closet, a small pistol she made me buy when we first arrived here. I would use it to put a bullet in my brain and end this hellish torment for good.

But I couldn't move. Any slight motion sent agonizing pain shooting up my spine and through my entire body. The best I could do was to snuggle next to my dead wife and pray to God.

The final movement began a few moments later.

I felt the pressure change inside me and the uterus vibrated violently. I gulped down a lungful of air and let out another screech as the vibration shook my body from head to toe. I leaned my head back, choking on my spit, when my uterus-wrapped prostate burst.

Seawater gushed from my exposed buttocks and washed across the floor. It smelled of salt, oil and chemicals. It stunk like the fish-men.

Spasms seized my body, jerking my spine and making me sit up. These spasms spread and forced me to stand, even though I didn't want to. I leaned against the wall next to me and held on for dear life as my hips thrust forward and back, my penis suddenly erect. I humped the air, an obscenity of lust and desperation. I felt the orgasm build inside me, boiling in the remnants of my prostate and then spurting through my testicles, erupting from the end of my penis. It burned, like icy acid, and I clenched my teeth and spat out a hoarse groan.

I ejaculated on the corpse of my wife, gobs of clear fluid splattering her dead body and coating her in thick goblets of goo. Inside each drop wiggled a small tadpole, squirming free of the fluid and crawling over Millie. My grip slipped on the wall as my orgasm faded and I fell down next to her, sinking into darkness yet again.

I wished I never woke up.

When I did, when my eyes broke the crust of dried tears and looked out on the new world, my heart crushed for the final time. A sadness so deep and profound wrapped itself around my heart like a wet, dark blanket that I could barely breathe.

The tadpoles had grown in that short time I was out to the size of grasshoppers. They crawled around, their bodies altering by the moment, growing tiny arms, legs, and tails. Gills formed on their necks, and their eyes—like the fish-men who came to our small town—were open wide and unblinking.

I had birthed the next generation of monsters and I was sure, in my heart, this same thing was happening all across town. By my quick count, there were over a hundred of them produced by mine and Millie's loins alone. How many would there be now, all over town, when this process repeated itself?

Thousands.

They would grow to man-size, I could see that. They would grow strong and powerful and move on to the next town to infect and impregnate those residents, and there would be nothing to stop them.

I sat up and studied my children. As I did so, their eyes, as one, turned to stare at me. It was then I noticed what those eyes looked like—big and brown and as wondrous as the night sky.

They had their mother's eyes.

I eventually managed to get to my knees and crawl from there. I'm bleeding profusely from both my rectum and penis and the flow won't stop. I don't care. I've made my way to the hallway closet and have managed to obtain the loaded pistol inside it.

Now I lay on my couch and compose this report, so if it's ever found and this monstrosity is ever defeated, people can know how it all began and what horrors those of us unlucky enough to be at the beginning of the mutation had to endure.

I pray humanity manages to win the day, but somehow I think we're all doomed. I could see it, as I stared into their tiny eyes—so like Millie's— that these creatures were the next phase of evolution.

Mankind was now officially outdated and past its prime.

I pray I'm wrong. I pray this message finds a people who have already won the final victory and humanity is free from the terrors of the fish-men.

In any case, it's all out of my hands now. Now I'm going to place the gun into my mouth and pull the trigger, and go far, far away.

Good luck and God bless you all.
Sincerely,
Tom Anderson

MAN'S BEST FRIEND

ANTHONY GIANGREGORIO

Barney Roosevelt ran as fast as he could down the dock, but he was too late.

"Damn it!" he yelled as the deep sea fishing tug chugged away. He dropped his fishing rods and bait to the dock and stamped his foot in anger.

"Looks like someone's not having a good day," a voice said from behind him.

Barney turned to see a man in his seventies with a bald pate and wire rimmed glasses. He had the classic beer belly most men his age had and he wore a t-shirt, shorts, and flip-flops.

"Yeah, you could say that," Barney replied, not wanting to be rude, though he still wanted to scream to the heavens in frustration.

Of all days to get a flat tire. By the time he'd changed it and was on the road once more, he had come in too late for the deep sea fishing trip.

"I had a deposit with them, too. It's nonrefundable."

The old man shook his head. "Gee, that's tough. Tell you what, I was going out myself in a few minutes. Got me a small twenty footer. It's nothing big but it gets the job done." He stepped up closer to Barney. "I could use some company if you don't mind listening to an old man talk about his life."

Barney's frown slowly disappeared. "Really, you'd let me go with you? I can't pay; I spent it all on that damn tug." He pointed to the fishing vessel as it rounded the bay and headed off to sea.

The old man waved his hand as if he was swatting a fly away. "Ah, that's not what I meant. I'm inviting you to come along. No charge, just bring your ears and we'll be good." He held out a hand to Barney. "The name's Charlie."

"Barney," he said as he shook the older man's hand.

Charlie smiled widely. "Well then, now that it's settled, get your stuff and follow me. I was about to cast off anyway, just like I said."

Barney did as instructed, and with his hands full, he followed Charlie to the opposite end of the dock, reveling in his good fortune. Barney had begun fishing in his early twenties and now that he was in his forties, he found he was a true fan of the sport. He tried to get out on a deep sea excursion at least once a month.

"*The Second Chance*," Barney read when he saw the writing on the hull of Charlie's boat. "Any significance?"

"Yup, there is. Had me a heart attack three years ago; almost died. Was right there at death's door, and at the last second, the doctors snatched me back from oblivion. After that it took a year to recover and when I did, I retired and bought this boat. Can't take it with you, Barney, so you might as well spend it, fuck it, and play with it while you're alive."

Barney chuckled at Charlie's words. "Amen, Charlie, I couldn't agree with you more."

They boarded the boat and ten minutes later were chugging out to sea.

"I can't thank you enough for this, Charlie," he said as he leaned back and enjoyed the sun on his face.

"Not a problem, son, there's room for two easily," Charlie said. "And I know the best spot to fish. Much better than where those damn fishing trips go to. You'll see; we'll be landing flounder, bass and tuna before you know it."

"You know, Charlie, I'm really glad I met you," he said. Charlie nodded, and with a grin, he opened a beat-up red cooler and tossed Barney a beer.

Catching it, Barney's smile went from ear to ear. "Damn, now I'm really glad to meet you."

The two men laughed as the boat headed out to sea.

Four hours later and Barney wished he had never met Charlie.

The old bastard would *not* shut up. All he did was go on and on, and no matter how many times Barney tried to deflect the conversation and make the man be quiet, Charlie would just keep going.

The old man talked about his time in the war, his dead wife, his two good-for-nothing-sons and a hundred other things.

"If we're lucky I can introduce you to my friend," Charlie said between speeches.

"Huh, what?" Barney asked. He was doing his best to tune out the old man's droning voice but the last sentence seemed to penetrate the cloud that was his inattentiveness.

"My friend; if we're lucky he'll show up. Don't know when he'll show but he always does."

"Sure, Charlie, whatever you say," Barney said, not caring at all. This day had turned out terrible. First he missed his fishing trip, then lost his money for the deposit, and now he'd ended up in the middle of the ocean with an old man who wouldn't shut the hell up. And then to add to the list, the old geezer was turning senile, and was talking about an imaginary friend.

What friend? They were in the middle of nowhere. The old guy was losing it.

Barney concentrated on his rod, gripping it tightly in his hands. The knuckles in both his hands were bone white and he was grinding his teeth in frustration.

Charlie walked up and leaned against the railing so he could look Barney in the eyes.

"So, as I was saying, my second son, he's the oldest, well, he goes and gets himself arrested. So he calls me and wants me to bail him out. I, of course told him no, that he should learn a lesson and stay there, but do you think he was all right with that? Hell no. He tells me if I ever want him to come visit me again, I better bail his ass out of jail. I told him not to blackmail me; that I was his father and he should respect me. He said it was my duty as a father to bail him out as he was my son. Can you imagine that? Like it was my fault he was in a bar fight and was arrested in the first place? So anyway, I told him..."

Barney had a headache—no, not a headache, a migraine. One that began behind his eyes and wrapped around his head and into his neck. It felt like a workman was holding a hammer, and with each tick of the clock, the man was hitting him on the head.

As his heart beat, so too did the pounding continue. Barney gripped the fishing rod in his hands so tight that it actually began to bend a little, the rod tough enough to battle a small shark, but unable to take the stress of Barney's aggravation.

"So you know what I did?" Charlie asked, not waiting for a reply. "I went down there and bailed him out. And the ungrateful bastard didn't even say thank you. Instead he borrowed twenty bucks for a cab and left me standing there like a fool. Now I ask you, did I deserve that? How can a son do that to his own father? Well, I tell you, I was so mad I turned around and went...."

Barney screamed as the world went white, then red.

Without realizing what he was doing, his mind shutting down from pure anger and rage, he dropped his fishing rod, picked up a long pole with a hook on it—the pole used to drag in fishing nets—and hit Charlie over the head with it like it was a baseball bat.

The tip of the pole, where the curved hook was, embedded itself into the top of Charlie's skull, severing the brainstem from his cranium in an instant. Charlie's eyes rolled up into the back of his head and his arms began to twitch. He dropped to the deck, a copious amount of blood pumping around the hook and onto the deck as his body spasmed as if it was flooded with electricity.

The end of the pole slid from Barney's hands and clattered onto the wooden deck and Charlie's boots made a staccato of drumbeats until finally slowing and then stopping altogether.

Barney stood perfectly still, blinking as he stared down at Charlie cooling corpse.

"I...I didn't mean to do that," he said to Charlie. "I just wanted you to shut the fuck up. Oh, Jesus, I didn't want you to die. Oh, Christ, what the hell do I do now?" He looked around the boat and then out into the ocean. It was absolutely quiet, with the exception of the water slapping the hull.

No one had seen him kill Charlie; no one knew what he'd done. He thought back to when they had left the dock. No one had been around. That meant no one had seen him leave the dock in Charlie's boat.

If he waited until nightfall and disposed of the corpse, he could sneak back into the harbor, wipe down the boat for fingerprints like he'd seen on that CSI TV show, and he would be in the clear.

He looked down at Charlie again, feeling guilty for what he had done to the old man.

But he couldn't take it back so the only thing to do was cover his ass.

With a sigh, he bent over and dragged Charlie's body closer to the railing. Though he wanted to just toss it into the water, he was smart enough to know it would only float. It had to sink.

Thinking hard on the subject, he came up with only one conclusion.

Like a balloon, Charlie had to be popped.

Pulling his fisherman's knife from its sheath on his belt, he knelt down, placed the tip of the six inch blade at Charlie's throat, and pushed down.

The blade slid in easily, and Barney winced as the flesh gave way. Only a small amount of blood pooled around the blade, as Charlie's heart wasn't pumping anymore.

With a deep frown of disgust, Barney began cutting downward towards Charlie's groin, gutting the old man like a fish. As he cut, clothing and flesh parted.

The rib cage was hard to slice through but Barney persevered, working at his chore with mechanical precision.

Sweat poured off his forehead as he sawed down to the corpse's belly button. Intestines popped out of Charlie's abdomen like they were springs forced into a small tube, then suddenly set free. The rank odor of blood and offal assaulted his nose and he had to fight off the temptation to vomit.

When he finished his task, he wiped his brow of sweat and used Charlie's pant leg to clean the blade of blood and bits of flesh. When it was clean, he put it away. He took a deep breath of clean air by turning his head to the side, then bent over, picked Charlie up under his armpits, and tossed him over the side of the boat like he was a piece of trash.

The body landed without fanfare, sinking into the ocean like a rock.

Barney stared at the spot where the body had sunk for almost a minute, then went into the wheelhouse to begin cleaning up any trace he was on the boat.

While Barney busied himself in the small wheelhouse, at the aft end of the boat, there was a small, steel, mesh, one foot step that was at water level. As if rising from the very depths like a monster from an old movie, the body slowly resurfaced.

It seemed to float on the water, defying the ocean current, until it drifted to the boat and slid onto the mesh step. It lay there, unmoving, still very dead, as the waves caressed the slack face.

Barney finished cleaning up the boat of his presence as best he could, and as the sky grew dark, he went to the aft end of the boat to pull in the anchor.

It was as he did this that he spotted the dark shape on the steel step, and as he moved closer, his jaw dropped when he saw it was Charlie's corpse.

Already the body was beginning to show decay from being in the water. The skin exposed to the air was a pale white and the intestines floated in the water, still attached, waving like red and brown streamers in the wind.

"What the hell?" Barney said to himself as he stared at the corpse.

He looked around the boat, wondering if someone was playing tricks on him. After all, he watched the body sink into the ocean. How the hell did it return?

He decided it was a fluke, somehow air had been trapped in the body and it resurfaced to end up back on the boat—a one in a million oddity.

Using the pole with the still bloody hook, he pushed the corpse back into the water, then poked it a few times to break the skin and allow more water into the body.

Once more the corpse drifted away to sink below the surface.

Satisfied the body was gone for good this time; Barney went to the wheelhouse and started the engine.

It turned over on the first try, and as he pushed the throttle forward, he began moving, deciding his ordeal was finally over.

So when he spotted the dark shape off the starboard bow of the boat, at first he didn't give it much thought. He merely assumed it was some debris, such as a log or perhaps the carcass of a large fish.

As the boat moved closer, he swung the bow to port and let the shape come abroad. There was a spotlight on the boat and he used it to illuminate the shape.

His eyes went wide when he saw it was non-other than Charlie's corpse, once more bobbing in the water, like the man had gone for a swim and was resting. The body was face down, the head tilted so that the entire skull was submerged. But there was no mistaking the clothing. Besides, what were the odds Barney would have another, different corpse pop up exactly where he had killed Charlie?

Once more the odds were enormous.

Deciding he needed to take more drastic measures, he used the pole and hauled in the corpse like it was the catch of the day. This time, he wasn't fooling around. Using a long-bladed carving knife taken from Charlie's deck cabinet, Barney began carving the body up like it was a turkey on Thanksgiving.

The blood in the body had congealed and was now a thick paste, and as he hacked and cut, he was having the hardest time slicing through the tendons connecting the bones to one another. By the time he was finished, he was covered in gore, and Charlie was in a dozen pieces.

One at a time, he lobbed the bloody parts into the ocean, satisfied when each one sank below the water line. Last was the head, and as Barney looked into Charlie's glazed eyes, he shook his own head sadly.

"Sorry about this, old timer, I just wished you hadn't talked so fucking much." He tossed the head into the water with a, "So long."

The head seemed to float for a few seconds, then tipped upside down so the jagged stump of the neck was pointed up, then it was lost in the water as it sank like a rock.

Barney quickly washed up, though he didn't do as good a job as he should have. He washed his face and arms, then wiped his clothes as best he could, but they were still soaked with blood. He decided he could explain it off as fish blood if he had to, on the off chance he was stopped by a straggler at the dock when he returned.

Satisfied the murder was covered up for good, he went to the wheelhouse, pushed the throttle all the way forward, and headed back to port, a sly smile creasing his lips.

He had actually gotten away with murder, something he would never have believed was possible, and especially not the act itself.

Humming a tune to himself, he steered the boat for the faint lights of the distant shore, feeling better than he had all day.

With night having fallen hours ago, 'The Second Chance' chugged into the harbor. Barney swung the boat around so the starboard side connected with the old car tires tied to the side of the dock to protect the hulls of the ships.

It was silent and empty on the dock as he tied the mooring lines and disembarked. He was confident he was in the clear when an armed security guard walked up to him from out of the shadows.

"Hey, there, how's it going tonight? Out for a little late night fishing?"

Barney nodded as he hid his face. If he could get out without the guard stopping him, he would be home free. If only he had known the dock had security, he would have come up with another plan.

"Yeah, something like that," Barney said curtly. He wanted the man to leave—now.

"Catch anything?" the security guard asked.

"Nah, no bites today."

"Too bad."

Barney didn't reply. He was about to climb off the boat and walk to the exit, figuring he could ignore the guard if the man called out him again, when there was a splash at the aft end of the boat.

No sooner did the splash echo off the docks then something flew through the air and landed on the deck of the boat. It was round and it rolled across the worn boards until it came up right between Barney's feet.

The security guard heard the splash and had seen the shape in the wan moonlight. As it thumped and rolled, he pulled his flashlight out and aimed it at Barney.

That was when he saw the blood covering Barney from head to toe.

As the beam of light played over Barney, it settled at his feet and the security guard's mouth went wide when he saw the decapitated head of Charlie.

"What the fuck? That's Charlie!" The guard drew his sidearm and aimed it at Barney. "Don't fucking move, mister!" The security guard aimed the flashlight at the aft end of the boat, reading the name of the vessel when it was illuminated. "This is Charlie's boat. I don't know what the fuck is going on here, mister, but you have a lot of explaining to do to the cops."

Barney was so scared he thought he would die right there and then, and he was about to make a break for it when the security guard shouted, "Don't try it! You move and I shoot!"

But Barney was in fight or flight mode and flight was the one he picked. With the dock out of the question, he dove over the side of the boat and into the water, hoping to swim around the boat and lose himself among the other vessels moored to the docks. If he was lucky, he could be long gone before the police arrived. The security guard didn't know who he was, no one did on the dock. All the police would have would be a sketch of his face, and if he stayed in hiding for a while, nothing would come of it. And even if it did, it was all circumstantial.

But no sooner did he hit the water and swim to the surface then he was hit from behind by what felt like a giant fist.

The air was knocked out of him and he let out a scream, sucking in water. Sputtering, he tried to swim away from what was attacking him, but when he tried, he was hit from the front, the air leaving his lungs in a *whoosh*.

He was knocked so hard he saw stars as he flailed in the water. Once more he was struck, this time from the side, and he could barely stay afloat.

As he floundered, knowing he was going to drown, he was struck on the side again, only this time he was pushed until his shoulders struck the tires lining the dock. He was just forward of The Second Chance and the security guard was right there waiting for him.

The man reached down, grabbed Barney by his collar, and hauled him up as Barney used his legs to get some purchase on one of the tires to pull himself up. He fell to the planks of the dock choking and spitting water, and as he laid there, helpless, weak as a baby, he felt his hands pulled around his back to be handcuffed. His clothing, though soaked, was still bloody and he knew, from that same show on the television that DNA or whatever could be taken from the diluted blood.

As he was pulled to his knees, he blinked water from his eyes, and as his vision cleared, he was greeted by his first look at what attacked him.

It was a bottle-nosed dolphin.

"What the hell?" he sputtered through a coughing fit.

"Looks like you met Earl," the security guard said as he called in to dispatch to report a murder and called for the police. His two-way radio crackled with a response seconds after he spoke into it.

"Who the fuck is Earl?" Barney gasped as he sucked in a breath of air. His front and back hurt from where he was struck by the nose of the dolphin.

"Earl was Charlie's best friend. Charlie would feed him fish when he was out in the bay. It got so that Earl was like a dog, always hanging around Charlie's boat. Charlie would toss a ball out to Earl and the dolphin would always bring it back. It's the damndest thing. Charlie used to say he thought Earl might have been in one of those aquariums or zoos, like a trained dolphin. Then they must have set him free."

"So that was the friend he was talking about—a fucking dolphin. But why did it hang around bugging me?" Barney asked.

The guard shrugged. "That's a good question, mister. Maybe it thought you were Charlie seems you were on his boat, or it didn't like what you did to its friend. Where's the rest of Charlie, you sick fuck, huh?" He gestured to Charlie's severed head still on the boat. "Either way, I reckon you're gonna have a long time to figure out why Earl stayed around you."

"What?"

The guard smiled slightly. "I liked Charlie, mister, and you should he glad I don't kill you right now and let the dolphin take your carcass out to sea. But as I knew Charlie well, I know he wasn't a violent man. See, we don't have the death penalty in this state, but I reckon you're going away for life. I'd bet my pension on that one." As he finished his small speech, the sound of a siren could be heard and moments later the red and blue lights of two squad cars approached.

Barney, still on his knees, let his shoulders sag in defeat, and he ignored the pain of his handcuffed wrists.

"Christ, I wish I never took up fishing," he said to himself.

As if in reply, the dolphin jumped up, did a spin, and let out a few choice squeals and clicks, then swam back out to sea.

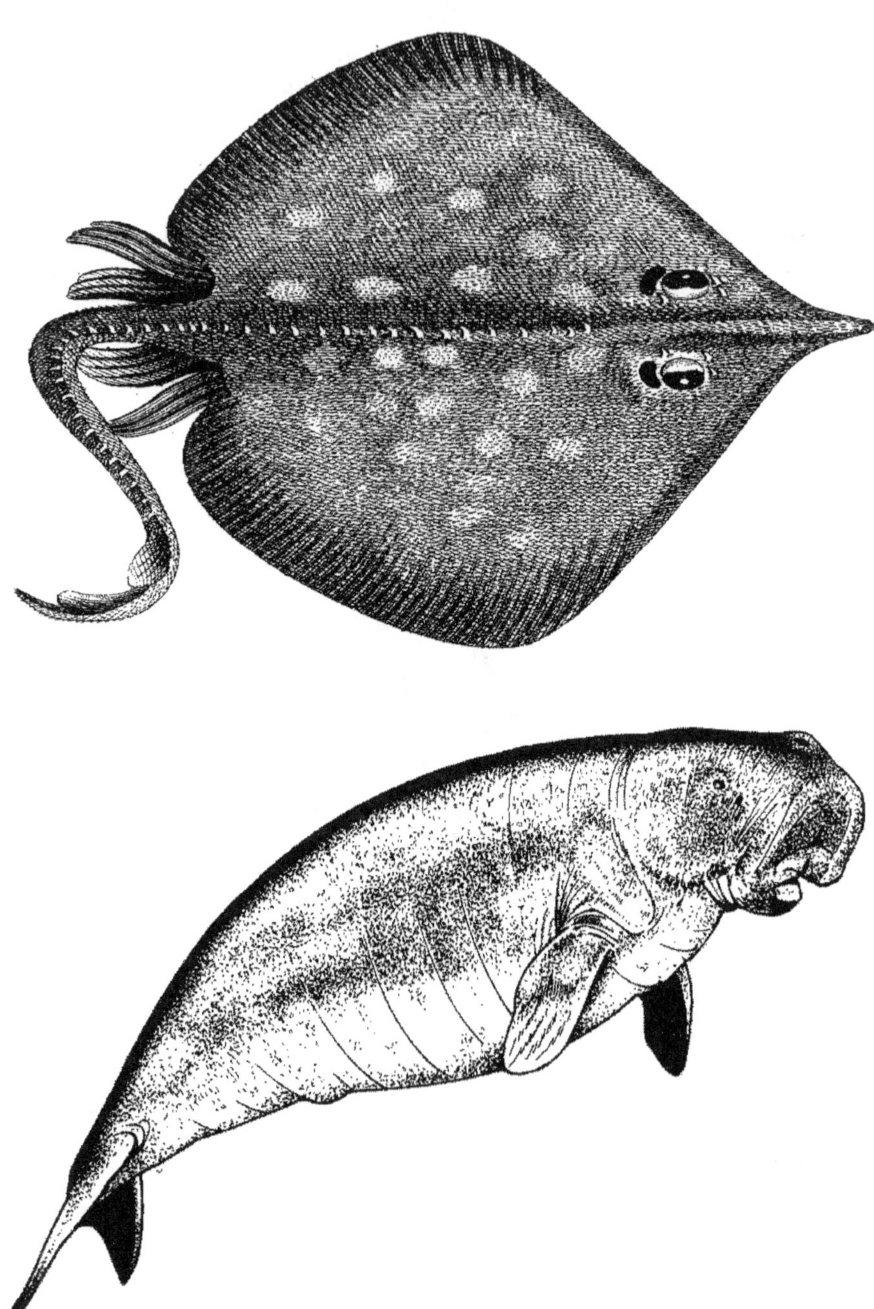

TIME AND TIDE WAIT NOT

DANE T. HATCHELL

"I saw her again, Mommy." Mikey stood next to the fake leather couch his mother was lying on. "Mommy, I saw the girl again." His almond shaped eyes stared at her through his coke bottle glasses.

"Mmmphh...," his mother twitched, the smell of vodka and BO hovering in her personal space that Mikey was invading.

"She was by the water and I saw her and I told her to wait and I ran to her but she was gone before I could get to her," Mikey recounted the story in the exact detail that he remembered. He grabbed her shoulder and shook it a few times.

"Mikey...child...it's not even noon. Why're you bothering your mama?"

Estelle rolled from her right side over to her left, facing Mikey. The faux leather grain pattern imbedded her cheek and a cushion seam left its mark down the side of her face.

He smiled, now having her attention, and adjusted his glasses on his flat nose.

"Why does she go 'way?" His smooth round face with his continually opened mouth reflected a constant state of confusion. When you're twenty-two years old with an IQ of fifty, there are always questions with mostly unsatisfactory answers.

"I don't know how many times I have to tell you this, Mikey, there was no girl on the beach. Real girls don't disappear when you run to them. It's just a manatee playing in the water. The sunlight and waves just make it look like a girl," Estelle's head throbbed, signaling it was time to have her orange juice and vodka.

"No, she walks on the beach. Manatee's just swim, they don't have legs and walk and don't look pretty," Mikey said.

"Whatever...whatever. Hey, where you running off to?" she asked as he skipped off to the back door.

"I ate me a peanut butter sandwich and put on my *sunscream* and my hat and shoes are outside and I'm going to walk the beach, bye-bye." The wooden screen door banged closed, sending new waves of pain through Estelle's head.

Mikey grabbed a bag of left over vegetables, and left the weathering old beach house behind him. He took long steps on short legs for the sandy beach of Crystal River, Florida, not more than a hundred yards away.

The house had belonged to Estelle's father, who earned his living as a fisherman for most of the sixty years that he lived. Her father had left her the house and a small amount of savings that supplemented the income from Government assistance for her and Mikey to live on. The land the house sat on was worth much more than the dilapidated sun cracked house, but Mikey had lived in the home all his life and she no longer considered selling it and moving into town.

Mikey loved everything about the beach. The waves crashing on the shore were a serenade to his ears and deposited a variety of treasures from the ocean on the white sand. Sometimes he would find whole sand dollars washed up. You could shake- shake- shake them and it would make a rattling sound. If you broke it open to see what was inside, five little 'doves' would fall to the ground. Mikey was fascinated by the little 'doves', and had over a hundred of them glued to a sheet of cardboard in his room.

"Hey, big guy, yeah you, watch where you're walking," a tiny sand crab called up from below.

"I'm sorry," Mikey said looking down. "I was just looking for shells and didn't see you."

"Yeah, well, I spent a lot of time digging out that hole. So, go around, got it?" the sand crab said angrily.

"Okay." Mikey didn't like the tone the sand crab was taking with him. After a few steps past it, Mikey turned around and asked, "Hey, do you want me to dig a hole for you? I can dig a big deep hole if you like."

The sand crab flicked another load of sand out of his abode and waved Mikey on.

It's just not fair, Mikey thought as he stepped to avoid the waves coming ashore. Everything seemed to have a purpose in life...but him.

Mr. Sand crab was always working on his house, and there was no one telling him what to do. Mikey's mom was always questioning him, always correcting him; he never seemed to make her happy.

He wanted to be useful in life, to be around where he was wanted. People didn't like to talk to him very much; they would always make the conversations short. They would talk slow and raise their voices. He didn't like that, he could hear just fine.

Even the sea creatures and birds didn't treat him very well. They were always busy-busy and wanted to be left alone. None of them would have a meaningful conversation with him.

No one that is, except for Mr. Manatee.

Mikey's one dream was to be the captain of a big ship and sail the world looking for gold and other treasures like in the stories his mom would read to him. He wanted a parrot too, but he didn't want a peg leg.

But mostly he wanted to feel love. Not like the love he felt for his mother, but like the kind of love that only a princess could give. Mikey had never kissed a girl, had never even held hands with one.

He wanted the girl that would mysteriously appear and disappear on the beach to love him. She was tall and thin with long black hair that draped down to her waist. She walked with such grace on the uneven beach that he knew she had to be a princess. But he could never meet her, never had a chance to even find out her name. He wanted to give her some of the little 'doves' from the sand dollar as a present. He would even give her his cardboard with the hundred 'doves' pasted on it; if he only had the chance.

Mikey finally reached the old pier that was all that was left from an ancient, beach-side motel. His mom had warned him to stay off the pier; she was afraid he might fall off and drown. Not that he couldn't swim, he could tread water with the best of dog-paddling swimmers. But swimming was best reserved for the pool or in shallow waters by the beach.

The pier was twelve feet wide and protruded twenty feet into the gulf. At high tide, it still kept fisherman four feet above the water. The swollen wood grain on the graying boards made the trek a cautious one. Nail heads popped up here and there and the wood splintered easily when it made contact with soft flesh.

Mikey reached the end, turned, and looked back at the beach. Not another soul to be seen, save for the gulls meandering about, looking for food by the shore.

"I'm here, Mikey," the voice of the manatee called from below.

Mikey spun around, somewhat startled. "I was looking for you Mr. Manatee. I brought you some carrots and some lettuce." He opened the bag and poured it out over the side of the pier.

The sixteen hundred pound gentle creature used its powerful tail to support its head above water. Its back was scarred with random slices and gouges from irreverent boaters that traveled in protected waters. He used his front flippers and shoved the crispy vegetables past his prehensile lips and to the molars in the back of his mouth.

"Thank you for the food, Mikey. You're a good a trustworthy person, aren't you," the manatee said.

"I try to be nice, so others will treat me nice. But I don't get treated nice all the time. Mr. Sand crab wasn't nice. I gave the gulls bread and they still pooped on me. Why can't others be nice all the time?" Mikey asked.

"Life is structured on how others interact, how others get along. But you can't control how others act. Only you can control your actions. You see, actions have consequences. You know that, don't you?"

"Yes. If I do bad I get in trouble," Mikey said with a nod.

The ocean started to bubble near the manatee and a large tri-angular shadow appeared in the water. But the shadow wasn't a shadow at all. On the surface emerged a giant Devil Ray. His black skin glistened in the light of the sun, and his harpoon-like tail floated to the top and moved up and down on the waves of the gulf.

The Devil Ray positioned himself by the end of the pier with his mouth above the water, its cephalic lobes dropping down. From tip to tip of his pectoral fin was twenty five feet.

Mikey took a step or two backward; he had never seen such an ominous creature in his life. Its mouth opened and closed like it was chewing air, and Mikey was worried that it wanted to chew on him.

"I was wondering how long it would take you to show up here," the manatee said to the Devil Ray. "Where have you been?"

"From going to and fro in the ocean, and from swimming up and down in it," the Devil Ray said. "What do you think I was doing? Whacking off to porn? Gees..."

"Ray, this is Mikey. There is no one on Earth as true as he," the manatee said.

"Pleased to meet you, Mikey, you can call me Ray," the Devil Ray lifted his right cephalic lobe and gave a sort of salute.

"Hel...hello Mr. Ray," Mikey said, uneasy with the new situation.

"Say, Mikey, ol' Mr. Manatee here says that you're a real straight shooter. That right?"

"Well...yes. I guess so," Mikey eked out.

"Come on, lad, don't be so shy. Now, you say that you're good to everyone, right?"

"Yes."

"But not everyone is good back to you, correct?" Ray asked.

"Yes."

"Then if you act bad to those who act bad to you, might they not in turn act good to you?"

Mikey's mouth opened a little wider, the wheels were definitely turning in his head.

"Think, lad, think! To get bad people to act good to you, you must treat them badly," Ray reasoned.

"But, but I don't want to be bad to anyone," Mikey whined.

"Mr. Manatee said that you can't control other people's action. He's wrong; he's just a big pussy. You can control how other people act," Ray said.

The pier started vibrating from the pounding of three pairs of running feet.

"Touch not his life," the manatee said to the Ray.

"I know the routine." Then the Ray disappeared into the depths below.

Three boys in their pre-teens tanned by Florida sunshine scuttled up the pier. One carried a fishing rod, one a pail of bait, and the other proudly brandished a spear gun that he held tightly with both hands.

Mikey knew the three boys, for they too lived nearby. Sometimes, when they were playing on their 'boogie boards' by the shore, they would let him take a turn. Try as he might though, he was never able to successfully glide on top of the thin layer of water between the board and the sand. Instead, he would slip backwards and land on his backside, or fall forward and scrape his hands and elbows. The three boys would laugh and laugh at him.

Sometimes when they would walk to a convenience store, they would give him money and he would go inside and buy energy drinks and cigarettes. The boys all brought him a note from their mothers, so Mikey knew it was okay for them to smoke.

Kenny, Kyle, and Blaine approached Mikey in a menacing manner as the crossed the pier. Their run slowed to a fast walk, and then the three surrounded Mickey.

"Look, guys, it's the 'tard," Kenny said. He was more or less the main instigator of the bunch.

Mikey's feeling were instantly hurt. He hated being called a 'tard. He didn't know why his friend would call him that name. "Don't call me 'tard. I'm not a 'tard," he lashed out.

"Oh, you're a retard all right. I bet you say it *wetard*," Kenny laughed. "Your face looks like a big goofy baby's. You got short arms, short legs, and short fingers. I bet it's true your momma slept with a manatee."

Mikey started to cry, his face turned crimson red in anger and frustration.

"Hey, look in the water, there's his daddy now," Blaine pointed to the manatee by the end of the pier.

"Hey, Mikey, that your dad? You came here to see your dad?" Kenny asked.

"Why are you being so mean to me?" Mikey cried. "That's not my daddy."

"Okay, Mikey, if that's not your dad, then I'm going to use him for target practice." Blaine pointed his spear gun at the manatee and made a *swooshing* sound as he pretended to shoot it.

"You leave Mr. Manatee alone!" Mikey screamed, snot dripping down his chin.

"No, he's gonna do it, unless..." Kyle thought a moment. "Unless you eat all of these shiners in this bucket." Kyle held the bucket up to Mikey.

"I don't want to eat that."

"Then I'm going to shoot him," Blaine said.

"But I don't want to eat that!" Mikey screamed.

Blaine raised the spear gun up and took careful aim.

Mikey yelled, "Wait, wait! Don't shoot Mr. Manatee. I'll eat the little fishes."

Kyle stuck his hand in the bucket and managed to capture three. He held his dripping hand out and Mikey begrudgingly took them from him. Mikey opened his mouth and shoved them in, making an awful face as they squirmed on his tongue.

"Eat 'em, you've got to eat 'em," Kenny demanded.

Mikey bit down and a salty-fishy-funky liquid squirted into the back of his throat. Mikey gagged and heaved two times before he fell to his knees, then threw up on Kyle's shoes.

"Oh, gross, you stupid 'tard," Blaine cursed. "Looks like you lose."

Blaine raised the spear gun and pulled the trigger. The CO2 cartridge propelled the arrow at several hundred feet per second, and it pierced the side of the defenseless gentle giant.

The manatee let out a cry of pain and anguish that none of them had ever heard before. The massive mammal of blubber and flesh went limp in the water, a ribbon of blood trailing into the Gulf.

Mikey was horrified and started to hyperventilate, being overcome with panic. Mr. Manatee was floating in the ocean, dead! His friends had killed him! But why? Why must they be so mean? Mr. Manatee didn't hurt anyone, ever!

The three boys were dancing and giving Blaine high fives for hitting the target. Mikey was shivering, still on his hands and knees on the pier when the image of a revolver materialized in front of his face.

He heard the Devil Ray's words in his head, as if the ray was whispering in his ear, *"To get bad people to act good to you, you must treat them badly."*

Mikey knew it was a gun, and something inside told him this one was real, not like the plastic guns his mom bought for him to play with. The voice told him the gun would make the boys treat him good. It would *force* them to.

They shot Mr. Manatee, they were bad. If he shot them, they couldn't do any bad things to him anymore, Mikey thought.

The shouting of the boys around him made him angry; they killed his friend and they were rejoicing about it. He knew if he went and found a gun like the one he was imagining, he could make the boys be good.

But something in the back of his mind reminded him what his mother told him. *Two wrongs don't make a right.*

His anger again turned to confusion. Mikey shook his head and the vision of the gun disappeared. He stood and wiped the vomit off of his chin with the back of his hand. Mikey was scared and felt like his soul had been violated. He wanted to run home and tell his mom, but the three boys stood between him and the shore.

"Looks like Mikey's got his sea legs back," Kenny laughed.

"Yeah, but he smells like puke, he needs a bath," Kyle surmised.

"He's the son of a manatee, he belongs in the water, anyway," Blaine said, and the three charged into Mikey.

Mickey panicked and he wrapped his arms around the boys. Instead of only him going into the water, all four of them went over the side of the pier.

Mikey hit the water on his backside and swallowed a mouthful of water as he went under. He flipped himself around and floated to the surface, struggling for air.

"Hey, I'm going to ride 'Mikey the manatee' to shore!" Blaine squealed. Mikey was holding his own, just barely able to keep his head out of water and finally getting enough air to breathe. Blaine caught up with him from behind, grabbed his shoulders, and pulled him back down.

Mikey's head went completely under; he kicked his legs frantically, and paddled with his hands in desperation. His lungs ached for air and he was about to give up and take an involuntary breath under water when he and Blaine were lifted from underneath; up to the surface.

The Devil Ray had them both on his back. Mikey laid coughing and gasping for air while Blaine was trying to figure out what was going on. With a flick of its pectoral fin, Blaine went flying though the air and splashed into the Gulf. And with a supernatural act that defied explanation, the Ray tossed Mikey out of the water and deposited him back on the pier.

The three boys were treading water, scared out of their minds over the giant Devil Ray. Kenny was the first to turn and swim for shore, the other two following right on his heels.

Mikey was on his hand and knees by the edge of the pier, his glasses and hat that had been knocked off him when the three boys plowed into him were on the pier and he put them on.

The three boys were swimming as fast as they could, but had a long way to go to reach shore. As Mikey watched, a pod of sharks overtook them and surrounded them in a circle. The sea gulls from the beach took to the air and hovered above as the circle tightened and the sharks began to feed.

The screams of the boys were drowned out by the shrill calls of excitement of the gulls. The sharks fed frenziedly, ripping meat off bone with their sharp teeth, the water boiling blood red. The gulls dipped to the surface for scraps of sweet flesh and gulped them down, then went back for more. It by far was the most terrifying thing Mikey had ever seen.

"Well, Mikey, things sure did get out of hand here," Ray said.

The splashing water was subsiding; the sea gulls were heading back to shore.

"They killed Mr. Manatee, and they were going to kill me." Mikey looked down at the pier, and then back at Ray in the water.

"Let that be a lesson to you, lad, life's simply not fair. You, my boy, were born a little…slow. Was that fair? Of course not. So you see, the key to happiness in life is to get ahead. Now, what would it take to make you happy in life?" Ray asked slyly.

"I want Mr. Manatee to be alive again."

"Heh, well, resurrections are not my department. But there you go, thinking of others and not of yourself. It's time to think of yourself, my boy. What would make your dreams come true?"

"Well, I want to be a captain of a ship, and sail the world and look for treasure," Mikey said, feeling selfish.

"Yes, oh yes, my boy! A ship! With three large sails and seven canons on each side. A crew to swab the deck and mend the sails, and an endless keg of rum," Ray exclaimed with excitement. "Follow me and I will give you what you wish for."

The ray swam along the pier and Mickey followed. He walked for twenty minutes, following the shore, the ray always within eyesight. Mickey found he was being led to the docks, where the ships were moored.

The ray led him to a sixty foot mast schooner, moored to the closest dock.

Mikey's eyes lit up and a broad smile exposed his jack o' lantern teeth. It was like a real pirate ship just like he had always dreamed of captaining. He imagined the Jolly Roger flying high from the deck and a parrot sat preening itself on the bowsprit.

"Now, Mikey, how would you like this to be yours?" Ray asked.

"I would like it very much, Mr. Ray."

"Obviously. But you see, Mikey, treasures such as these come with a price. Are you willing to pay that price, Mikey?"

"How much does it cost? I don't have a lot of money."

"Oh, pish-posh, my boy, money cannot buy such treasures in life. This is one of those opportunities that only comes around once. And it can be yours if you do just one little thing for me," the Ray teased.

"What do you want me to do?"

"Kill your mother, Mikey. I want you to kill your mother," Ray said in a cold voice.

"Kill Mommy? I'm not going to kill my mommy, you're crazy, Mr. Ray."

"No, my boy, I'm just trying to protect you. Your mother is un-fit, and she will be the death of you."

"She won't kill me, she loves me, she says so all the time."

But a large black void appeared in the water next to Ray as images of Estelle in various stages of inebriation flashed like pictures on a movie screen before Mickey. All his memories came back to haunt him.

"She's a drunk, Mikey. Every day and every night she lives in a bottle. She's not caring for you properly. One day she could be so drunk that she could give you the wrong medicine and kill you. Or get so drunk out of her mind she could cut your throat while you slept and wouldn't even remember it the next day."

Mikey stood speechless, but shook his head no.

"Your mother is certainly popular with men, isn't she, Mikey?"

Mickey remembered the times he had seen Estelle naked and in all sorts of sexual positions with a countless number of different men.

"Quite the harlot I would say. That's what she does when you go to bed at night, Mickey. Right after she gives you your medicine. I hear she really likes it doggy style on the couch. I warn you that if you find any deflated 'balloons' lying about, stay away from them," the Ray said sarcastically.

Mikey remembered in silence as the sexual visions played before him.

"What if she meets a man that wants her and not you? A few extra pills before you go to bed at night and you'll never wake up. That's why you must kill her, Mikey. Not just for the ship, but for your very life."

"No! No! No! Why do you say these things? You're mean, Mr. Ray, you're mean!" Mikey was pulling handfuls of hair out of his head.

"The truth hurts, my boy. The truth hurts. You know what she says about you when she doesn't think you can hear her, right?"

Mickey nodded as he saw Estelle in a collage of images and in her own voice spoke of Mikey. "He's such a retard... Mikey's a retard... so fucking retarded, retarded is as retarded does."

Over and over again to his friends and neighbors his mom kept referring to him as retard. She would say retard this and retard that; *retard, retard, retard!*

Mikey closed his eyes and let out a wail from deep within his soul.

The Ray swam up to the side of the ship. "You're so close, Mikey, so close to all of this being yours. You can be the captain of this ship. Just think what it would be like."

Mickey imagined he was standing on the deck of the pirate ship, a two foot silver saber in his hand. He was dressed in a puffy-ruffly white shirt, covered with a long black leather jacket. His black boots came up to the knees on his black pants, and a triangular captain's hat adorned his head.

"Imagine your mother was before you, Mickey. What would you do?" Ray asked.

Mickey imagined a large table in front of him, his mother laid on it in her underwear, bound at her hands and feet, unconscious.

The cruel words she had said hung in the air, the word retard repeated over and over again. The ray could sense Mickey's inner turmoil and said, "She'll kill you, Mikey. You better get her before she gets you. You have to do it, Mikey! Kill her! Kill her!" the Ray demanded.

Estelle eyes opened wide, and her lips moved to mouth the word 'retard'.

Mikey's anger grew to the point that his sanity was now in question. These images were too much for him. The memories were ones he didn't want to face.

"Retard...retard...," Estelle said angrily. "You're a fucking retard, do it! Do it! You fucking retard! Kill me!"

Mikey cried out and raised the blade high into the air. Estelle was spitting like a rabid animal demanding him to kill her. Mikey closed his eyes and screamed at the heavens; then turned and jumped off the side of the ship, plunging the silver blade into the head of the Devil Ray.

*　*　*

The ship disappeared as did the ocean, the sky and the dock. Like a television being turned off the world went black, then came back on again.

Everything was how it had been before the three boys had arrived to harass Mickey; the Devil Ray was unharmed and unmarked, and it swam over to the manatee. The spear that was in it was gone, and the manatee floated in the water, unharmed and healthy.

"I told you there was no one more honorable, as kind, as Mikey," the manatee said to the Devil Ray. "To him, this test has all been a bad dream."

"Yada, yada, yada. You win, I get it. You don't have to rub it in," the Ray sighed. "I guess my bid for winning in 'the garden of Eden' will end soon enough. Imagine, a new world with eons of peace and happiness; no disease, or hunger, or malformation. How dull, how overwhelmingly and utterly dull..."

"You'll get another chance to have things your way some day," the manatee said. "It will be here before you know it. Just like this ending has," the manatee reassured.

* * *

Mikey woke flat on his back on the beach not far from the pier. The sun was nearing the horizon and looked like a giant orange ball descending into the Gulf. His shoes were gone and his feet with the unusually large gap between his big and second toe were wet from the reach of the waves. His hat partially covered his eyes, and when he sat up and adjusted it, he realized his glasses were on his face, too.

He stood cautiously, waiting for a full command of his balance, and walked out into the Gulf waters to wash the clinging sand off his exposed skin and clothing. His glasses had an oily smear coating them, so he dunked them in the water and wiped them with his shirt. He waved them back in forth in the air and dried them as best as he could as he made his way back to shore.

He put his glasses on, and as his eyes focused, there she was. It was the girl by the water, the mysterious, beautiful girl that had taunted him over and over; his beloved princess.

He stood frozen, afraid to move. Afraid that if he did one thing wrong, had even one wrong thought, she would disappear again, he opened his eyes as wide as he could make them and ran towards her. He didn't look down to see what hazards the beach offered for him to trip on. His eyes didn't blink, for in a blink, she could go away. His heart raced as he grew closer and closer.

She looked up from the beach and away from the shells that she was gathering. Mikey saw her look at him, look directly at him, and his heart jumped a beat when she gave him a smile.

She stood looking his way as his pace was slowing the closer he got to her. Mikey was panting and in somewhat disbelief that she was still there, he almost expected this time to end like the others.

The girl held a Triton shell in one hand, and stretched out the other to receive him.

He came to a complete stop, and stood silently before her. He wanted to reach out and touch her, but he was afraid. Afraid of doing something wrong, it was a feeling that he couldn't explain.

97

His genetic gift of a protruding tongue felt dry and sticky in his salt-dehydrated mouth. He wanted to speak, but he didn't know what to say.

The girl handed him the Triton shell, it was upside down and full of water, "Here Mikey, drink this. It will refresh you." Her lips were full and a light red in color, Mikey felt a curious attraction to them.

Without question, without words, he took the shell and drank the mouthful of liquid, never once blinking or looking away from her. When he finished, he let the shell drop to the sand, as warmness engulfed his whole being. His vision blurred and he removed his glasses, thinking he needed to wipe them again. But as they came off, the world around him came into a new focus, and the beauty, his princess, was still there.

"You see, Mikey, I told you that you would feel better," she said.

"I do...I do feel better. And I don't need my glasses anymore," he said with his usual confusion.

"All things have a reason, but all reasons are not evident. You do understand that don't you, Mikey?

"I guess so," Mikey thought a moment, "I know that you have a reason, that's why I see you, but I don't know what that reason is."

"All reasons aren't revealed, and those that are, are known at the proper time. How would you feel if your mother read you the end of a story first, and then wanted to read it to you from the start?" she asked.

"Well, that might be okay, but then I would know how it would end and it wouldn't be as much fun," Mikey said.

The girl took Mikey's hand and sat him down on the beach. Mikey's heart fluttered with emotions that he had never felt physically before. A shy grin crossed his face and he blushed a spotty pink.

"Lay next to me, Mikey," she said.

He stretched out on his back and the girl laid on her left side next to him. She reached out her right hand and rubbed her fingertips on the left side of his face. Her fingers felt soft like the satin pillows on his mother's bed.

She bent her face forward and Mikey could feel and smell her breath as it lingered over his lips. It was an earthy, arousing smell, nothing unpleasant at all about it. It unlocked things hidden in his brain and his body was once again flooded with unfamiliar feelings. Passion, a wanting, and animalistic urges of desire.

Mikey became aware that his penis was hard, and was pulled away from his hormonal clutch, "Oh no!"

"Mikey...Mikey, what's the matter?" she asked reassuringly.

"My pee-pee is being rude...when my pee-pee is rude, Mommy tells me to run cold water on it."

The girl lowered her head and gave Mikey a tender kiss on his lips. Mikey's tense body immediately relaxed, and all thoughts of his embarrassing anxiety melted away.

She gave more kisses to his mouth, kissing him longer and deeper with each one. He kissed her back in kind. And he tried to match her slow methodical pace, being careful to do as she did so he could do it right.

The girl worked off his swim trunks while continuing to soften his protest with her passionate kisses. The hormones flowing though his body sent a slight buzzing through his head. He was totally lost, drifting in a dimension that he had never new existed.

A sudden warmth engulfed his swollen member and he opened his eyes to see her sitting on top of him, and felt the slow movements of her hips as she took him deep inside her.

She rose above him, moving her long black hair away from her breasts and behind her back. This was the first time he realized she was naked, and that it was her hair that partially covered her all the times he'd seen her. He watched her through his partially opened eyes as her mouth opened and soft moans of love-making oozed out.

Mikey was caught up in the enchanted rhythm, their bodies moving as one. His breathing increased and he felt an urge that both excited and scared him.

His release sent waves of pleasure through the girl, her body quivering and she cried out in orgasmic triumph.

Mikey was lost in orgasmic pleasure, his body shaking slightly as he let the rapture of sex fill him to his very soul.

The sounds of the waves crashing on the sand pulled Mikey back to the present. The girl's head lay on his shoulder and her hands touched his chest. He rolled on his side and gave her a soft kiss, and watched the top of the sun disappear over the horizon. He had never felt this way about anyone...ever.

"Mikey, it's time for you to go back to your mother," the girl said in a soft voice.

The beach, the sand, the thoughts of his mom, all came flooding back to him. But he didn't want to go, he wanted to stay with her. It was like holding on to a dream when you first awake, like holding water through open fingers.

She stood up and took Mikey by the hand, the two walking into the Gulf to wash in the ancient waters.

"You must go now, Mikey." She stopped ankle deep in the surf as he retrieved his swim trunks and hat on the beach.

He put on the trunks and adjusted the hat on his head. "I have something that I want to give you."

"You can give it to me the next time you see me. Now goodbye."

"But your name, I don't know your name," he said.

"I am the Ocean, Mikey. I am the mother of all. Now, please, go, it's you destiny."

He turned and left, feeling compelled to leave, as if he had no control of his actions. He glanced back a time or two and the girl still stood unmoving, as if waiting for him to be out of sight.

The light was fading fast, and Mikey quickened his pace home, he knew his Mom would be angry if he was late.

When Mikey was gone, the girl took a big toe and etched a long single line in the wet sand underneath her feet, as if she was doodling. She pulled her long black hair back behind her head, and stretched her arms up to the sky.

As the light faded, the salt waters of the ocean caressed her flawless skin. Her flesh below her waist began to change, to morph, as the waves crashed against her. When the most recent wave receded, the girl's legs were gone and she stood on a pair of glorious fins. With the next wave she dove into the surf, then swam out into the Gulf, leaving the beach empty once more.

* * *

Mikey's eyes snapped open as he struggled to breathe.

There was something around his throat!

He tried to suck in one more lungful of air, but no matter how hard he tried, his air passage was blocked.

It was dark, well past midnight, and the light of the moon pierced the edges of the shade covering his window as he lay in his bed.

In that dull light, his shocked eyes beheld his mother, sitting on his chest, her knees on both sides of him. In the gloom of the room, Mikey could see her face and he knew that look well. She was plastered out of her mind, so deep into the bottle she was basically sleepwalking. She would never remember the action she performed this night. As he gasped for air, he could hear her mumble something.

"Fucking retard, no good retarded bastard. Ruined my life..."

The darkness was closing in and he tried to speak, to tell his mommy that she was killing him, that he didn't want to die. That he loved her, no matter what she thought of him. That he was sorry he was born 'slow'.

But her grip was like iron, and try as he might, he was helpless to stop her. As white spots crossed his vision from lack of oxygen, his dream flooded back to him. He saw Mr. Manatee and Devil Ray, both frowning at him. They had warned him about his mother and he hadn't listened.

The girl was there, her arms open wide to him, and even as he lay dying, he felt the wetness of his underwear from his wet dream of making love to her.

But though it had only been a dream, to him the sea creatures and the girl were the most realistic entities he had ever met in his life, and though he wanted to live, he accepted his fate.

As his mother applied enough pressure to entirely block off the oxygen to his brain, Mikey's eyes glazed over and he fell into the dark abyss of the hereafter.

But as he did, he smiled, for in the abyss was a magnificent, sixty foot schooner, filled with cannons, booty and even a parrot for his shoulder.

He had found his pirate ship and he was the captain.

He was happy.

LITTLE MURMUR

RICK MOORE

He knew before he entered the house the suffering he was soon to endure. It was Friday, after all. When he stepped inside his worst fears were confirmed. The whole place reeked of fish. And that could only mean one thing: his mother's fish stew.

Trevor set his school bag down beside the doormat and took off his shoes. These rituals were so drummed into him that he completed them without thought. The last time he'd forgotten and entered the house wearing shoes, even though he had unconsciously wiped them on the mat, his mother had spanked him until the belt dripped blood. He walked through the house, heading for the kitchen, and opened the door. His nose wrinkled as the full force of the stench assaulted his nostrils.

His mother stood at the cooker, stirring a large pot on the stove. She leaned forward, inhaling the aroma. How could she stand it?

Before being told, he went and washed his hands, hoping it would please her. She said nothing, but took a bowl from the cabinet and began filling it. Trevor sat at the table in his usual place and waited.

"Smells delicious, Mom," he lied.

Trevor was thirteen years old and a notorious bully at school. His only friends were two other bullies he had beaten in fights that later came to recognize him as their natural leader. Only one thing really scared him and that was his mother.

"Enough talk," she said. "Eat."

The bowl she placed before him stank. She stood with her arms folded, her eyes narrowed, waiting for him to object.

Looking at her, with her single joined eyebrow, fleshy nose and hairy mole on her cheek, he wondered not so much why his father had left one day to buy cigarettes and never returned, but what had ever drawn the man to her in the first place. She often berated the man, calling him a worthless drunk, and perhaps that had something to do with it.

Trevor's attention returned to the fish stew.

Daily, Trevor suffered at the expense of his mother's culinary shenanigans. But while most of her stomach-churning fare could eventually be swallowed so long as it was chased down by copious quantities of water, her fish stew barely needed to touch the inside of his mouth before he was ready to blow it back out with a torrent of bile. Inside the inky bowl of liquid before him, many a scaly chunk of bone-filled meat awaited. A stir with his spoon to explore what else might be lurking within the bowl revealed several fish heads.

"What's the matter?" she asked. "Don't you like it?"

Experience had taught Trevor, that the best thing to do was to hold his breath and get started. If he waited too long, the broth would cool, and the only thing worse than a hot bowl of his mother's fish stew was a bowl gone cold. He didn't dare leave any of it. Somehow, he managed not to puke. Somehow he forced it down. When the bowl was empty, he asked if he could go to the beach to play. This was another ritual. Every night Trevor washed and dried the dishes, Friday being the only exception. In a rare instance of mercy, his mother allowed him one night off. One time, several years earlier, knowing he was about to vomit all over the kitchen table, he had begged her to let him go play on the stretch of isolated beach their house was located a quarter mile from. She had relented, and had continued to do so every week thereafter. If she knew he ran to the beach to vomit, she said nothing. But whenever he returned there was always an amused twinkle in her old gray eyes, so he had to wonder.

"Very well," his mother said. "But only for an hour. First go put on your clothes for play."

Trevor raced upstairs, changing his clothes in a matter of seconds, willing the fish stew to stay down a few minutes longer while he hung his school uniform on hangers and put on a pair of old jeans and a faded t-shirt. Then he left the house and ran to the beach.

Soon, he was crashing through the wild grass and leaping over the first sand dune. He slid down the dune, his feet digging up sand. He glanced backwards, just to be sure his mother couldn't see him from the house. Then, clutching his stomach, he leaned over and spewed. When he was finally purged of the noxious stew, he pawed at the sand, covering the evidence.

He was just about finished when a sound like none he had ever heard filled his ears. It was a woman's voice, singing, but like no singing he ever knew existed. The type of song and its language were so foreign to his ears. Trevor stood, wiping a thread of puke from his chin. The voice was so entrancing he broke into a run to locate whoever might be creating such incredible sounds.

"Hello, Trevor," the woman said when he stood before her.

She was positioned on a rock, the sea crashing all around her.

"You're a...a..."

"My name is Ariela," the mermaid said. "I was sent by my father to deliver a message. We know how deeply you hate to eat fish. How the taste makes you sick to your stomach. And my father wants me to tell you, if there were more little boys like you in the world, the oceans would be far happier places."

"I'm not a little boy," Trevor said, pushing out his chest. "I'm thirteen."

Ariela giggled, covering her mouth with her hand. Her tail slapped against the rock. "You still have much growing to do, young Trevor. But any boy with such consideration for the other creatures of this world, will a fine man one day make. It is in recognition of your fine ways that I come here today to extend the hand of friendship."

Trevor moved closer. Ariela's face was beautiful. The blue of her eyes was deeper than any he had ever seen. And her hair, golden and long, hung down past her shoulders, covering her breasts.

Suddenly, he became aroused.

He held out his right hand, meaning to take Ariela's in his. He didn't remember picking up the large smooth stone he held in his left hand, but as he neared her, and her stench hit him, he acted without thinking, the repulsion chasing away his attraction.

He smashed the mermaid in the side of the head and she dropped off the rock on which she was so artfully positioned and fell to the sand. Trevor jumped down and knelt over her. The blood from the wound seeped into the sand, turning it dark.

"Trevor..." Ariela said, sounding confused. "I came to...offer our friendship. Why are you..."

"Shut the fuck up, fish-bitch!" Trevor yelled in her face, and giggled.

The mermaid's tail thrashed the sand, but Trevor wasn't looking at her tail. Ariela's hair had moved away from her breasts when she'd fallen and he immediately felt the impact of getting his first proper look at them.

He had seen boobies before, in a magazine another kid brought to school. The magazine showed other things as well, things he hadn't really understood—until now. Trevor used his left hand to pull down his jeans and his right to reach into his pocket and remove his pocket knife.

Until now the knife had only been employed to dig shells and stones from the sand and for stabbing pieces of driftwood and performing surgeries on crabs. He opened the knife and pressed the tip to just below the point where Ariela's human upper half met the start of her scaled tail. The tip punctured her flesh and she gasped.

"Trevor...please don't do this...."

He stabbed her repeatedly, opening a hole and digging out chunks of flesh. When he had made a big enough opening, he pulled his pants the rest of the way down and stuck his member into the hole. The mermaid's tail thrashed between his legs. He picked the bloody stone and gave her another whack on the head. He had only intended to calm her down a bit, but must have used too much force, because the blood flowing out of the second wound was a torrent, while the first had only been a trickle. Ariela's blood pooled around them as Trevor thrust away, grabbing her breasts with hands that were barely big enough to hold them. If what was between a normal woman's legs felt anywhere near as good as what he was experiencing, then sex was very soon going to become his number one priority.

A sudden overwhelming urge to taste her flooded his mind. He pulled out and reached into the gaping hole. His fingers closed around some of the meat inside the bloody wound. He yanked as hard as he could. When he removed his hand, he saw it contained a lump of flesh that dripped blood through his fingers and splattered the sand. He shoved the meat into his mouth, smearing his lips, and chewing with his eyes closed. It was disgusting and glorious all at the same time. He mounted her and put himself back inside her, harder than ever, and fell into a steady, thrusting rhythm.

Ariela raised her head, eyelids fluttering, to look up at him as he thrust again and again. "But you...you hate that you... have to eat fish..." she said. We...saw it...in your dreams..."

"True," Trevor said, hitting Ariela's human belly and breasts with a spray of her own blood as he spoke, bits of food falling from his mouth. "But you ain't a fish," he said, building towards climax. "You smell like one but you taste like, like... Well like a mermaid, I guess."

Before long he was finished. It only took a few seconds before he knew what he intended to do with her next.

The other thing Trevor always brought along when he went out to play was a book of matches, but until now he had only used them to start fires or burn insects. He left Ariela where she lay, her tail beating feebly against the sand, splashing in her blood as it pooled under her. He walked back up the beach, going above the tide line, gathering wood that had dried out from exposure to the harsh sun. It took several trips, but before long he had a nice little pile gathered. Carrying the last armful back to the site of his intended bonfire, he found the mermaid trying to crawl back to the safety of the sea. He dropped the wood in his arms, selected a sturdy looking piece, and followed her bloody trail down to the shore.

"Trevor," Ariela gasped, looking back as he raised the driftwood. "I'm not mortal in the same way as you. You can't..."

"That's what my mom always tells me," Trevor said, clubbing her about the head until she fell face first into the wet sand. "Can't do this, can't do that. But she's not here." He threw the driftwood into the sea. He grabbed Ariela by the tail, and walking backwards, dragged her back towards the pile of wood. "I'm going to get into terrible trouble for staying out late," he said. "But I know it's gonna be well worth it."

The skewer was actually a rusted iron pole he'd found on the strip of beach years earlier. He kept it hidden in the wild grassy area behind a dune he thought of as his den. Ariela regained consciousness just as he was shoving it into her mouth. Using all his strength, he pushed and pushed, watching the iron pole disappear into her body. Blood flowed out of her mouth as he pushed the iron pole deeper inside the mermaid. The blood made the pole slippery, and the task more arduous, but at last the other sharpened end popped out of a section of her tail. She remained conscious the entire time. Trevor thought that after the pole had been rammed through her from end to end, and after the flames had finished burning away all her yellow hair and had blackened her skin to a crisp, that she would have died. But amazingly, the fish creature was still alive. He knew she was cooked right through because he had cut off chunks of her—both fish and human—and had eaten them.

But still the mermaid's tail kept thrashing, and she went on making a gargling noise in the back of her ruptured throat. Sated with the cooked flesh of the mythical creature, Trevor sat by the fire and watched her continue to cook. Long after her eyes popped, the mermaid's tail continued to move. The sky darkened, the stars came out, and with a full belly, Trevor slumbered.

He was woken by a whack to the head.

He looked up and saw his mother looming over him.

"So this is where you got to, is it?" she said. "I should thrash you blind for staying out so late."

Had it all been a dream? And why was there a gentleness to his mother's tone, almost like she wasn't really angry with him at all?

"The next time you catch and kill a mermaid, boy," his mother said. "Be sure to gut the little bastard first."

"Mom?" Trevor asked, sitting up and rubbing the sleep from his eyes. His mother walked to the blackened body positioned on its pole over the fire's dying embers.

"And you're supposed to keep them raised up over the fire. That way they'll cook but won't get burned." His mother looked at him, shaking her head, and peeled off a strip of arm meat, the fingers at the end of which continued to twitch. The little mermaid made a little murmur.

"You'll learn," Trevor's mother said, tilting her head back and dropping the strip of meat into her mouth. "And when there's no mermaid to be had, you'll get to like that fish stew of mine. You'll see." His mother chewed, nodding her approval. "Tasty bit of mermaid that is," she said. "Needs salt, though."

CAREFUL WHAT YOU WISH FOR

TONIA BROWN

To be fair, Timmy never asked for a goldfish.

He just came home one day from school, and the fish was sitting on his dresser, in a little glass aquarium, as if it had been there for the whole of his twelve years on earth. After a full five minutes of staring at the thing and it not disappearing, Timmy ran back down the stairs to find out what he'd done to deserve a goldfish. Because whatever it was, he planned on doing it again and again. Or at least until he got a dog, which was what he really wanted.

"There's a goldfish in my room," he said when he reached the kitchen.

"That's nice, honey," his mom said. She was making dinner, which meant she wasn't paying him any mind.

He whined, "For real, Mom, a real live fish."

His mother stopped chopping onions. He had her attention now.

"What?" she asked.

All at once, Timmy felt like he had exposed some grand secret of the universe, but to the wrong person. He stammered, "A f...f...fish. In m...m...my room."

She narrowed her eyes as she wiped her hands on a kitchen towel.

"Show me what you've done this time."

They were in his room in moments, where Timmy's mother stared wide-eyed at the goldfish in the small aquarium on his dresser. "Timothy Michael Pearson! Where on earth did you get that?"

"I got it for him," Dad said. He was standing behind them, wearing a wide and knowing smile.

Mom wasn't smiling. She wasn't even frowning. She looked really, really mad. Madder than Timmy had seen her in a good long while.

"And when were we going to talk about this?"

"What's there to talk about?" his dad asked.

She tipped her head at Dad, a sure sign she was hornet-mad. "We can start with who's going to clean that tank because if you think..."

"Timmy will clean it. Won't you, champ?" his dad asked.

"Yeah," Timmy said. "Yeah! I'll clean it every day."

Dad chuckled as he ruffled Timmy's hair. "You won't have to do it that often, silly Billy. Once in a while should be fine."

"Mark?" Mom groaned.

"Sorry, Martha," Dad said, then kissed her on the forehead. "I suppose I should have asked you first. But it was kind of a spur of the moment thing. I bought it for a song from some street vendor. And I reckoned if Timmy could prove to us he can keep up after that little guy, then maybe we could talk about a dog later."

Mom nodded, the beast of her anger satisfied by Dad's offering of a kiss and a lame excuse. Timmy didn't understand old people, but he understood fish even less. Now dogs, those he understood. Or at least he thought he did. He wanted to. And if this fish was the only way to get to a dog, then understand it he would.

Timmy had to eat rice that night. He hated rice. And he knew it was rice even before he saw it, despite the fact his mother tried to hide it in that stupid ceramic dish shaped like a chicken—as if that made it any easier to eat. Rice and...what was that? Broccoli! Ugh. It was as if she didn't want him to eat at all.

"People are starving in China," Mom said. "They would kill for that rice."

"They're starving 'cause rice is all they have to eat," Timmy mumbled.

"All right, mister, you can go to bed without anything to eat at all."

He knew it! She didn't want him to eat!

Timothy went to bed with a rumbling belly and a sour attitude. As he lay on his side, hungry and angry, watching the fish, he wondered how long it was going to take to get that dog. His stomach rumbled in the quiet of his room. Even the fish seemed to hear it. Goldy stopped in its circle and swam to the edge of the tank, nearer to Timmy and his grumbling stomach.

"I wonder," Timmy said aloud, "if the chicken plate was gone, would Mom ever make rice again?"

The next morning his dream came true. Well, sort of.

When he went downstairs, seeking sustenance after a long night of being so very famished, he discovered the scattered remains of the dreaded ceramic chicken plate. Sometime in the night, it had slipped from its spot on the dish rack, and busted to a dozen pieces on the tiled kitchen floor. He toed the shards and smiled. There was no chance of a plate that broken ever getting fixed!

Timmy couldn't have been happier. "Yes!" He pumped his fist into the air, laughing and dancing around among the broken pieces.

"My dish!" his mother cried as she entered the kitchen. With a gasp, she pushed him aside and rushed up to the mess. She turned back to Timmy with a terrible, sad look. "How could you, Timmy?"

"What? But I didn't..."

"How could you do this? You know I love this plate. Your grandma gave me this dish."

"So," Timmy said, not understanding.

She thought he did it and for once, Timmy wasn't to blame, unlike all the other times when he *did* do it.

"But...I didn't break it, Mom, I swear."

His mother didn't believe him; he could see it in her tear-filled eyes. She collapsed to the floor crying, cradling the pieces of the broken plate to her like she had broken her arm. Dad tried to comfort her, but she shrugged him off and ran upstairs. The sound of a door slamming reached father and son as they stared at the broken plate together.

"Why is she so sad?" Timmy asked in a whisper.

"Because," Dad said, "that plate was the last thing your grandmother gave us before she passed on. Your mom thinks of her every time she uses it."

"Oh." Timmy didn't know that. He wouldn't have wished the plate broken if he had known it was special to his mom. He felt kind of sick inside, like he had broken the thing himself. But he didn't. Did he?

"But I didn't break it, Dad."

"We can deal with that tonight."

"But I didn't break it! I swear!"

"And I said we'll deal with it tonight." Dad checked his watch. "Get your clothes on, son. I'll run you to school. It'll put me behind, but I don't think your mom is up to it today."

Timmy groaned. "If I rode the bus, you wouldn't have to be late."

"Stop your grousing and get your duds on."

It was the same thing every morning. Why couldn't he just ride the bus like the rest of the kids? His parents were such worry warts. Timmy had heard such awesome stories about the bus. The things the kids talked about. The things they did! He felt like a little kid, being driven back and forth to school by his mom or dad. He wished he could pretend he was a rich kid with a chauffer, but no. His parent's beat-up station wagon snatched away that illusion.

"Geesh, Goldy," he whined as he changed clothes in his bedroom. "I don't know why I gotta go to school at all. I wish I didn't!"

The fish stopped its swimming and headed to the side of the glass. It was like the fish was really listening to him, which made him feel a little bit better. Not much, but a little.

Until he heard his dad honk the car horn and holler up at him. "Timothy Pearson, get your behind down here now!"

Timmy put on his shirt and shoes and raced to the garage, wondering what he had done now. He found his dad looming in the garage doorway, fuming about who knows what.

"Explain yourself, son," his dad demanded.

"Um," Timmy started, not knowing what he was supposed to explain. "I was just getting dressed, like you said."

"Very funny." Dad grabbed him by the shoulder and pulled him into the coolness of the garage, dragging him to the car. Once there, he pointed at the passenger tires. Both of them were sitting on their rims, they were so flat.

Timmy gawked at the huge gashes that ran the length of the rubber rings. "What happened?"

"That's what I'd like to know, Timmy." Dad had that look in his eye, the same one Timmy's mom had just moments ago. The look that said, *You did this. You're to blame.*

"You think I did this?" Timmy asked and pointed to the tires. "I didn't do it!"

"I didn't say you did." Dad raised an eyebrow. "Do we have a guilty conscience?"

Timmy crossed his arms and stuck out his lower lip. "No, 'cause I didn't do nothin'."

His father gave a tired sigh as he checked his watch again. "I don't have time to argue about it. Just go to your room. You're staying home today."

"All right!" Timmy shouted before he could stop himself. Great, now it looked like he really did cut the tires.

Dad pinched the bridge of his nose between his fingers. That wasn't a good sign. It meant he was angry. "Go to your room, Timmy. Now."

He did as asked, bounding out of the garage like a frightened deer. His father called out to him before he could escape. "And you're grounded until I say so," his dad said.

"Aw," Timmy whined. "But I didn't do anything."

"No television."

"Dad!"

"No video games."

"But..."

"Just go, before I get really mad and revoke your privilege to breathe."

Timmy screwed up his face in frustration as he ran to his room. Parents were so unfair sometimes. From the sanctity of his bedroom, he could hear his parents' low mumbles.

Dad was telling Mom it would all be okay, but Mom kept crying anyway. A horn honked from the driveway, and Timmy pulled the curtain in his room aside to see a rusty old taxi parked on the roadside. It had come to pick Dad up for work as he couldn't drive with two flat tires. Timmy would never hear the end of it now. He didn't know how much a cab costs, but he knew it must be a lot, because Dad always complained if he had to call one.

Timmy did his best to stay out of Mom's way that day. He kept quiet, in his room, just like a good boy should. He even cleaned the aquarium, from top to bottom. Well, sort of. But mostly he just sat and stared at his new fish. It was the only bright thing in his life right now. Sure he got a day off from school, but that would just put him behind on homework. And besides, what good was a day off when he couldn't play video games or watch TV? A boring day, that's what.

After several hours, he started to get really hungry. With no dinner last night and no breakfast this morning, by noon his belly was really grumbling. His mom, bless her soul, came to his rescue. She placed a plate, complete with a sandwich, potato chips and a pickle spear, on his desk without saying a word to him.

"Mom?" Timmy asked as she turned to leave.

She gave a tired sigh, then turned back to him. "Yes, son?"

"I really didn't break it. And I'm sorry I was glad it was broken. I didn't know...I didn't know it would make you so sad."

"It's okay." She smiled, weak and sad. "I believe you. I know it must seem silly to a boy like you. But that plate was very important to me. Do you understand?"

"Yeah." He furrowed his brow as he asked, "Am I still grounded?"

"Your father will talk to you about it after dinner."

"Okay."

"And be sure to clean up. Your Aunt Betty is coming over."

No sooner had she closed the door than Timmy collapsed onto the bed. Aunt Betty! Ugh! This was getting worse and worse.

"Why Aunt Betty?" he asked no one in particular, though Goldy seemed interested in his question. The fish swam to the edge of the aquarium and stared at him. "Out of all of the loud and annoying people in the world, why do I have to be related to her?"

Goldy didn't answer, but it did eye him in a funny way, as if to say he was a bad kid for dreading his aunt's visit.

Timmy stuck his tongue out at the fish. "You don't know what she's like. She isn't just way too loud or way too annoying. She also likes to kiss people, on the cheek. People as in me. Yuck! Who does that anymore? I'm almost thirteen. I'm almost a teenager!"

Goldy swam in place and kept staring.

"I wish she couldn't visit," Timmy said. "I wish...I wish she just couldn't come over."

Goldy seemed to tire of his whining. The fish swam away and left him alone with his wishes. Which, of course, he kept right on wishing.

Dinner came and went with no sign of Aunt Betty. Mother worried, jumping at every sound, running to the door at every car that passed their driveway. When the phone call finally came, Timmy almost knew without being told. It was Aunt Betty, she had been in a car accident. She was alive and in good health, save for a pair of broken ankles.

There would be no visit tonight, or for quite a while.

It took everything Timmy had not to squeal aloud at the news.

No more visits from Aunt Betty for a whole month at least! How cool was that? And his parents seemed to forget all about the grounding, which was just a bonus. He rolled about on his bed in silent glee. This was awesome! First no rice, then no school, and now no Aunt Betty.

He stopped his rolling and sat up as a thought struck him hard. Three things he wanted to happen had happened just after he wished for them. Not very big things, but wishes none-the-less. What was happening here?

He supposed it was just a set of…what was the word he'd just learned? He closed his eyes and sounded the word out in his mind, slowly.

Co-in-ci-den-ces.

This brought a smile to his lips. Sure, it was just a series of co-incidences; nothing to get excited about. He looked up to Goldy with a goofy grin on his face.

"It's not like I could wish for something impossible. Like for Sarah Hollis to kiss me or something; though it sure would be nice if she did." He lay back on his bed and dreamed of that wish coming true, nice and slow, under the apple tree just outside of school.

School was boring and stupid, typical of an average day. He still didn't get to ride the bus, and everyone asked why he missed the last day, but all Timmy wanted to talk about was his new pet, Goldy—his golden ticket to a dog.

Sam Peterson was royally pissed that Timmy had a pet and he didn't. "My dad will get me a dog before you'll ever have one. This afternoon if I ask," Sam said. "Anytime I want one, I could have one. I just don't like dogs."

"No," Timmy corrected him. "You don't have one 'cause even dogs don't like you!"

The kids all laughed and Sam turned the exact shade of Sarah Hollis' pink blouse, which Timmy had spent all morning staring at. He had loved her from afar for an entire school year now, but she would never notice a boy like him, three grades under her. But here, on lunch break, he blended in with the crowd. And he always lingered long enough to be near the door when she went back to class. It was the one time in the day she passed close by him; close enough for him to smell her sweet shampoo and wonderful per-fume.

As he stood with his goofy grin and dreamy eyes, he was sur-prised by the sight of his lovely Sarah tripping over a loose brick in the walkway. Timmy pushed the others out of his way as he rushed up, arms outstretched, in an effort to keep her from hitting the ground. He arrived just in time to have her topple atop him instead of the ground and, miracles of miracles, her lips landed exactly where his happened to be at that very moment.

She kissed him!

She may have done it by accident, but it happened!

He held her close, for two or three heartbeats, his lips latched to hers by pure accident, but he didn't care. When she realized what was happening, she pushed away from him, took on a terrible look of disgust, then slapped him. Right across the jaw, she smacked him, and for what? Breaking her fall?

"Keep your hands off of me!" she shouted as she scrambled back to her feet.

"Looks like he had more than his hands on you," Sam laughed.

They all laughed, every kid who heard Sam. And they were laughing at both Sarah and Timmy. Sarah stamped her foot in frustration before she pushed her way through the crowd and disappeared. Timmy was left alone, starry-eyed and blushing.

The kiss stayed with him all day, as did the slap. His classmates teased him wherever he went, and for once he was glad he didn't have to endure a bus ride home.

When his mother arrived to pick him up, she asked, "What's eating you, son?"

"Nothing," he said. And yes, it was a lie. But so what? It wasn't like she really cared.

They both fell quiet as she drove the long route home. At length she said, "I got a call from school today."

Timmy recognized her tone. "What did I do wrong now?"

"Mr. Adkins says you've been tripping girls, then groping them."

"I did not! Geesh!"

"Okay, okay, how about you tell me your side of the story?"

Timmy did. He told her exactly what happened, minus the important part, of course. He didn't tell her that he had, just the very night before, wished for the kiss. It was terribly exciting, this idea that he could wish for things and they would happen. Even if the results were unpredictable. He would just have to figure out how to word his wishes better.

As he explained to his mother the humiliation of his day, he noticed they weren't driving home at all. Mom was pulling the car into the hospital parking lot. They were going to visit Aunt Betty! This was just awful. Not only did he have to go into the hospital, which he really hated, but he had to see Aunt Betty after all. He was really going to have to perfect his wishes, and soon.

He decided to give it a try, right now.

"I wish," he whispered under his breath. "I wish I didn't have to see Aunt Betty. I wish we would just go home instead."

But it didn't work. They went right in and spent almost three hours listening to the cackle of that horrible woman. Timmy's ears were ringing and his cheeks were swollen with kisses by the time they left. At least he got to eat fast food on the way home, but it was little consolation for such a terrible trial.

He flung himself on his bed and eyed his goldfish as he contemplated his problem. Why didn't his wish work? What had he done wrong?

Goldy swam about without a care in the world. No laughing kids. No annoying relatives in hospitals that smelled like antiseptic. Timmy sighed as he watched her. "I really wish we didn't have to go back to that hospital. I wish we never had to see Aunt Betty again."

Maybe she could move or something, he wondered. Or maybe his parents and him could move. That would be fun! Then he wouldn't have to see Aunt Betty or go back to school and have all of the kids make fun of him for trying to grope Sarah—even if he didn't.

It was three in the morning when his mom got the call about Aunt Betty. She had suffered from a massive brain clot that sprang up overnight. Sometimes these things happen, the doctors tried to explain to his crying mother. Sometimes they don't catch all the injuries from car wrecks. Sometimes people die.

Timmy didn't know what to think. He was almost numb with disbelief. Sure he had wished that Aunt Betty was gone, but not this? He didn't wish for this, for her to die. And why did it work the second time, when his wish about visiting her didn't? Timmy felt shame settle on him when he realized he almost wished his mother's last three hours with her sister away, just because he was so selfish. He would have to learn to control his wishes, as well as wish for better things.

Could he wish for Aunt Betty to come back? Probably not. He had seen one too many movies where some fool tried that, with disastrous results. No, until he learned what made the wishes happen, he promised himself he would stop wishing all together.

He tried to keep his promise. He really did.

Two days after the funeral, which also got Timmy out of school, though he was far too sad to care about that, he was sitting in his room late in the night, contemplating both the idea of wishing and his yearning for a dog. He thought about wishing for one, but what if the wish backfired? They seemed to go terribly wrong with such ease, and he wasn't willing to risk something as important as a dog on bad wish.

A pebble hitting his window grabbed his attention. Timmy peeked out to see Sam standing on his lawn, in the moonlight, smiling up at him.

"Hey, loser!" Sam yelled in a hoarse whisper. "I just came by to show you this."

Beside Sam sat a puppy, and not just any puppy. It was the cutest, bestest puppy Timmy had ever set eyes upon. It was exactly the kind of dog he wanted. He didn't know the name of the breed, but he knew he wanted one. And there was Sam Peterson, all smiles and rich parents and puppy owning before Timmy could prove to his parents he could do it, too.

"My fish is better than that stupid dog!" Timmy shouted in as close to a whisper as he could manage. "Twice as good!"

"Whatever," Sam hissed back at him. "Can it do this?"

Sam wiggled a little rubber newspaper at the puppy, who looked like it couldn't care less about newspapers, rubber or otherwise. Yet the moment Sam tossed it away, the puppy leapt into action. It ran across the dew-covered lawn, and snatched the toy up. The puppy brought the toy back to Sam, who received it with the grin of a greedy master.

The dog could fetch! Great, Goldy couldn't do anything but swim. Timmy slammed the window on Sam's wild laughter and whipped around to eye his lame pet. "Why can't you fetch? Stupid fish!" He slapped the side of the aquarium, as if he could strike the source of his worry.

Goldy swam in furious circles, and in the weak glow of the nightlight, the fish looked very angry that Timmy had slapped the tank. It was as if he had slapped the fish itself.

Timmy felt bad for taking his frustrations out on Goldy. "I'm sorry. I just wish...I don't know. I just wish I had Sam's dog, you know? I wish he couldn't have it anymore and had to give it to me."

Goldy calmed down, and so did Timmy.

Three days came and went, and with them sad news arrived.

"Have you seen my Sam?" Mrs. Peterson asked Timmy when he was playing in front of his house.

Sam's parents were carrying papers with Sam's face and their phone number on it. Mrs. Peterson's eyes were red with grief, like she had been crying for ages. "He went to bed three nights ago, and when I went to his room the next morning, he was gone."

"No?" Timmy said, though he could hear the doubt in his voice. But he couldn't tell her that he had seen Sam outside his window the very night he went missing. Everyone all knew how much he and Sam fought. They would blame Sam's disappearing act on Timmy, which is probably what Sam was planning all along.

"Can you do us a favor?" Mr. Peterson asked.

Timmy nodded.

"We just bought him a dog, the day before he..." the man paused, as if too sad to say the truth. "Anyway, we don't really have time for the puppy now. Can you take care of him for a bit?"

Timmy nodded, very slowly, and tried hard not to grin.

The wish had worked—again. He didn't know how or why, but he knew it was his wish that sent Sam away. Timmy wasn't upset about it. He didn't like Sam anyway. Why should he care where the boy went?

But his dog.

Timmy cared about that with all of his heart.

The puppy's name was Bruno and he came to the house that very evening. Timmy pretended to take on the job of watching the pup with a heavy heart. On the inside, he was cutting cartwheels and singing hosannas and strutting like he had won the Kentucky Derby. Once he got Bruno to his room, Timmy let all of his joy out in one big squeal of laughter.

"Welcome home!" he shouted as he squeezed the little ball of a puppy. The dog was no bigger than a kitten, but was much fatter, with folds of skin hanging off of his chubby frame. Most kids, Timmy reckoned, would want a big dog, like a Retriever or a Dalmatian—but not Timmy. He liked this little fat fur ball because it could sleep with him and follow him around and never be in the way. He also knew it would attract the girls like flies to honey.

Who could resist the adorable face of Timmy's new dog?

When he turned out the light, Timmy was reminded of Goldy by the soft glow of the aquarium. Now what was he gonna do with the goldfish? He had a dog now and he didn't need the responsibility of taking care of a fish too. And he certainly didn't want to clean the tank if he didn't have to.

Something would have to be done.

"What do you think, Bruno?" he asked in a whisper.

Bruno licked his nose, which was an excellent suggestion.

Timmy would just get rid of the goldfish. In the morning, when everyone was still asleep, he would flush the fish down the toilet, then tip the tank onto the floor. When it crashed, he would jump back in the bed and shout "Bad dog! Bad dog!" but it would be far too late. Bruno would have 'eaten' the fish, and all would be well.

It was the perfect plan. Goodbye one goldfish, and hello one wonderful dog!

He fell asleep with the idea in his mind, just like a wish.

Six in the morning came early, but Timmy was ready. He woke to the first rays of the sun, ready to enact Operation Get Rid of Goldy. But a crucial piece of the plan was missing. Bruno was gone. Where had the puppy gotten off to? No matter, he would just find him, carry him back to his room and begin the scam.

Timmy crept all over the house, whispering the puppy's name over and over but to no avail. As a last resort, he cracked his parents' door, just to make sure the dog somehow hadn't snuck through into their room in the middle of the night. But Bruno wasn't there either. He wasn't anywhere. And Timmy was beginning to worry.

"Timmy?" his dad called out from his bed, Timmy's mom lying beside him. "What's wrong, son?"

The plan abandoned in the face of this new worry, Timmy told them, "Bruno's gone. I can't find him."

His parents looked at one another for a moment.

"Who?" his mother asked.

"The dog. Sam's dog. He wasn't in my room when I woke up," Timmy explained.

"Aw, son, I'm sure he's fine. Let's look for him, okay?" his dad said.

And they did. They looked in the kitchen, all the cabinets, in the bathroom, in the garage, and even in the attic. But again there was no sign of the dog.

"You know," his dad said. "There's a good chance he slipped out of the house somehow and just went home. Some dogs do that."

"But this *is* his home!" Timmy whined.

"For now, but it's a real possibility he went back to the Petersons. Let's go back to bed for a while, and when it's a decent hour, I'll call them myself. Deal?"

"Okay," he said but it really wasn't okay for Timmy. He hated the idea of the puppy going anywhere near the Petersons. Bruno was his now.

Dad helped him into his bed, tucking the covers nice and tight, just like he liked them.

"Besides, you still have a really great ..." Dad paused as he turned to look at the tank. "My God, son, what have you been feeding that fish?"

Timmy sat up and stared at the tank. He rubbed his eyes in disbelief, but it didn't help. The fish in the tank looked like Goldy, swam sort of like Goldy, but it was way too big to be the same goldfish whose ruination he'd plotted just the night before.

This goldfish was enormous, almost too big for the tank. The fish looked swollen in the belly, as if Timmy had indeed been feeding it too much. But of what, he had no idea. Timmy stared unabashed at the bloated fish. It was just so large. So very, very large. Far too large to flush down a toilet now.

"Wow," his dad said. "It's like the damn thing swallowed a dog."

Timmy's eyes widened as everything fell into place. And he realized that from now on, whenever in Goldy's presence, he should be very careful what he wished for.

THE CAVE

MARC SHEMMANS

The dripping didn't cease. It continued into a puddle beneath, where the drops broke the shiny surface at a rhythmic pace. Each pelted the water with a thick, coagulated-like plop, the way melting ice cream falls from a cone.

If anything, the dripping grew faster.

Carl Manning opened his eyes. So accustomed to the darkness, he blinked uncontrollably. The fresh light stung. While adjusting to the light that filled the small room, he felt the cold slab of stone that lay underneath his left cheek. Pulling his arms against the rough surface below his head, he pushed his palms against the floor and lifted his body to his knees. After gaining his balance, he checked his body thoroughly. The front of his clothing looked filthy, layered with a chalky dust from the rock floor. He swept the dirt from his double-breasted suit as best he could. His dark jacket hung over his shoulders and revealed a handsome, raspberry dress shirt. Opened at the collar, the shirt made him seem much younger than he truly was. This style not only gained him youthful appearance, but glances from young women as well. Friends and family advised him to wear a tie, especially in the courtroom, but he always refused: Ties made him feel much too old.

Carl's hazel eyes began to absorb the room around him; however, he quickly discovered the room was not a room at all. With its rocky walls and stalactites, which hung like icicles, the room was nothing more than a round cave. The walls curved vertically around, connecting with the floor and ceiling at inclines. The sloping angles gave the appearance of a disfigured bowl.

One of the first things Carl noticed was the height. The cave was very shallow, the ceiling hanging barely a foot above his head. The stalactites were so low that Carl had to be careful not to collide with one.

Only inches away from where he stood, that same dripping fell into a puddle. The liquid looked milky-white in the soft glow of light around him. This was the only sound in the cave.

It took only a few moments for him to assess his current situation. A sudden terror seized him, and his heart began to race at once. Nowhere around the cave could an opening, a doorway, or even a small fissure be found.

He was trapped.

Avoiding the hanging rocks, Carl hurried toward the wall opposite him. He pressed his weight against it, hoping the wall would shift, allowing him an exit. But it didn't budge. In fact, the pressure he applied rebounded upon him and a sent a shock through his arm.

Ignoring the pain, he ran his hands along the uneven surface of the wall, looking for a gap or crack. His hands brushed along the walls like a psychic looking for a spiritual connection. Maybe if he found some sort of slit in the rock, he could chisel away at it until it grew big enough to make an exit.

After many long minutes, Carl finally gave up. The rock wall was completely solid and intact. Not one fissure to be found. He even rapped his knuckles against the rock wall, checking for any hollow places which could be found. However, the dull thud he achieved could only mean that the walls were thick.

He couldn't understand it. If there was no way to get out, then how could he have gotten inside? Even if someone sealed the wall after enclosing him, he should have been able to find the mended line where the rock junctions conjoined.

However, these thoughts fled his mind as he considered a more disturbing idea. If he had been put in here, surly he would have remembered. Instead, he had no recollection whatsoever of anything prior to waking up on the cave floor.

But that wasn't entirely true. He remembered his friends' constant persistent cajoling to wear a tie in the courtroom.

The courtroom!

He had been in the courtroom before waking on the stone floor. Hadn't he? He thought hard. If he had, how did he end up here? He couldn't vanish from one room and wind up in a cave, lying lamely on his stomach. That wasn't possible. He'd seen some impressive stunts, but nothing like this.

Another thought seized him. A trick! This must be some sort of trick. He was probably on one of those prank TV shows or something. Maybe even one of his friends had set this up. He knew enough pranksters who loved pulling this type of thing. However, logic told him if this was a prank, the tricksters had paid a hell of a lot of money setting it up.

"Think, dammit!" Carl hissed to himself.

How had he gotten here? How had he gotten here?

He sat on the floor next to the puddle. He clinched his eyes shut and probed his mind as deeply as he could.

I'm in the courtroom. I've got Judith on the witness stand. She's recounting the day her husband, Ryan, was murdered. Her alibi is solid. I've saved her, and I'm going to reap the benefits. That's what happened, right? What else? Something must have happened. Think! You can do this. Just remember.

The courtroom was crowded. This was the trial of the year. Billionaire murdered. Wife suspected of killing him. Carl Manning, the best damn lawyer in Birmingham, in charge of the wife's case. But I was going to get her off. The contract had millions to be paid out to me if we won. And I had it. I had it beat. But look at me now. I'm in some godforsaken cave.

"Where the hell am I?" he yelled to the ceiling, which ricocheted off and bounced around the thick walls, echoing his hostility over and over until finally fading away.

Still staring at the ceiling, Carl saw dim light reflected feebly against the rock. The light convulsed and shattered, then repaired itself repeatedly. Searching for the source, he found that the light was shining off the small puddle beside him.

He stared at the puddle as it caught a new drop of the chalky water, and even more rivets cut through the puddle in circular shapes. He held his right hand, palm up, for the next drop. It fell in the centre of his palm and at once sizzled as it burned his flesh. He jerked his hand away and furiously wiped the water on his trousers. He feared immediately thereafter that his trousers would singe and a hole would burn through. But it didn't. Instead, a dark stain appeared where he had touched them. Carl looked back at his right hand. A red, irritated dot had appeared.

"Son of a bitch," he said incredulously, rubbing his palm with the left index finger. The water must be acidic or something. Whatever it was, he wasn't going near it again.

While rubbing his burned flesh, Carl thought about the reflective light on the ceiling. If this cave was completely sealed, if there was no way in or out, then where was the light coming from?

He stood up at once, his neck arched. His eyes searched the corners of the wall near the ceiling. He must have missed these spots. If light was flooding the cave, then there must have been either a hole where light was penetrating or an artificial light powered by a lamp.

He used the inclines of the wall to lean against and crawl up as close to the ceiling as possible. Once again, he groped at the wall, hoping to find some hole or crevice. As if blind, his outstretched hands slid across the rocky surface to no avail. The wall was as solid as ever, and just as cold.

He dropped back onto the floor, careful to avoid the obtrusive stalactites. He halted where he stood and picked at his chin, where he felt the bristly hairs. He agitated it roughly with his fingers in deep meditation. He furrowed his brow as he summed all of his logical and deductive reasoning skills.

The cave he occupied was completely shut off. Nothing was getting in or out. He sure as hell wasn't. However, light was somehow managing to seep into the cave. And any idiot knew light couldn't exist without a source.

So, he had to be correct in thinking this light—this pale, white light—was either surrealistically magical, or he was having a bizarre and incredulous dream.

However, as best he could remember, he had never known he was having a dream while in the process. He believed every dream was real, until he woke up and realized the truth. And to be honest, a particularly bland cave was no normal dreamscape. Most of his dreams took place in royal, billionaire mansions with hundreds of beautiful girls awaiting his return to his nocturnal imagination. He even dreamed of himself addressing an enormous courtroom with reporters, camera crew, famous celebrities all around, aroused and intrigued by his prowess as a lawyer and his devilishly handsome features. Never in his memory could he recall dreaming of a barren, cold cave, alone and trapped. If anything, this was a nightmare—something with which he was very unfamiliar. Men like him didn't have nightmares. Men like him didn't fear, or worry enough to conjure a restless night, imprisoned in their own heads. No, he slept more than perfectly every night.

Could this, therefore, be years of unhindered rest unraveling at once by a dream-like form of karma? Possibly. But even if this was the case, karma was not at her best: This nightmare was boring and pathetic. There was nothing extremely frightening about it. His only real concern was escaping. And he was sure if he had gotten in, he could certainly be able to get out. It was only a matter of time.

His wife Corinne would probably worry if he didn't show up soon. She would become suspicious once more. His late nights at bars with clients kept her restless at night.

Carl chortled silently to himself.

Corinne hardly ever got any real, solid hours of rest. Carl, on the other hand, slept soundlessly.

A perfect balance.

The water didn't stop dripping into the puddle. Never would it stop, he thought irritably. It annoyed him greatly, especially in his quest to think clearly and precisely. It was as if an enormous lake was above the cave and it poured ceaselessly through the stalactite.

Then something moved within the water.

He frowned, leaned closer, and gazed into the puddle.

Nothing.

Then a splash as another drop of water hit the water.

Carl spun around at once.

The water was coming from somewhere. Maybe not a lake, he thought, but somewhere above him. Meaning there had to be a hole near the stalactite, or in it.

He grasped the hanging, pencil-like rock.

"God dammit!" he shouted into the cave, retracting his right hand from the stone as if it were a stick of emblazoned flame. The echo reverberated for much longer than before.

He examined his hand. The small dot in the centre was no longer discernible in the vast redness that pulsed heatedly off his entire palm. As though painted crimson, the palm of his hand shone a bright, red pigment.

The same acidic water that dropped from the tip of the rock must have covered the entire stone. If he tried to attempt to break it, he would burn both his hands.

Suddenly, near his left ear, he heard a soft, hissing sound. He could have sworn he heard his last name, but when he looked back up in front of him, he gasped in horror. The stalactite that had burned his hand raw no longer hung stiffly. In fact, the entire stalactite had vanished. In its place, a long, thick, dark emerald fish hung. It was like no fish he had ever seen before in his life. It had long, razor-like teeth and its smooth scales were the color of leaves on a moonless night with designs of black stripes, much like tree roots in the dark, running diagonally around its body.

Its slender form swiveled like a rope, flicking rhythmically at the ends. Its pointed, sharp face rose on a kind of neck which curved upward, like a U-bend of a sink. A pink, thin tongue slid quickly from its mouth and tasted the still air. Forked at the end, the tips almost grazed Carl's right cheek.

Instead, the fish continued to lick the air, for Carl had stumbled backward, bumping his head into solid stalactites behind him. In fear, he crouched low, looking up to check whether other fish had appeared, but he found it the same; only cold stone.

He jerked his head back around and saw the fish drop to the ground unceremoniously. For a brief moment, Carl prayed to God that this thing had killed itself from its rough landing. However, the giant aquatic creature didn't seem bothered. Ignoring its fall, it slowly, silkily, slithered toward Carl on its ivory scaled stomached. The tongue never stopped jerking. The teeth never stopped chattering.

Carl couldn't speak. His heart seemed to be lodged tightly in his throat. Why was it not dying? Fish couldn't breathe out of water, could they?

He felt like crying, he felt like screaming, most of all, he felt like running. But he couldn't. He knew it, of course. He was trapped. He was trapped in a cave with a huge fish, and its burning, sun-yellow eyes looked viciously murderous.

In his attempt to put as much room as possible between himself and the enormous creature, he must have tripped over a rock or his own feet, for he toppled onto his back— hard. Unlike the fish's resilience, his thunderous crash resulted in severe bodily consequence. A blinding spark of pain shot up his back.

The fish didn't hesitate. It didn't pause to see what had happened to Carl. It didn't look frightened of his sudden movement, or any more dangerous. It continued smoothly on its long belly toward Carl—its supper. Ready to feast, the fish unhinged its jaw and opened wide.

Carl didn't care where the fish came from at this point. He was too fixated on the long, sharp fangs that now hung from the fish's open mouth. The pale, pink mouth stretched wider and wider, until finally he could see inches inside its throat. For a quick second, he thought he saw an apple core stuck deeply inside, but once he blinked, the core had vanished.

Instead, he saw only a dozen or so long fangs that curved to a venomous point. The fish slithered inches closer to him. It would strike at any moment.

It began to raise its head high into the air.

Carl scooted helplessly backwards, hoping beyond hope that a doorway would suddenly open up in the wall and allow him his freedom. But this didn't happen and he hit solid wall at last.

This was the end. The fish's head rose at least three feet into the air and then paused.

Carl's face poured profusely with sweat. His raspberry shirt was soaked to a maroon.

Then the fish did something that shocked him. He almost forgot his own fears for a moment because of it.

The fish's head jerked down, as if bowing to Carl.

It was a quick bow, almost curtly and formal. But it was there.

Then, just as quickly, it pulled back its head and launched forward at him.

Carl, caught off guard by this, pulled his arms before his face—as if this would have protected him—and clinched his eyes shut tightly.

However, he felt no pain. He felt no stabbing of teeth into his flesh. He felt nothing, except for the dull pain in his buttocks where he had chipped his tailbone.

He opened his eyes cautiously and slowly dropped his hands.

The fish was no longer present. At least not in front of him anyway. As a precautionary measure, his eyes searched the stalactites above him, thinking the fish may have slid up an arm of stone and now waited for Carl's self-assured safety, so that it could attack at his most vulnerable time. As if this just now hadn't been it!

Carl clutched his chest, which ached horribly from his trembling heart. He applied a great amount of pressure, as if hoping to calm his heart by letting it know he was okay and nothing bad would happen, rather like someone would treat a small, petrified puppy.

He attempted to stand up, but a lightning bolt of pain soared from his bottom up his spine. The pain overwhelmed him. He saw the flash of light flicker before his eyes, and he fell onto his back, which, unavoidably, sent another white-hot stab of pain through his body. A whirring of constellations streamed before his eyes as he fought the throbbing.

If this wasn't some sort of nightmare, how could a fish morph from a stone stalactite? But it couldn't be a dream; he was in far too much pain to be sleeping silently and safely in his bed. Nothing made sense. Fear began to grow hot around his face.

This was just some strange hallucination, that's all.

He'd taken drugs before—several times for that matter.

Acid. Dope. X. 'Shrooms. Blow. You name it.

His drug-abusing clients usually offered him the best after he cleared them of narcotic charges. His reputation as a man whom criminals could trust to free them of prosecution gained him supporters of the filthiest breed. Club owners granted him VIP status, where he would spend his well-earned pounds late into the night for 'business meetings'. He'd even met his current client at one of those clubs, though he didn't have to insert a dollar bill between her panty strap and ass for a 'business meeting'

Judith Carlisle, the alleged murderer of her billionaire husband.

'Alleged'.

Carl smiled despite the pain.

Of course she'd done it. He'd even helped her.

After their many trips of acid, Carl and Judith had concocted a plan to collect her late husband's fortune and move away together.

They had been sleeping with each other for months even before the trial started. Carl had everyone fooled—especially his wife.

When he finally won Judith her case, he was going to divorce his wife. He would tell her that he had fallen out of love with her— her jealousy had pushed him away—she had ruined their marriage.

He didn't worry about his money, his savings. Carl wasn't stupid. He'd made his wife sign the prenuptial at their engagement.

Yes, the plan was full proof. However, Carl always had an inkling of a suspicion that Carlisle's son, Judith's stepson, knew something about their clandestine plans. But Carl had never been able to prove it. He had worried of course. The young twenty-something-year-old college dropout had already been convicted of two indictments. One for armed robbery, the other for grievous bodily harm.

He could be a problem. He was definitely unstable, but brainy enough to uncover the truth? Doubtful.

Carl always thought he might be just a little paranoid.

Was that happening now? Was he just being paranoid? Maybe he imagined the fish. Maybe he had taken something, passed out, and woken up in a dream state-of-mind. The ultimate trip, he thought sardonically. To confuse the world of hallucinations for the real world.

The panic inside him was building. He felt the heat steam from underneath his clothes, rise up through his shirt collar, and encase his face. He was consumed with the fear of the unknown. For so long, he had lived in a world set by his rules, his decisions. But now he was in a place where control was out of his hands.

He felt sick. His throat grew dry and tight. He began to choke.

Falling to his hands and knees, he choked and sputtered. His eyes bulged from their sockets and tears began to leak from their ducts. His nose ran heavily of thick mucus. He couldn't stop himself. Ironically, the idea of his disgusting appearance frightened him more so than his fear of the cave.

When the choking had reduced to a stuttered coughing, he wiped his face with his hands and rubbed the tears and mucus onto the cold floor. His stomach wretched, but he didn't vomit. He had nothing to vomit. But he needed water. He needed something to quench his dry throat.

The puddle lay before him, its milky-white color glistening in the soft glow of the cave. The rippled marks of the falling drops confused him in his desperation to find water. The slow, minuscule waves reminded him of an oasis in the desert.

He crawled lamely to the puddle, cupped his hand, ladled out a handful of water, and drank it ravenously. When his hand didn't burn, he continued to drink and drink, until his thirst was quenched.

His coughing had calmed, and his breathing had slowed to an almost normal level. He ran his index finger across his forehead where it collected a pool of sweat, which he flicked with a snap away from him. He sat gingerly on the back of his heels, careful not to put pressure on his bottom.

His stomach roared within him. How long had he been in here? He probably hadn't eaten for a while. Not since lunch. Whenever that was. If only he could...

His stomach growled once more. But this time, a sharp piercing joined it. He screamed in pain, in agony. Something inside his stomach had bitten him!

He clutched his stomach as another horrendous growl erupted from inside his abdomen. There was no bite accompanying it this time, but the lingering pain of the first bite still burned within him.

Suddenly, he felt his chest tighten and then bulge under his shirt, as if he were growing fat or was being pumped with air. His esophagus burned as if he was swallowing a giant hot pepper—only in reverse. A long, warm object tunneled up through his chest and halted within his throat, where he lost all source of air and collapsed on the floor, groping at his neck, which felt twice as wide as normal.

He couldn't choke. He couldn't sputter. His throat was completely shut off by the thing inside. The monster inside! He knew it must be a monster, for he saw—by magic or by a hidden psychic ability he unknowingly possessed—two great crimson orbs attached to a dark, unrecognizable creature inside him.

Just as Carl almost lost consciousness, the monster began to move once more, as though only teasing the notion of death with Carl, until he could no longer take it.

The monster began to pour from his throat, up into his mouth. The object was tasteless, but his tongue ran across the millions of stiff little hairs wrapped around it. Carl turned onto his stomach and heaved it out.

Covered in his saliva, or perhaps its own mucus, the monster fell onto the ground like a helpless baby animal, newly born from its mother. Carl's eyes burned with tears and sweat from the ordeal. He blinked them clear to see what he had produced.

A football-size fish lay staring at him. A thick, shiny coat of slime plastered its shiny scaly body, its red eyes staring into Carl's. At once, Carl began to dry-heave from disgust. The pain was excruciating. After a few heaves, blood splattered out of him, the blood that oozed from the fish's vindictive bite.

His gagging must have scared it, for it slithered away toward the puddle, sliding head first into the dark water to disappear.

Carl, ignoring his pain, hobbled toward the puddle. The damn thing had escaped! Oh, how he had wanted to stomp on it. To squash its spine! To crunch it under his foot until there was nothing of the damn thing left except slime that he could wipe off at his leisure.

He pushed his hand through water and felt around for the creature. Nothing. He continued to feel around until his hand hit solid rock.

Enraged, Carl climbed to his knees and scattered the puddle with both hands, hoping to find the fish. But underneath the water, there was nothing. He quickly stood and walked around the cave, wanting to find a means of escape.

He went back over to the huge puddle, hoping to find a hole that led somewhere but there was none.

Above him, another droplet fell onto the crown of his head, where it sizzled and burned as it had done before. He grasped the back of his head and yelled in fury.

"What the hell is happening to me?" He gazed around the cave frantically, looking for some sort of explanation.

"What is this place?" he yelled at the top of his lungs. "Is this Hell? Am I in Hell?"

A soft chuckle rattled between his ears.

It was at that moment that realization finally struck and time became frozen within the cave. Visions flashed before his eyes at an amazing speed, as if trying to catch back up from its icy lag.

He hadn't been in the courtroom last before he found himself in the cave. The trial had ended. He and Judith Carlisle had won. They had gone back to her house to celebrate.

Bottles of champagne were strewn around the room. Half were empty. Some opened, but not touched. Who cared? They could afford it now. They were now wealthy beyond their imaginations!

Their clothes were scattered across the furniture. Her bra lay in tatters after he ripped it off with his bare hands. Judith had torn open his suit, the buttons having popped off.

However, presently, as he ran his fingers down his shirt in the cave, the buttons were securely sewn on.

The scarlet, satin bed sheet covered Judith's bosom and his waist. They had just finished making love, or at least compensating for the lack thereof—he had never known.

She rested on his bare chest. He ran his fingers across her beautiful, exposed, butter cream back—his fingertips caressing like rain drops. She was expounding on their plans to move to the beach, maybe somewhere in the Caribbean. He had closed his eyes, imagining all the places she described. He had felt relaxed, at peace with the world. Then he heard her scream.

His eyes flashed opened, and he saw with tremendous horror Judith's stepson at the foot of the bed. His clothes were wet with the rain outside. His hair stuck to his forehead. And though his face was wet from the rain, Carl could tell he was crying. His eyes were puffy and red. He looked so feeble—feeble like a child.

Then he pointed the gun. It appeared like a magician pulls a colorful scarf from his sleeve. It hadn't been there until he revealed it.

One shot, without warning. Judith's blood sprayed onto Carl's chest and face.

He froze. Had not tried to protect himself, to defend himself, or even to shut his eyes from the fear.

He watched the son turn the gun towards him. Carl had watched the bullet leave the barrel, watched it fly through the air, and watched it enter the left side of his chest. He looked down at his chest. At the puncture wound. At the life fluid that poured from the hole.

The pain wasn't as bad as he thought. The pressure of the bullet hurt more than the process of death seeping behind his eyes like when a theatre curtain closes, ending a dramatic scene.

As Carl's eyes drooped and blurred, he saw the son point the gun at himself. He pushed the muzzle inside his mouth, and pulled the trigger. The last thing Carl remembered seeing was the son's brains shooting out the back of his head and striking nightmarishly onto the wall behind him.

And then all Carl saw was darkness.

And now he was in this cave.

Had he died? How could he be sure?

He felt alive.

How could he hurt, choke, cry?

He sure felt alive.

Despite the doubt that had begun to form, he knew the truth. He knew where he was. All the mistakes he'd made to earn him this eternal punishment. He pushed his doubts away and admitted the truth.

He had died and was resurrected in Hell.

He sat limply on the floor, ignoring the pain from his tailbone.

He heard a noise. A quiet splash. Then saw the face in the puddle.

He crawled over to it, and when he reached the edge, he felt something shove him from behind.

He hit the water and immediately his lungs began to fill with the cold, dark liquid. Then a pale shape began to float towards him and he was entangled by something. He tried to brush it free, but all he managed to achieve was to come face-to-face with Judith's late husband Ryan's, ghastly and decomposed face.

Ryan's eyes opened and his skeletal hands reached out for Carl, who tried to fight free. He hit the corpse time and time again until he had no more energy.

Then something strange happened.

Ryan's pale and mottled face burst open. It shattered into a dozen large creatures—a dozen fish. Fish with deathly sharp teeth that immediately began to slice into Carl's exposed flesh, as they began to eat him alive, causing him agonizing pain.

The last of Carl's air bellowed out of him in a scream as he scrambled to the surface.

He tried to climb out of the puddle but several of the fish pulled him down.

And suddenly, the light from the cave went out like a burnt bulb. A telltale of the acknowledgement of his demise.

The cave was silent except for the sound of dripping. The dripping didn't cease. It continued to drop with thick, fat plops, like congealing blood.

If anything, it appeared to grow faster.

THE ONE THAT DIDN'T GET AWAY

MATT NORD

"**W**hy the hell does he have to come along?" Chris complained.

"Because he's my cousin," Tom said. "He's family."

"Well, with family like him, who needs enemies?" Chris mumbled.

Tom rolled his eyes and said, "That doesn't even make any sense."

"Neither does bringing along that loud-mouthed bastard..." Chris snapped and immediately regretted it. "No offense."

"Look, I don't really like the guy, either," Tom said, placing his big hand on his friend's skinny shoulder.

It wasn't meant to be intimidating, Chris knew. Tom Henry was the kindest man he had ever met. The type that everyone who knew him would say he wouldn't harm a fly. And it was true. In all of the years he'd known him, Chris had never seem him threaten another person or get in a fight.

The truth was he really didn't need to. His size was enough to deter even the most belligerent drunk from picking a fight. In fact, Chris, who was known for having a bit of a mouth, had been saved a beating on more than one occasion by simply walking up and asking said potential beaters if there was a problem. The answer in all cases was a meek 'no', followed by several proverbial tails tucked snuggly between multiple pairs of legs.

As grateful as Chris was for being saved from getting an ass-kicking, he dreaded the inevitable tongue-lashing he'd get from Tom, who would reprimand him on the need to treat everyone with respect. He would finish by telling Chris how he couldn't always rely on Tom to pull his behind out of every fire.

"It's just," Tom went on, "Jerry is my Aunt Maggie's only son. She was my favorite aunt, and when I was ten and Jerry was seven, I made a promise to look out for him."

The big man's eyes got a spacey look to them and he stopped talking. He was obviously off in a memory and he wasn't thinking what he was doing when his grip on Chris' shoulder became tighter.

"Hey!" Chris squeaked.

Tom came back to reality and snatched his hand back like he had touched a hot stove.

"I'm really sorry, man. I didn't mean to hurt you," he apologized profusely. He had a worried look on his face.

"I know you didn't, Tom," Chris said, massaging his shoulder.

"It's just, I made a promise to my aunt," Tom said. "And ever since she died, Jerry's just been so lonely."

"That's because nobody else can stand being around him," Chris mumbled.

"Come on, Chris, be nice," Tom said. "Besides, Jerry loves fishing." Chris rolled his eyes and crossed his arms in a huff. Their fishing trips had become a yearly tradition over nearly two decades. It had always been the two of them. Chris might be mouthy when he was at the bars, but he knew one thing about fishing.

You needed to be quiet if you wanted to catch anything, and if there was one thing he knew about Jerry, it was that he had no concept of what it meant to keep quiet.

Chris glanced over at Tom, who still had a sullen look on his face. "Fine," Chris finally said and Tom brightened immediately.

"But you better keep him in check."

"Sure, sure," Tom said, clapping his hands together so hard it hurt Chris' ears. "This is gonna be fun!"

* * *

Chris gritted his teeth and tried to hold his tongue, not that it was helping. Since they set out early that morning, Jerry hadn't shut up, and none of them had gotten so much as a nibble. Chris had promised Tom on the way to pick up his cousin that he would make every attempt to be cordial. Tom had agreed to try to keep Jerry at least somewhat quiet.

Unfortunately, one of them wasn't able to keep up their end of the bargain.

"I'm fucking telling you!" Jerry bellowed. "I was fishing on Seneca Lake and I caught this fucking trout! It had to have been at least fifty pounds!"

Chris had stayed quiet for most of the morning, only giving Jerry a half-hearted, "good morning" when they picked him up at his trailer and answering Tom if he asked Chris a question. Chris had been bombarded all morning with a constant stream of wild fish stories, disgusting jokes, and too much information about Jerry's past sexual exploits.

The jokes were bad enough. But the other two topics? Chris wasn't sure which were more unbelievable.

"Can you believe it?" Jerry rocked the boat as he spread his arms wide to show the other two men just how big the fish had been. "Fifty pounds!"

"Whoa!" Chris nearly dropped his fishing rod trying to keep his balance. "Watch what you're doing, dumbass!"

Jerry shot him an evil look. Tom steadied the boat simply by grabbing either side with his massive hands and settling his center of gravity to the middle of the rocking vessel.

"You got a problem, asshole?" Jerry looked like he was about to jump on Chris.

"Uh, yeah," Chris shot back. "I came out here to fish, not to take a dip!"

"Oh, I'll give you a dip!"

The two men seemed to be ready to jump on each other when Tom laid a big hand on each of them. Both immediately quieted, but the tension remained. The big man had a sad look in his eyes.

"Come on, you guys," he pleaded. "We're out here to have a good time, right?"

"I'm having a blast," Jerry said. "It's this prick that's trying to put a damper on the trip!"

"Jerry!" Tom roared.

Chris knew Tom rarely raised his voice in anger, and if he did, someone had really pissed him off.

"I invited you along because I knew you were lonely," Tom said. "You don't have a lot of friends, so don't push away anyone who's willing to reach out a hand of friendship."

He took his right hand off Chris and turned his massive body to face Jerry. It wasn't a threat, but from Tom, a lot of innocent gestures seemed menacing.

"I promised your mother I'd look out for you," he said. "That promise didn't die with her."

Chris started to feel a little guilty. He knew how Jerry was and could have simply kept his temper in check. He hated the fact that he'd upset Tom, not because he feared him, but because he was his best friend. He had been for years and years, and if Tom could bail his sorry ass out of the situations he had, then why couldn't he swallow this nasty pill and try to do his best to keep the peace?

It was obvious that Tom's words hadn't affected Jerry in the least. Jerry still glared at Chris and he couldn't believe the hate he saw in the man's eyes.

Time to swallow that pill, Chris thought to himself.

"I'm sorry, Jerry," he said.

Jerry's looked changed from anger to suspicion. Tom turned around and gave his friend a hopeful look. Chris nodded at Tom, giving him a genuine smile.

"We've been going on these trips for a long time, Tom. We've always had a good time, and I'm not going to be the reason that this year was different," Chris said, looking back and forth at the two men. "So, let's just try to get along."

He held his hand out past Tom's bulk towards Jerry. Tom looked expectantly at Jerry, who regarded Chris' outstretched hand like it was covered with dog shit.

"Jerry?" Tom asked and Jerry seemed to snap out of a trance.

"Yeah," he said, grabbing Chris' hand for a quick shake. "Fine, whatever."

"Okay, then," Tom said with an enormous grin on his face, clapping both men on their backs and nearly sending both in the water. "Let's fish!"

The next hour went by uneventfully, other than the fish that were caught. Not many words were exchanged other than by Tom, who quietly told Chris how much fun he was having every few minutes.

"Me, too," was always Chris' response. And, truth be told, he actually was. If he kept facing the water from his side of the boat, he could pretty much imagine it was just him and Tom.

But it was too good to last.

"You guys want to hear another fish story?" Jerry asked over Chris' shoulder. Chris rolled his eyes. Tom saw this and nudged him with an elbow. Again, while not meaning to, the blow caused Chris to wince.

"Uh, yeah, sure," Chris said, rubbing his tender ribs.

"Hey, Tom," Jerry began. "Did I ever tell you about the fish woman I met?"

Tom's smile disappeared and his face went white. Chris didn't notice the change but thought it was strange when he didn't answer.

"Right here in this very lake," Jerry continued.

Chris wasn't sure what he should prepare for: an obnoxious joke, a fish tale, or another one of Jerry's sick sexploits. Maybe a little of each.

"I don't want to hear that story," Tom's cold reply came.

At that, Chris raised an eyebrow. After all of the stories Jerry had told that morning, and all of his jokes that Tom laughed at, why the change in his demeanor?

Jerry let out an evil sounding chuckle that made Chris' skin crawl. Apparently, another game was being played.

"I haven't heard it," Chris said, tossing his chips in the pot.

"You don't want to, either," Tom said with a hint of finality in his voice.

They all sat in uncomfortable silence for a short time. Chris nearly jumped out of the boat when Jerry spoke.

"Well, I'm going to tell it, anyway," he said.

Tom looked like he wanted to argue, but kept his mouth shut.

Satisfied that he wouldn't be interrupted, Jerry began his story. "It was ten years ago. I was out here fishing by myself."

"Surprise, surprise," Chris mumbled.

Jerry shot him a dirty look but Chris had an innocent look on his face. "What, can't a guy clear his throat?" Chris asked.

Jerry snorted and hawked a disturbingly large loogie towards the side of the boat, but it didn't quite make it to the water. Tom didn't say anything but gave the puddle of snot and spit a disgusted look as it dribbled its way towards the deck of the small boat. Jerry ran his sleeve across his mouth to wipe away the string of spittle hanging from his lower lip.

"Anyway," Jerry continued, satisfied that all attention was on him and his antics. "I was out here, probably close to this very spot, and I had my cast out. I was just chillin', minding my own business and drinking a few beers."

Chris raised an eyebrow to that. He'd watched Jerry single-handedly down nearly an entire case of beer that morning, not that Jerry had paid for it or even so much as offered to chip in.

"Okay, maybe a few more than a few, smart-ass," Jerry sneered. "But I wasn't drunk!"

Chris decided against saying anything or even batting an eyelash in Jerry's direction for the duration of his storytelling session, or he feared it would never end. He made his best attempt at an attentive but neutral face. He almost laughed out loud at the thought of how ridiculous he must have looked, but managed to hold it together.

Chris glanced over at Tom, who simply sat with his head down and his hands clasped between his legs. It made Chris a little uneasy to see his large friend look so ill at ease.

What the hell is bugging him so much? he wondered.

"So, I'm kinda' just relaxing when all of a sudden," Jerry paused in an attempt at a dramatic effect, "my line goes tight and I nearly get pulled out of the fucking boat! Whatever this thing was, I knew it was huge and strong as hell!"

Tom didn't seem to notice the 'excitement' of the story or he was simply ignoring it. Chris just made a 'wow' face, so Jerry wouldn't be disappointed.

"So I fight this thing for at least three hours! I'm exhausted. I can barely hold on to the rod," Jerry said, clearly excited. "Then I just lose it. I was done, anyway. I knew I wasn't taking this thing in!"

Chris was starting to wonder if he'd misunderstood Jerry when he said something about a 'fish woman'. Maybe it really *was* just a fishing story.

"Then it came up..." Jerry said.

Chris waited for more of an explanation. He was actually interested, now.

"What came up?" Chris asked.

Tom looked up, now, a slightly pained look on his face.

"The fish woman," Jerry said calmly, as if it was no big deal.

Again, Chris needed clarification.

"What are you talking about?" Chris asked. "You mean, like a mermaid?"

Jerry chuckled. "Not quite," he replied. "You ever see that old movie *The Creature from the Black Lagoon*?"

"Uh, yeah, back when I was a kid," Chris said. "They used to play it on *Midnight Theatre*; old and cheesy horror movies."

"Yeah, that's prob'ly the one," Jerry said, nodding profusely. "Now, picture that fucking thing grabbing a hold of the side of this boat and pulling itself aboard."

More dramatic pausing to allow it to sink in and Chris smirked slightly. Tom still had a concerned look on his face.

"Now, picture this fish bitch has tits like a playboy centerfold and an ass that's perfect!" Jerry shouted, laughing slightly.

Chris had no choice. The thought was in his head now, and it wasn't even remotely appealing.

"Well, this thing pushes me down on the boat and I'm nearly pissing myself!" he said, getting more and more excited. "I figure I'm done for, that it's gonna rip me open and eat my guts!" He paused to take a swig of warm beer. The amber liquid dripped down his chin as he belched and tossed the can overboard. "But no! This thing tears my clothes off!" He yelled. "I mean, I got a little scratched up, what with its claws and all, but nothing like I thought it was going to do."

Chris didn't like where the story was going, and his face must have told as much.

"What's wrong?" Jerry asked. "You don't like my story? It involves my two favorite things: fishing and fucking!"

He laughed as he stood up in the boat, causing it to rock again. Chris grabbed the side of the boat to steady himself. Tom didn't bother. He wasn't going anywhere.

"Well, I'd been with enough ladies in my life that I could tell by the look in her fishy eyes where this was going." Jerry licked his lips at this.

"Okay," Chris said. "What's the punch line?"

Jerry stopped and sat back down. "What do you mean, 'punch line'?" he asked. "I swear it's the truth! It really happened!"

"So, you had sex with a fish?" Chris asked for clarity.

"Fish *woman*," Jerry corrected him.

"Whatever," Chris said. "Did you kiss her?" he chided.

"Heh, hell no!" he replied. "She had these fucking razor sharp teeth, like, um, like a piranha."

"Of course," Chris said, rolling his eyes. "But wasn't she all scaly and shit?"

"Well, on the outside, maybe..." Jerry looked out over the water and smiled. "But shit, I mean, black, white, green fucking scales; they're all pink on the inside, am I right?"

Neither Chris nor Tom returned the high five Jerry went for. He lowered his hand and grabbed another beer. As he cracked it open, he looked deep in thought.

None of them spoke for a while. Then Chris decided it was his turn to be the joker.

"Well, I suppose I'd buy that story more than the one about the fifty pound trout!"

He slapped Tom on the knee and laughed loudly. Tom feigned a small grin. Jerry, who hadn't taken his eyes off the lake since the silence had begun, slowly looked over at Chris.

"You don't believe me?" Jerry's tone sent shivers down Chris' spine. Jerry took a small sip of beer and placed it on the seat next to him. Then he pulled a boning knife from a sheath that Chris hadn't noticed under Jerry's pant leg. It was rusty and covered with what he hoped was old, dried fish guts.

"I still come out here to visit her, once in a great while," Jerry said, boring his eyes into Chris'. "But sometimes... she gets hungry!" He shoved the knife towards where Chris sat.

"No!" Tom screamed as he moved into the path of the blade. It slipped between his ribs and punctured his left lung before Chris knew what was happening.

"You fucking idiot!" Jerry shouted, pulling the blade out of his large cousin. Tom fell over the side and into the water, splashing the other two men in the boat.

"Shit, shit, shit!" Chris shouted, moving as far from the knife-wielding maniac as he could on the small boat. "You fucking killed him!"

"Damn it," Jerry said. "Not what I meant to happen, but..." he shrugged. "What can you do?"

Chris wanted to try to help Tom, but he seemed to be paralyzed with fear. He looked overboard at his friend. Tom's back was up and it was obvious that he wasn't moving on his own. Chris willed himself to reach over, hoping to roll him over, but before his hand reached Tom, he pulled it back in shock.

An enormous clawed, webbed hand reached over Tom's wide back and pulled him underwater. A few seconds later, Chris gazed on in awe and horror as the water began to bubble furiously, turning a bright red. Shreds of Tom's flannel shirt and a couple of beefy fingers floated to the surface.

Chris leaned over the other side of the boat and emptied his stomach, cheap beer and beef jerky splashing the water.

The water calmed and Chris heard something large surface. The boat tilted as whatever it was grabbed the side of the boat. Chris looked over his shoulder. His eyes widened and he let out a loud gasp as he soiled himself.

"Hey, baby," Jerry said, caressing the thing's bald, scaly head as he stared right at Chris. "Ready for some *dessert*?"

ONE LAST SWIM

KELLY M. HUDSON   *For Tim*

Terry knew it was a bad idea to go out for one last swim, but it was the end of her vacation and she was damned if she was going to let an approaching tropical storm rob her of a final dip in the beautiful, warm water of the Gulf.

Now she was out in waves twice her size, pushing her away from the beach and towards a small cliff wall, with no hope of swimming against the tide. Above her, the sky turned dark purple and pissed rain. The clouds—once fluffy and white, billowing like fat dandelions—were black now and spitting long streaks of hot lightning. The air had changed, growing colder by the second, the usual humidity fleeing from the new, icy breath of the storm. The change came quickly, before she even had time to really register it, and by then, the Gulf grabbed her and tossed her around like an abused wife.

She screamed, hoping someone would hear her. The storm, as if wanting to toy with her further, reached out and snatched up her cry, swirling it into the howling winds and tossing it out into the churning waters. To add injury to the insult, the waters punched her side and slammed her against the small cliff face, bouncing her off the sheer rocks and sending her spinning in a circle.

With the breath knocked out of her, she tread the water, fighting against the push and pull of the currents, hoping to find a spot where she could hold on to the rocks. Her fingers slipped, scraping the smooth surface. Another wave battered her into the rocks and she jounced off, her shoulder throbbing from the impact. She had to get someplace where she could slow down and catch her breath, where she could lean against something or hold on, because at that moment, it was like she was thrown into a washing machine with the lid slammed shut.

She thought of her husband, Evan, and Sammy, their four year old. They were inside, safe and warm, probably wondering what had happened to Mom because she hadn't told them she was going. If she could hang on, if she could stay afloat long enough, surely they would come looking for her.

The waves pushed her back towards the rocky cliff and this time, she was ready. She rolled onto her back and struck the stones with her feet first, using the force of the wave to thrust her up and flat against the rock. Her fingers scrambled along the surface, finding long cracks two inches deep. She held on for dear life, suspended by her fingertips, as her toes scratched just above the water level, searching for some purchase. Miraculously, she found one, and she dug in her digits as far as they would go.

Water splashed up and smacked her backside, hitting so hard she almost let go and slipped back down into the depths. But she held firm, her arms and legs already aching from the effort. She had to stick here, stay where she was, and wait for help to come.

She tried to put her mind on other things, thinking of their trip.

For Evan and Sammy, it was their first visit to Sanibel Island off the coast of Ft. Myers. She had spent many summer's out here when she was a kid and always talked about how beautiful the area was. Finally, a nice vacation earned after all those years of hard work at the firm.

Evan had proposed they come out and finally make a visit. Both husband and son hadn't been disappointed, and they had a great week of sun and swimming. Out here, it was like they were finally free of all the worries back home. There was no mortgage to worry about, no electric bills or cable or garbage or water. There were no in-laws or friends, always demanding time, and there were no pressing pressures of any sort. There was only time spent together and it had been wonderful.

Terry's father used to live nearby, in Sarasota, after he divorced her mother. She remembered the spent summers fondly, a time of swimming and new boys and friends; not a lot unlike her time she'd had with Evan and Sammy. She was glad they came and even happier things hadn't changed much on the island. She hoped Sammy was having the same experiences she used to have. That the sense of wonder and awe at nature and the Gulf that were so important to her were now imprinting themselves on him. It seemed so, because every day he was eager to get out to the beach, into the water, or play in the sand, building forts with Evan and then crushing them, pretending to be a giant monster.

Water smacked her again, colder than before, shocking her from her reverie. She was stuck on the rock, and she had to think of some way out. She looked up the face of the cliff but couldn't see any other cracks or potential hand-holds. The top of the cliff was forty feet away, and there was no way to scale it. Those forty feet might as well have been five hundred.

The muscles in her forearms burned and she could hardly feel her hands anymore. It was amazing she'd only been hanging there for a few minutes and already her body was about to give out.

Knots of pain shot up her calves and her hamstrings cramped. She trembled, on the verge of letting go and plunging back into the water, when a face popped over the edge of the cliff up above.

"Hang on!" It was a man, with a sunburned face and a big, walrus mustache. He was chubby, with three chins ringing his neck and holding his unwieldy head aloft. The man had wispy gray hair on top of his head, battered to and fro by the unrelenting winds of the storm.

"I'll get help!'" he yelled, and then disappeared.

Please hurry, she thought. She didn't know how much longer she could hold on.

Another wave crashed the rocks to her left, missing her but slapping something against the stones with a wet smack. She stared as a creature stuck to the rocks for a moment before sliding down and back into the brine. It had a nearly translucent sack for a head with a bluish tint to it and a vivid red line splitting it down the middle. Tentacles flowed from the sack, thick and blue, about twenty feet long.

It was a Portuguese Man o' War.

Her gaze followed the sea creature as it tumbled down, splashing into the churning water, dead.

Lightning slashed the sky, flashing the area in a bright blast of incandescence. As she stared down where the cliff met the water, just a few yards away, she saw hundreds more of the Man o' Wars, all floating in the general vicinity.

Her fingers ached and her toes hurt as she tightened her grip as best she could. She knew if she fell into the water, it was all over.

Her father had told her about Man o' Wars. She remembered the day vividly, when she was ten years old and several dozen had washed up on shore, dead. She walked around them, studying their long tentacles and bizarre heads. Her father had been walking behind her, slow catching up, but when he did, and saw what she was in the midst of, he called out to her, fearful.

"Don't touch them!" he shouted. He was still young then, probably the same age she was now. He was tall and rangy, with thin limbs and a swimmer's build. His hair was just starting to go gray then, but he didn't seem that old to her.

She froze, bent over with a stick in her hand to poke the bladder of one of the creatures. Her father picked his way carefully through the carcasses until he reached her side.

"You have to be careful," he told her, taking her elbow in his hand and standing her up. "They can still sting you, even if they're dead."

He led her up to the rocks just a few feet away. They sat down and he pointed to the water. She could see more of them floating, dozens upon dozens.

"They always travel together," her father said. "Sometimes in the hundreds."

"Are they jellyfish?" she asked.

"No. They're actually four different organisms, all living as one. Each part does for the other what they can't do for themselves," he said. He'd spent a lot of time studying the sea and always looked for opportunities to teach her something. "See that part on top, the clear part with the blue in it? That's called the bladder. It fills with gas and lets it float on the water. It also acts as a sail."

"Like a boat?"

"That's how they got their name. The bladder resembles the tri-angular sails on old Portuguese ships."

"Huh," she said.

He told her of their tentacles, and the venom they contained, and how badly they could sting. If she ever saw one when she was swimming, he said to her, she'd best get away as quick as possible. Where there was one, there were dozens.

And now she hung on the rocks, battered by the wind and sea, with nearly a hundred of the creatures floating around just a few feet from her. How had this happened? How had she been so stupid to come out and swim when the storm was on its way? One last swim, she'd thought. How dumb was that?

Her toes slipped from the crevice. She screeched and almost fell, her fingers barely hanging on as her feet scrambled along the slick, wet surface of the rock. She couldn't feel her toes anymore, they were so cramped and bent, but she managed to stick them back into the holds, regaining her place.

She couldn't hold on forever. How long had the man been gone? Half an hour? It seemed like forever. Spasms rippled down her forearms, shaking her biceps and shoulders. Her fingers were about to give out, and if they went, there was no way to hold herself up anymore.

A wave slapped her back, stinging her with its smack, and that was all it took to knock her from her perch. Terry plummeted down into the churning waters, splashing and sinking like a stone. Salty water shoved itself into her nose and down her throat as she thrashed about, coughing and choking. She paddled her way to the surface, breaking clear and hacking away, her lungs on fire and her body aching so hard she was afraid she would be too tired to stay afloat.

Something soft brushed her arm. She froze, moving her legs as minimally as possible, as a Man o' War floated next to her, its sack bumping into her shoulder.

Another wave smashed through, pushing the creature away from her at the same moment it slammed her against the rock wall again. She barely had time to get her hands up to protect her head before she ricocheted off and went splashing backwards.

Tentacles scraped her left forearm. They stung her, the pain so intense and bright-hot she nearly passed out. It slashed her skin, burning and lancing, as she jerked her arm back, pulling away. More tentacles touched her kicking legs, stinging and lacerating her flesh. Panic exploded in her chest as she cried and thrashed, managing to swim away from the Man o' War for a second.

The waves heaved and rolled, sending four more of them sailing towards her, their bladders erect and full of gas.

She lashed at the water in front of her as lightning creased the sky, flashing like a strobe and sending the world around her spinning into a surreal swirl. The waves crashed and boiled, rising and falling in stuttered glances. The Man o' Wars drifted closer, their heads shining in the light. The roar of thunder filled her ears. It shook her bones and everything spun together into a stammering blink.

The water slammed her against the rock wall again, knocking her from her brief moment of unreality. She bounced off and swam as hard as she could away from the Man o' Wars, heading towards the open Gulf. But the water was having no part of her escape as it buffeted her back towards the cliff wall and the tentacles of the dangerous fish.

Terry treaded water, trying to keep away from them to no avail. They were too many surrounding her, almost as if they were stalking and pinning her in like she was their prey.

"They don't think," she heard her father say to her, remembering when she was a child. "They float and sting and eat fish and sometimes, humans get in the way."

It didn't seem like that to her at the moment. As she looked out, spitting up water and trying to stay afloat, they seemed like demented demons hell-bent on killing her. It was hard not to take it personal when they surrounded her, their bladders gleaming like the brains of some Martian invader.

"You have to be careful when you're out in the water," her father had said to her. "It's not like going to the zoo. It's the real world. It's nature. And you always have to respect nature."

She hadn't done that. At some point in her flawed decision-making, she'd decided she could go out for this one last swim before the storm hit. She thought she had plenty of time. In her arrogance, she didn't tell her husband and now here she was, alone, about to drown or be stung to death by a floating armada of jellyfish.

"They're not jellyfish, honey," her father had said.

None of this was helping her now. Her father's memory, while soothing, was not getting her out of her predicament. She had to act now.

Terry let the water push her back towards the rock cliff. If she could get up into the holds again, she could hang on until the man she saw returned. Shouldn't he have been back by now? He'd been gone an eternity.

Something grazed her leg and she froze. A Man o' War floated just two feet from her. She thought for sure she'd been stung again but, as her leg was rubbed again with no sting, her father's voice returned.

"Some fish live in them," he'd told her. "They're immune to the sting and they swim around the tentacles, unharmed."

It must have been one of those fish.

She was brushed again. This time, she heard a scream so loud and distant she looked up, hoping rescue had arrived. Piercing pain burned her leg as a tentacle wrapped around her ankle, holding her tight.

It felt like it was burning through to the bone; the agony was indescribable. As she pulled away and her fingers raked the sheer rock in front of her, the screams grew louder, echoing back into her face. She realized then it was her own screams she heard. No one was up above. No one was there to rescue her.

Another tentacle found her right thigh. Everything went black for a moment. She was shocked from her unconsciousness by the scraping of another tentacle, this time across her ribcage. She kicked and fought, but the pain was too much, and she felt herself slipping away.

With one last, desperate try, she clawed the rock in front of her, searching for support. She tore fingernails off, beyond thinking now; just a wounded animal fighting to stay alive. Bloody streaks scarred the rocks where her shredded fingers fought to hold on, marking her doom. She was going to die down here, stung to death by an army of Man o' Wars.

She spun, freeing her legs from the stingers, and faced what was behind her. At least a hundred of them rode the roiling waves, spilling towards her, their bladder-heads honed in and shining blue. More lightning lit the sky and flashed off the water. Thunder boomed. Salty brine splashed her face and eyes, gagging and blinding her.

It was over.

A tentacle hit the top of her shoulder and Terry screamed again, terrified. It tapped her again and brushed her face. It took her a moment to realize it wasn't stinging her, that it was the end of a rope.

From up above, she heard a chorus of voices. She tilted her head back and there was the rope dangling just over her and, at the other end of it up top, at least a dozen people. They screeched and pleaded, their faces hovering over the edge of the cliff.

She grabbed the rope, her strength fading. She wouldn't be able to hold on, she realized, so she wrapped the end of it around her arm until all they had to do was pull and she would be lifted out of the water.

She was going to make it.

Tentacles lashed her legs. More struck her sides and back. Still others burned her buttocks. She felt one tighten around her left breast and squeeze. She blacked out. She woke up, dangling from the water, and looked down.

Several Man o' Wars hung from her, their long tentacles wrapped around her legs and torso just like the rope around her arm. She couldn't feel their stings anymore.

The rope pulled her up.

The Man o' Wars and the thrashing Gulf weighed her down.

Somewhere, in the back of her mind, she heard her father again.

"You have to be careful when you're out in the water," her father had told her. "It's not like going to the zoo. It's the real world. It's nature. And you always have to respect nature."

She smiled at her daddy and promised she'd always pay attention and respect nature. She was there with him, on that beach again, a young child, wrapped in his warm and loving arms. It was the happiest she'd ever been and now, being back there again, the rest of her life faded away into nothingness.

And as she died, the tourists of Sanibel Island hauled her body from the water, thirteen Man o' Wars clinging to her. Her body was so bloated from swelling, they later said, she didn't even look human any more.

She died grinning, though, and to a man, they all testified it was the creepiest thing they had ever seen.

INNOCENT BLOOD

REBECCA BESSER

Rachel Baker sat in the car, watching her husband in the café, having lunch with a woman she had never seen before. For weeks she suspected he was keeping secrets from her. Now she knew the truth. He was cheating on her.

She watched them talk and laugh, with her heart aching in her chest. What had she done to cause him to seek out another woman? Why wasn't she good enough?

As she sat there, her hurt turned into anger. She would show him she was a force to be reckoned with.

Starting the engine with a violent twist of the key in the ignition, she sped away with an idea forming in her head. She had just a few hours to get things ready. He would have the surprise of his life waiting when he came home from work.

* * *

Rachel pulled into the garage and waited for the door to close behind her before getting out. She had a lot to do and time was growing short. She also didn't want some nosy neighbor ruining things before they began.

Getting out, she started to unload everything she had bought. She was especially careful with the white plastic container of leeches, and the small aquarium of electric eels in the trunk, which she had purchased at a local specialty fish store. She had worked there part time a few months ago and had learned a lot about aquatic life.

Living by the ocean definitely had its perks. She could find almost anything at the local markets, things that had been caught, and others that were used for bait. That was how she had found two, good-sized live lobsters. The boat was docking when she finished loading the eels.

After those were safely inside, she went back out and extracted the largest of her purchases from the back seat—the stuffed and mounted sword fish. It was wrapped in brown paper and was very heavy.

Once everything was inside, she stood for a moment, grinning. If anyone had been there to see her, they would have noticed the demented look in her eyes.

* * *

Jason came home right on time.

"Honey, I'm home," he called as he came in from the garage. "I smell fish. Are we having fish for supper?"

Dropping his keys on the counter, he frowned. Nothing was cooking. Usually she had something started when he came home.

"Honey?" he called, heading toward the hall.

He stopped dead in his tracks when he finally spotted his wife. She was standing in the archway leading to their bedroom, wearing a red velvet teddy and nothing else.

"I've been waiting for you," she purred and walked slowly forward. She wrapped her arms around his neck and kissed him.

He grinned and kissed her back.

She pulled back, bit her bottom lip, and pulled him by his hand into the bedroom. There were candles sitting on every available surface, casting a warm, seductive glow across the bed.

"This is a nice surprise," he said, pulling her to him and kissing her again.

She pulled away and shook her head when he tried to lay her on the bed. "Not yet, I have plans for you first."

"Okay, I'm all yours," he laughed.

"Take off your shirt and lay on the bed," she said.

Grinning, he did as he was told.

Rachel climbed on the bed and straddled him. Taking his wrists, she pulled them above his head and tied them to the headboard with silk scarves.

"Feeling frisky, are you?" he asked, getting a great view down the bodice of her teddy as she leaned over him.

"Something like that," she said, grinding on him before climbing off.

"Where are you going?"

"Not far," she replied, picking up the remote and turning on a video she had ready in the TV. "I thought you might like some extra stimulation."

A tingle of excitement went through him as he watched the adult movie on the TV, their naked bodies grinding and sweating. His wife had never shown signs of being *this* kinky before.

Maybe she got some ideas from one of those women's magazines she was always reading, he wondered fleetingly. Mentally shrugging, he decided he might as well enjoy it.

Rachel climbed back on the bed, careful not to block his view of the TV. She skimmed her fingers down over his chest, until she reached his belt, unbuckling it. She grinned in satisfaction when he groaned and closed his eyes. Unzipping his pants, she giggled as he raised his hips, trying to get her to touch him.

Before long she had him stripped naked.

And that was when she pulled out the little white plastic container.

"What's that?" Jason asked with curiosity and excitement in his eyes.

"A surprise for you," she laughed.

Something about the sound of her voice seemed off to him; it held a touch of harshness, and a lot of crazy. Warning bells went off in his head. He tugged at his wrists, trying to free them, but they were tied tight.

"Rachel, untie me," he insisted.

"Hmm, I don't think so," she said, smiling and opening the container. "We've just begun our fun for the night."

Getting up on the bed, she straddled his legs, sitting back on them with all of her weight. Extracting a black worm from the container, she quickly laid it on his erection.

"What the hell is that?" he asked, trying to buck and wiggle his hips to throw it off.

"It's a leech," she said calmly, adding another.

"Get them off me!"

"Darling, I thought you liked to be sucked. Doesn't your girlfriend suck it for you? Might as well let them suck it, too, since you like to share."

"Who? I don't have a girlfriend! What the fuck is wrong with you?" he screamed. "Get those damn things off of me!"

"What's wrong with me?" she yelled back. "Who was that woman you were having lunch with? You've been cheating on me and now you're going to get what you deserve!"

Hurriedly, she added the rest of the dozen leeches.

"I haven't been cheating on you!" he screamed, still trying to shake the leeches off. "I would never cheat on you! I love you. Please take those things off."

Rachel laughed and slid off the bed. "I don't believe you. I saw you with her. I saw how she tossed her hair, how she looked at you. I saw the way you looked at her, how you touched her hand. Nothing you say will change my mind. You can't convince me that what I saw with my own eyes isn't the truth."

"You're crazy!" he screamed. "She's…"

She picked up the remote and turned the TV up full volume, drowning him out.

He thrashed and kicked as she pulled a heavy pair of rubber gloves out from under the bed and put them on.

She calmly walked over to the closet and pulled out a pair of lobsters. Bringing them back over, she took the rubber bands off their claws and laid them on his chest. They started pinching him, cutting his skin, and pulling off chunks of flesh.

Jason screamed as one of them pinched and tore off his nipple.

Rachel just stood beside the bed, watching with a demented, gleeful look in her eyes as he suffered. The sounds of moaning and flesh meeting in sensual pleasure on the video covered everything else. She started getting excited as his blood flowed from the wounds. She had never realized that torture could be so arousing.

When the lobsters would start to wander off, she would pick them back up and lay them on his chest again. They kept pinching and pulling his skin, and he kept screaming.

After a while, she decided the lobsters weren't enough fun anymore, then she started to pick off the leeches, dropping them back into their container. She enjoyed the look of fear in his eyes as he watched, waiting to see what the leeches had done to his dick. The spots where they were connected were bleeding, and there had been enough of them that his genitals were covered in blood. It flowed freely at first, because of the leech's saliva that caused the blood not to clot. But, after a few moments, the bleeding started to slow.

Jason wasn't paying attention to Rachel. He was too busy worrying about the damage to his manhood. So when she reappeared beside the bed holding a dripping, hissing electric eel, he jumped and struggled to escape his bonds.

Shaking his head, he tried to kick her away, but he missed and kicked the eel's tail instead. The numbing buzz of its electric charge stunned him, causing his leg to become useless. He continued to kick at her with the other leg, and she simply touched the eel's tail to it as well, rendering him immobile long enough for her to put the eel back into the small aquarium and get another.

She had a hard time carrying the second one, it was wriggling and the rubber gloves didn't have any grips on them. But she finally got the wet creature under control and carried it to the bed.

Jason could feel the cold water dripping on his skin as she bent over and quickly wrapped the eel's tail around his genitals. His entire body jerked as electricity coursed through his blood stream. It didn't last long, but it was enough to stun his entire body.

Rachel put the eel back in the aquarium with the others, then turned off the TV. The room was completely silent as she sat on the edge of the bed and looked at her husband. His eyes were vacant as they starred off into space. She feared the eel might have killed him, and then she wouldn't get to have any more fun, but he was still breathing.

Lovingly, she stroked one of the lobsters as she put it down between his legs, hoping it would grab onto something sensitive.

Something inside her broke loose as she sat there and she began screaming at him. She loved him so much. Why had he cheated on her? What didn't she give him that he needed? Why did he have to go out and find another woman?

All the hurt and anguish came pouring out of her, and before she knew it, she was pounding on his chest, yelling incoherently at him. Begging him to love her, then yelling at him for hurting her.

By the time she calmed down, he was starting to stir. She decided it was time to finish this, now tired of the whole thing.

She trudging over to the closet, the adrenaline rush her anger gave her was now gone. She was drained from her emotional outburst and no longer felt anything. It was all mechanics now. What was planned had to be done; she just wanted to get it over with.

Kneeling down, she unwrapped the small sword fish she had bought. It was stuffed and mounted. She hadn't been able to find a live one. Besides, a live one would have been too heavy for her to lift and use for what she had planned.

Walking over to the bed, she raised it up and forcibly slammed the sword beak of its upper jaw into his chest twice, puncturing one lung and then the other.

Standing beside the bed, holding the board with the mounted fish, she watched her husband struggle for breath. Pink bubbles rose from the holes his chest and his mouth.

She jumped when the phone rang.

With a sigh, she answered it. "Hello?"

"Hi," a feminine voice replied. "Is Jason there?"

Anger surged from the depths of Rachel's soul; this had to be the woman.

"No," Rachel snapped. "He's not. Would you like to leave a message?"

The woman was silent for a moment, as if she was thinking of the proper response. "Well, I guess I could talk to you. Or is this a bad time?"

"You can talk to me," Rachel said flatly as she watched Jason take his last breath.

"I don't know if he did yet, but Jason was supposed to tell you about me," the woman said. "I'm Joyce, a friend of his from college."

"Oh, really?" Rachel asked.

"We lost touch and I found him on *Facebook* a couple weeks ago. We've been talking and meeting for lunch every once in a while."

"Oh," Rachel said. "Why didn't he tell me?"

"He wanted to, but I asked him not to. I've been having some personal issues from a bad break up. I had a stalker and I didn't want to bring anyone else into it. Everything was cleared up today and he was going to tell you about me when he got home. He said something about meeting for dinner or something sometime. My girlfriend was all for it."

Rachel couldn't breathe. All she could hear was the thump of her heart as her blood pumped through her body. Jason hadn't cheated on her. The woman was a lesbian! She'd just tortured and killed her husband and he had done nothing to deserve it.

When she hung up the phone, Rachel started to cry. Guilt and loss weighed heavily on her. She couldn't undo what she'd done. What was she going to do now?

She began to panic, looking down at her husband's dead body. She had to get him out of here. His very presence was making her uneasy. Quickly, she put the lobsters away and dressed.

She wrapped his body in plastic and dragged him out to the SUV. Luckily for her, the plastic made it easier to move the body, at least until she reached the garage. But since it had gone so well on the carpeting in the house, she grabbed the welcome mats she had in front of the door and laid them in a path to the hatchback. After that, it was a bit easier.

Once she returned to him, after putting the mats back, she put his legs up in the cargo area, but wasn't able to lift his torso at the same time. He was too heavy and bulky.

Panting and sweating, she leaned her hip against the bumper and tried to calm down and think rationally. While she was looking around, she noticed a length of yellow nylon rope hanging on the wall.

It gave her an idea.

Taking it off the peg, she quickly uncoiled it and tied an end around Jason's ankles, then climbed into the cargo area of the SUV. She crawled over the back seat and out through the left passenger door, still holding the other end of the rope. Wrapping it around her arm, she put all of her weight into pulling him up and into the SUV. Once she had most of his body loaded, she tied her end of the rope to the handle of the door that led into the house. Rushing around the back of the vehicle, she pushed him the rest of the way in, and after untying the rope from the door, she coiled the slack and put it on the backseat. She went back in and got the eels, lobsters, and leeches, putting them in the back with the body. After closing the hatch and making sure it was secure, she slid behind the steering wheel and pressed the button to open the garage door.

The darkness of night was welcome. She hadn't realized how much time had passed since Jason had come home, and she began torturing him. As she drove to the pier to dump the body, she cried and lamented what she had done. She was so upset that she almost drove off the road a couple of times. Luckily, there was no one around to notice.

She was happy to see that the pier was deserted; it was probably because of the overcast sky. No one wanted to be around the water when it was about to storm.

As fast as she could, she dumped Jason's body and the water creatures she'd used to torture and kill him into the ocean. She hoped with the wind kicking up they would all be washed out to sea and no one would ever know what happened. She planned to file a missing person's report in a couple of days, figuring it would be enough time before saying anything was wrong.

It only took five minutes to dump everything, but it seemed like an eternity to her. She kept glancing over her shoulder, expecting someone to be standing right there and catch her red handed. No one did.

As soon as she returned to the SUV, the sky let loose a torrent of fat rain drops. They made driving home difficult. Between the blurred windshield and her blurred visions from tears, she could only drive thirty-five miles per hour.

Once she was home, she took the rope, the blanket, the sword fish, and the clothes she was wearing and burned them in the living room fire place. As flames consumed them, she thought about her life and how the heat of jealousy had destroyed every-thing.

Lying down on the couch, she watched the fire until she fell asleep, her cheeks wet from her tears.

* * *

A few days later, Rachel called the police and reported Jason missing. She decided to say he had come home from work, and then decided to go for a walk to the pier. It was something he frequently did, so it wouldn't raise suspicion with the neighbors if they were questioned.

Joyce kept calling.

After Rachel made the report, she told Joyce he was missing. Joyce was upset and said to please let her know as soon as she heard anything.

* * *

A full month after filing the missing person's report, the police showed up on Rachel's doorstep.

"Yes," she asked upon answering the door. "Have you found anything out? Have you found my husband?"

She was thinking she should get an acting award for what a good job she was doing when the tall, balding officer took off his hat and shuffled his feet.

"We've found his body, ma'am," he said nervously, glancing at his partner. "He washed up on shore and was discovered yesterday morning."

Rachel gasped, covering her mouth with her hand for added effect. "His body?"

The other officer stepped forward. "I'm afraid so, ma'am. It looks like he'd been in the water a while, too. Fish bites all over him. He's at the morgue now; we'll need you to stop by and identify the body. If you'd like, we can take you now and bring you home. I don't think it would be wise for you to drive right now."

Rachel nodded, real tears sliding down her cheeks. She knew the officers thought it was because she was in shock and upset because she just found out that her husband was dead. But she knew it was from guilt, remorse, and loss.

She went with the officers and did what she needed to do. She signed a paper for them to do an autopsy and went home. She didn't sleep that night, too worried they would find something that would trace it all back to her.

It was days before she heard anything more.

The autopsy reported there was no water in his lungs and there was bruising on his wrists. They suspected foul play, but had no more evidence to go on. It was ruled a homicide. Rachel was questioned but ultimately released. Without proof it was all conjecture and she played the act of the grieving widow to a T.

There were no other leads and the case eventually went into the cold case files.

* * *

That was when weird things began to happen. Rachel would come home and there would be wet footprints on the floor leading to the bedroom, and the bed would be soaked with sea water.

One morning, there was a pair of lobsters crawling around on the kitchen floor. They were still wet, like they were just taken out of the water.

Leeches had filled the sink in the bathroom while she was out for the day.

Each time, she had destroyed the evidence, not saying a word to anyone.

She didn't know why, but she *knew* Jason was haunting her.

Rachel needed to get away, to leave the house where she had killed him.

So she put the house up for sale and in days had an offer.

* * *

Rachel came home from signing the papers at the realtor's, relieved that the house was sold. She had sixty days to move out, which was fine with her, she already had half of her stuff packed.

With a sigh of relief, knowing she would be far away soon and the haunting would end, she went to take a hot shower.

She turned on the shower and took off her clothes. Without looking, she stepped into the tub. A sudden jolt of electricity coursed through her body. In a moment, her eyes took in the bathtub half full of water.

It was swarming with electric eels.

With all of them combined, she died almost instantly, and as she fell, she hit her head on the toilet.

* * *

When her body was found three days later by a neighbor coming over for a visit, the eels were gone and the shower was still running. Her death was declared an unfortunate accident. But, it wasn't. It was revenge.

Innocent blood had been spilt, and a soul couldn't rest until retribution had been taken.

FISHECSTASY

ANTHONY GIANGREGORIO

It was Friday night and the college dorms were hopping as usual.

Keggers were going full blast with many students already unconscious from over indulgence. On the second floor, room 15, three college pals were taking shots and trading stories.

"So, what's the strangest sexual experience you guys have ever had?" Mark asked his two buddies, Chris and Jeff.

Chris took a moment to think. His swayed back and forth as he tried to stay conscious. Alcohol poisoning wasn't far from the truth. "I did it with a piece of liver once."

"You what? How?" Mark asked as he sipped his beer. He was the sober one of the bunch. He had learned more than a year ago that if he stayed sober, or less drunk than everyone else, he could find out all sorts of interesting things about his friends; information he could later use against them.

Chris belched as he formulated his response. "It's not hard really. You take a piece of raw liver, and put it in some saran wrap. Then you heat it in the microwave. Not too much, just enough to get it warm. Then you slide your dick in it. It's just like a nice warm, moist pussy."

"Oh, God, that's so fucking gross!" Mark yelled as he laughed.

Chris belched again, drank half a beer and shrugged. "Did it with a loaf of fresh baked bread once, too. Almost burned my dick that time, as I rushed it and didn't let the loaf cool enough."

"Oh my fucking God, no way, that is incredible!" Mark yelled, loving all this great stuff. He couldn't wait till he needed something from Chris and had this info to use later to make him cooperate.

Jeff gulped half his beer and said, "I did it with a dog once."

Both Mark and Chris turned and stared at their friend.

"You did what?" Mark asked, not believing what he just heard.

"Yup, right in the pooper. I was horny as fuck and the family dog was right there. Hey, a hole is a hole. I even think the bitch enjoyed it," Jeff said, his words slurring from all the alcohol he'd consumed.

"No fucking way. You're bullshitting us," Mark said.

Jeff shrugged again, finished his beer, and went for another one from the cooler beside him.

"Nope, did it three times after that too when I was too horny to just jerk off."

"So why'd you stop?" Mark asked.

Jeff smiled. "That's when I got me a girlfriend and got to fuck the real thing."

Chris let out a burp so loud and smelly the entire dorm room smelled like old, regurgitated beer. As Mark waved his hand before his face to clear the air, Chris said, "Oh, come on, Mark. You never gave it a thought at the aquarium?"

"What do you mean?" he asked.

"The fish, Mark, the fish!" Chris yelled. "You never were there one night, all alone, horny as hell and the idea never crossed your mind?"

Mark stared at Chris, not fully understanding his question.

Chris seemed more lucid after his burp and he waved his hands in the air as his eyes went wide. "The fucking fish, Mark! You never thought about fucking any of the fish?"

"That's sick, of course not," he replied, making a disgusted face.

"But what about the dolphins, Mark?" Jeff interjected, liking where Chris was taking the conversation. "Technically, they aren't fish, they're mammals. Bet they got a nice warm pussy, too. And to do it in the cold water, only your dick nice and cozy. Shit, I think I'd try it if I had the chance."

Mark stood up, realizing he was now the center of the topic. "I gotta go guys, thanks for the beer."

As he turned to leave, Chris called after him. "Just think about it, Mark! All alone in the aquarium, those nice soft and warm fish pussies just waiting for you to fuck them!"

"You two are sick fucks, screw you," Mark said, opened the door, stepped through it, and slammed it behind him.

The two friends stared at one another, neither having anything to say.

Finally, Chris spoke up. "So you really fucked a dog?" he asked Jeff, wanting to get the conversation going again.

"Shut the fuck up and give me another beer," Jeff said in reply, the two going back to drinking.

Ten minutes later, the conversation about screwing this and that was a distant memory, and neither would remember in the morning.

But Mark did remember as he wasn't drunk, and though he didn't want to admit it, Chris had planted an idea in his head that no matter how hard he tried to forget, he just couldn't shake it.

That night he went on the internet, trying to see what he could find about men fucking fish. There wasn't much there, some women with eels and the like. Other than the typical barnyard porn, the aquatic stuff was missing.

He went to bed that night thinking about work, how easy it would be to do exactly what Chris said.

Finally, as the college dorm partied long into the night, Mark fell asleep.

Tomorrow was another day. A day he would be working...at the aquarium.

Mark showed up for work at six p.m. sharp. He worked the night shift, after the customers had gone home. His job was to feed the fish, clean the tanks and make sure the filters had been flushed and cleaned. He worked until two in the morning and he enjoyed it. With his headphones on, he listened to music and had the place to himself. He did his job well and his supervisor liked him.

The customers left at nine, and by ten the place was all his. The last fellow worker was gone by ten thirty, leaving Mark to do his thing.

He worked diligently, moving from tank to tank, dropping in food where it was needed. It wasn't a large aquarium, as it was a small town, but it was one of the only attractions in the area and so had enough business to keep afloat financially.

Mark finished with the shark tank and moved to the dolphin tank.

It was set into the ground with a four foot glass wall surrounding it. There were two adult dolphins in the water, Matty and Mary.

Matty had been rescued from the ocean after becoming hurt by a boat propeller. Mary had come from another aquarium when it had closed due to lack of funds.

"Hi, guys, how are you tonight?" Mark asked as he carried a bucket full of raw fish to feed them.

Matty swam up and let out a few squeaks, then back flipped into the pool. Mary swam up to him and floated, watching Mark as he walked around the pool.

When he was near the small diving board set up for the announcer during shows, he dropped down on it and began scooping out the fish, letting it fall into the water. Matty and Mary quickly ate, enjoying the last meal for the day.

As Mark fed them, Chris' words came back to him. *"Come on, Mark, you never thought about it? Even once?"*

He shook his head to clear it, trying to concentrate on his job, but the more he watched Mary play in the water and eat, the more he began to get aroused.

By the time the two dolphins were done feeding, his pants were tight in the crotch area.

He hadn't had sex for more than three months and as he was nineteen, his hormones were raging and he would have killed to have a female right then and there to screw.

But there was no female there...well, not a human female anyway.

The more he watched Mary, the more he realized how horny he was and Chris' words still rang in his head, prodding him on.

He had to admit, Chris had a point. Dolphins were mammals and so were warm blooded. He knew he was crazy but his drive to have sex was too much for him, and despite his better judgment, he decided to go for it.

Quickly stripping off his clothes, he stood on the edge of the diving board with his boner protruding ahead of him like a stubby flag pole.

With a tingling in his belly in expectation of what was to come, he dove into the pool.

Swimming to the surface, he slapped the water and Mary and Matty swam to him. He pushed Matty away, wanting only Mary, and Matty rolled in the water, not happy at being snubbed. Mark sucked in a great big breath of air and went under the water as he held onto Mary's dorsal fin.

His first try failed miserably, but the second time he adjusted his position, and with him hugging Mary and his belly pressed to hers, he positioned himself and penetrated her.

As he slid inside the dolphin, his cock was surrounded by warmness and he had to fight to keep from groaning in pleasure, not wanting to suck in water.

Mary never stopped swimming and as Mark held onto her, she slowly moved around the pool. Mark was in heaven as he slowly slid in and out of her. Each time he pulled back, his dick would be surrounded by the cool pool water. Then he would push in and the warmness of the dolphin would surround him. As if she knew he had to breathe, she even moved to the surface so he could suck in a breath of air.

He stroked her in and out, back and forth, until he had an orgasm that shook him to his core. As he let her go, he floated in the water, realizing Chris had been right.

Fucking that dolphin had been incredible!

As Mark treaded water, his face wearing a look of contentment, he never saw Matty swim up behind him. Dolphins were well adept at mimicking their human masters and Matty was no different.

Before Mark could so much as cry out in surprise, Matty plowed into him and wrapped his fins around Mark, holding him in place.

Mark screamed to be let free, sucking in water, and a moment later felt blinding pain in his ass as Matty began mating with him, just like Mark had done with Mary.

Mark began to scream as his backside exploded with fire, the larger dolphin trapping him like a child would a kitten.

Mark fought the best he could but he was no match for the dolphin, and as he sucked in a lungful of water and began to choke, he realized he was dying!

He imagined what would happen the next day, when his naked corpse would be found floating in the pool. What would people say? What rumors would be spread? After all, how does an employee of the aquarium end up naked and dead in the dolphin pool? And when the autopsy was performed and they found out he'd been raped by a dolphin, what then?

He imagined the look on his father's face at hearing the news, or his mom's!

And he would have died right then and there if not for Mary bumping into Matty playfully, causing Mark to become dislodged. There was another blinding pain as Matty withdrew from his ass and then he was sinking to the bottom.

With his last seconds of air, Mark kicked up to the surface and sucked in the best tasting air he had ever had the pleasure to breathe.

Coughing and spitting, he swam to the ladder and pulled himself up and onto the edge of the pool. As he lay there naked, he saw diluted red pooling under his ass and realized he had gotten the pounding of his life.

When he looked back into the pool, he saw Matty and Mary were now mating, going at it like two lovesick teenagers.

Coughing and vomiting water, Mark pulled himself together and got dressed, feeling humiliated and sore.

He was shaking so badly he could barely get dressed, and when he had his clothes on, he limped away from the pool.

Matty sent a few squeaks his way but Mark didn't look back. He didn't want to think what those squeaks might have meant.

Hey, Mark, thanks for a good time...call me!

His sexual escapade had turned into a disaster. For the rest of his life, he would have to live with the knowledge that he was raped by a dolphin.

He finished his shift on auto pilot that night and went home early, leaving his keys on the supervisor's desk along with his resignation.

He didn't want to work around fish any longer.

The following week, the college dorm was hopping once more.

Keggers were once again in full swing and Mark was with his friends, drinking again. He was pretty quiet, though, and had been like that since the previous week.

As the three friends drank and laughed, Chris slapped Mark on the arm.

"So, Mark, did you ever do it with one of the fish like I suggested?"

Jeff laughed hard but Mark said nothing. Mark turned and looked at Chris, frowned deeply, and then punched Chris right in the face.

"Fuck you, asshole," Mark snapped as he got up and walked out of the room.

Neither Jeff nor Chris noticed that Mark was walking funny, and had been for a week.

Chris was knocked onto his ass and he rubbed his jaw where Mark punched him. He looked at Jeff with an odd expression and said, "What the fuck did I say?"

Jeff shrugged. "Who the hell cares, just give me another beer."

The two friends continued to drink without Mark, and as time went by, Chris looked at Jeff and asked, "So, what's the strangest sexual experience you ever had?"

HOOKED

ALAN SPENCER

The lighthouse at the edge of St. Margaret's Bay flashed a series of intermittent warnings, and looking on, the source of the distress was obvious. From the harbor, the group stood together in their rain slicks, huddled waist-deep in the water, not moving. Aiden Wesley knew they were his fellow workers, all fishermen, who lived on the outskirts of the bay. They resided in quaint, picturesque houses located near the docks that were notorious for being covered in stacks of wooden lobster traps and used-up fishing gear. It was near sundown, the end of the workday, a time when many of his co-workers should've been enjoying an ale up the road at the private pub, but instead, they waded in the water, purposeless.

Aiden kept scrutinizing the fishermen, arriving near the shore in his commercial boat. It wasn't but seconds later that the throng became alerted to his appearance, each jerking their heads in his direction.

It was then that their hands lifted up from the water and revealed the rusted steel hooks clutched in their grasps.

And then the S.O.S. signals from the lighthouse abruptly ended.

A bloated corpse bobbed low underwater, cut up by the many sharp riverbeds it had traveled over. When the body arrived in St. Margaret's Bay, it was bloodless, but like the rest of the human corpses the tributaries and channels washed up over many decades, the sardine-sized stickleback fish partook of the feast anyway. They gathered in schools of hundreds of thousands to gorge on the flesh and fat left on the remains...

Leaping onto the dock and charging inland, forgetting his boat and how it veered off-shore to inevitably crash, Aiden speedily escaped the twenty some fishermen's advances. He could hear them tramp onto shore, their rubber boots squeaking as they treaded sharp rocks and climbed through the hilly terrain to reach him.

Increasing his stride, he was much too fast for them. He was too scared to blast the biggest question on his mind: why were they carrying those menacing hooks and coming after him in mob fashion? The men he'd known for years were now cold to him—strangers. Their eyes were yellow, shining like pennies under murky depths. The strange-looking orbs kept glowering at him, proving the men weren't themselves but something else, and they couldn't be reasoned with.

He'd evaded them after half a mile of running, and up the road, he met Mr. Jeffries, a retired fisherman, who was dressed in a yellow rain slick and clutching a kerosene lamp. It was misting heavily; the sky had transformed into a foreboding gray in what seemed only minutes. A storm was coming in, and it was going to be a mean one.

Mr. Jeffries served up many questions, the words bursting from his mouth. "What in blue fuck is that signal about, Aiden? Who's up there? The lighthouse signal's only for emergencies. And I've been watching those fishermen. The bastards just let their boats float into the bay like it was nothing. It's like they've gone crazy."

"I...I...I don't know what's wrong with them," Aiden spit out, trying to catch his breath and answer the man's queries. "I came inland by boat, and they were all in the water just standing there. Then they came out and were right after me without a reason."

"Drunks, all of 'em!" Mr. Jeffries cast his judgments, staring down his nose at the next generation of unworthy fishermen. "Fishing ain't what it used to be. People used to take pride in their work. People wanted to do a good job, not fuck about like they do now. Christ, things are going down th—*aaaaaaaarggggggggghhh!*"

The man was violently interrupted by a flying object that attached to his face.

Without sensing their arrival, all Aiden heard was the rattle of chains and then Mr. Jeffries was snagged by a hook, the prong catching him in the nose, and with a tensing of the chain's slack, the edge ripped through it, the breaking of cartilage like wet sticks snapping underfoot. Gone were his nostrils, and in its place

gleamed exposed raw sinuses that gurgled and churned out bubbles of red.

Before Mr. Jeffries' screams took on new heights, another hook
caught him across the belly, and he was dragged towards the group
of fishermen, who clotted the road a few yards from his stand-
point.

They'd caught up with him, or they were ahead of him the entire time, he realized.

By the time Aiden understood what had occurred, he had no
choice but to keep on running. The rain was pounding down much
harder now and obscuring the road into town, but he saw one of
the fisherman remove the same knives they used to gut their fish
and jammed the blade into Mr. Jeffries belly. Wielding it violently,
the man dug it into his guts with three practiced swipes and then
the punch of his fist through the slit's opening. As the wailing old
man continued his notes of agony and his viscera were uncoiled
roll by roll, two more fishermen picked up the bawling old man
and carried him off back to the bay.

Then the others continued pursuing Aiden, motioned onwards
by an unknown imperative.

Aiden had to warn the others what was coming despite the
danger he was in.

And more importantly, he had to reach his wife.

Racing ahead was all he could do.

*Flensing the scattered bones and the leftovers of greater feasts
that had collected on the bay's bottom, the sticklebacks used their
numerous teeth to waste nothing of their catch. Over hundreds of
years, their hunger was finely cultivated, and with that cultiva-
tion, came new strength, new abilities, increased thought proc-
esses and ambitions, and at the top of the list, ravenous appetites.
And one day, they'd come up with a way to gain access to more
meat...*

Blind to the scene ahead of him, Aiden nearly collided with the
two police vehicles, their front doors open, parked awkwardly in

the middle of the road. The rain was pelting the inside interiors and giving him the idea the cars had been abandoned for a time. A police issue revolver was on the ground, and he was about to pick it up when he caught movement near the trigger guard. It was a fish the size of a minnow, though it was a deep burgundy with orange stripes flanking its sides. Its maw was open and trying to suck in air as it waded in the rain- saturated puddle of blood.

But it wasn't trying to breathe.

It was desperate to ingest the blood.

The fish's eyes were the same strange yellow as the fishermen.

Disbelieving the sight of the demonic-looking thing, Aiden caught activity in his peripheral vision. It was a pair of legs jutting out from the edge of the road. He ran to them, sensing distress in that direction by the low mewls he made out over the spattering of rain.

But it wasn't mewls he was hearing. It was the scraping of steel against bone many times over. It was Sheriff Bullford on the ground, already dead, and when Aiden caught sight of the man's face, he backed up in horror as the three hooks embedded in the skin were suddenly pulled in different directions, completely removing the flesh over his entire face. Each tissue section was dragged down the road like wet potato skins, reeled in so fast.

New chains rattled all around him, and from a distance, he couldn't see them at work, but they were out there. The evidence of that arrived when another hook pierced the corner of the sheriff's mouth and dragged him onwards, his limp body whisked away into the increasing darkness of nightfall.

Not knowing where to retreat to next, his eyes adjusted to the night, and he found that he was standing in town, where houses were scattershot among the deep sloping hills.

His house was only a short distance off.

He did his best not to get snagged by the fishermen on his way there.

The taste of blood, the flesh, and even the marrow of bones was so concentrated in their mouths, the need for it ran in their bloodstreams, and with that circulation, came deeper realms of intelligence. It was with this knowledge they learned that the boats floating overhead and the legs standing in the water harbored the same meat they craved, and the sticklebacks began making their plans...

Jilted screams, shattering windows, kicked in doors, the blasts of firearms, the roar of screeching tires against the pavement only to crash recklessly off-road, all of it was a constant din as Aiden arrived at his house. His wife's face was in the window, casting a smudge in the thickening rain, and opening the door for him, she drew him close, grateful for his presence. Mariel ran her hands up and down his face, smothering him with kisses.

"Do you know what's happening? I keep hearing screams. It's like everybody out there is being attacked. Did you see them? My God, did you see who's doing this?" she asked, her voice filled with fear.

You don't want to see who's doing this, he thought, taking her by the arm and guiding her to the living room. He tried the phone, but the line was down.

"I tried that already," Mariel commiserated, working a strand of yellow hair out of her eyes. She was pacing, her body visibly shaking, and he didn't blame her. He knew no matter how deep he reached within himself, there would be no reassurances he could offer to equal the threat outside.

"It's no use. Cars keep driving away, but they don't seem to be getting very far," he said.

The words seemed to fall out of him now that he was unable to filter the information for the sake of her calm. "All the fisherman are carrying hooks, and they're... they're... they're snagging people up and doing God knows what. I saw the fishermen standing in the water—just standing there. And then they came after me, and I ran, and then I saw the sheriff's dead body in the road, and my God, they ripped his face off with their damned hooks!"

She threw him up against the wall with two hands pressed against his chest, ending his babbling spell by yelling, "Stop saying those things! It's not true. The sheriff's not dead. There's nobody with hooks. I refuse to believe it!"

He was deflated against the wall upon hearing her reply.

He was known for being strong. Strong-backed. Strong-minded. Strong-willed. Lugging lobster cages and fish nets with unflinching work ethic for a thankless job. Committed to work that would kill off most men, but now in the midst of these events, he was a miserable version of his former self after witnessing such gruesome deaths.

And all he could say to her was, "I know it's impossible to believe, but I saw it with my own eyes. The fishermen are out there right now, and they're killing everyone."

Hunger gave way to new innovations. How else would they gain access to human meat but to be able to control the humans? All it took was a few changes in their strategy, and their feast would be unending...

The first step was turning off all their lights. Then they locked and double checked each entrance. They barricaded their furniture against the windows, and when all of that preparation was done, they waited on their stairway. Aiden clutched his low caliber rifle, and Mariel hugged him tight.

The screams kept happening, ricocheting off the hills, each pitch constantly in flux, from infernal and ear-splitting, to pulse-boiling baying, to crackling death rattles.

Death was being refused when the victims needed it the most.

There were even moments the two of them could distinguish the hooks penetrate flesh and peel open wounds. Subtle, but pronounced enough, especially when the prongs scraped teeth and unlocked jaw bones.

"Why haven't they come here?" Mariel finally whispered to him. "They haven't treaded near our house."

The question was logical. The closest houses were a block east and west of them, and those homes had been invaded, the inhabitants forced out, carried off and murdered in brutal fashion.

So why not them?

Instead of answering the question with more guesswork, he marched to the window in the living room where a square of glass could be looked through despite the barricade of furniture. The rain was settling down, the darkness shielding the fishermen from view, but their eyes, their cast-iron hot orbs, burned in the night for more prey. The fishermen were spread out, and it seemed like the town was filled with moving fireflies. They scouted and searched, and a sliver of hope made its way home against Aiden's better judgment.

They had been overlooked.

All they had to do was be patient.

And then they would be gone.

The plan was executed, but the wait was much longer than they intended, and it wasn't only the thirst of blood that tripled with each passing day, but the need for the hunt, to relish in human suffering, to hook in their prey like so many of their brethren had been hooked...

Hours ticked away, and they remained safe. Aiden checked and checked again out the window. The yellow eyes moving in the night were absent.

"They're not out there anymore," was all he said to her.

"How can you be sure?" Mariel whispered.

He shook his head no, he couldn't be sure.

"So we stay here." She spoke to herself, still sitting on the stairs. "Help will come. Someone will be here eventually. They have to. It can't be too much longer now."

He agreed, though silently, and he sat back down with her on the stairs, and once again waited for their hopes to pan out.

For the first time in the six years Aiden had been fishing for a living, he couldn't sleep. He stared out the window as if expecting a pair of yellow eyes to peer in at him at any moment. Mariel was asleep out of sheer exhaustion, though his protection seemed to have its sway over her, and she slept like a baby. He stayed in position, doing his job as a husband, the protector, until he felt the migraine form in his head. Slow at first, then pounding.

Aiden rubbed his temple, trying to soothe that strange ache into submission, when it exploded into excruciating pulses like two sparks going off behind each of his eyes. He lost control, giving in to the elevated throes of pain, and he shoved Mariel aside and launched himself into the bathroom.

He slammed the door closed and locked it, not wanting to be disturbed. The pounding continued, growing more intense by the second, as if the fleshy material behind his eyes were dissolving, being eaten by acid. He tasted many things on his tongue unknown to him, sea salt being the most pronounced.

Throwing open the medicine cabinet, he retrieved a bottle of painkillers and downed a handful, forgoing the task of counting out the pills.

Banging her fists on the door, Mariel's urgency surged out her ailing voice, "Aiden, you unlock this door! Tell me what's wrong? Are you hurt? Please, baby, answer me!"

His throat was locked up as if someone had shoved a stopper down into it. Working through the unknown bodily seizure, his fingers were digging into the sink fixture for a grip over his self-control, but he lost that battle to the new wave of agonies billowing behind his eyes. Building stronger, a series of molten hot tears trailed down his cheeks and landed loudly in the sink, wet and heavy like sodden rags.

Before he could distinguish anything else, he gazed at himself in the mirror's reflection as the small bodies of the stickleback fish squirmed around the circumference of his eyes. Now he couldn't see anything, only feel their wet, fishy bodies writhe. Worse yet, they swam in his brain, and filling up his face, he couldn't fight back against them, not even for a moment.

The door to the bathroom had been shattered, the pieces left behind in jagged shards. Aiden could see again now, though it was so yellow bright, everything tinged with golden hues as if he were looking through a car's taillight.

Unable to react, only watch, he saw Mariel's body strewn on the floor, her mouth and eyes gaping wide, each orifice squirming and active.

And without a shred of mourning or concern, he was out the door after peeling away the barricade at the front door, and marching out into the dawn, he walked with new purpose.

The rattling of chains was all that mattered to him. Their continuation, the reassurance the work was done and nearing its completion. Aiden dragged them on and on without need for rest, no matter how badly his muscles knotted up and ached.

He powered on until he returned to St. Margaret's Bay.

Along the bay's edge, the waters frothed with their busy bodies, the millions of sticklebacks swarming each other. They were in such a thick mass it was impossible to see through what used to be clear water, each fish lining up for another taste from the gory, floating pieces.

Aiden stopped treading towards the bay, finally arriving on shore. He then turned around at the two corpses he was dragging behind him, each with hooks in their mouths, the edges shoved up through their chins and jutting out their cracked and open lips. The other fishermen were poised with corpses behind them as well, the bodies they'd picked up from the sidewalks, roads and houses, the payload of last night's kill. Mariel was among the workers, lugging a corpse of her own.

The fishermen, including Aiden, each helmed various bladed implements, and one-by-one, they went to work gutting the dead, cutting them up into servable pieces and lobbing them into the water, adding to the feeding frenzy that would continue for several hours until every dead male and female in the close-knit town was turned into food.

The sticklebacks implanted their eggs into the local fish used for commercial product. Once processed and eaten, the inevitable would occur. Possession. Control. Sustenance.
The feast of flesh would finally be brought to them.

By afternoon, the gathering of fishermen had grown in numbers. Random townspeople had been added to the roster, each wielding hooks and chains. Feeding time was over and there was more work to do. Walking from the bay, the collection of people advanced to the next town, and by the time they reached the edge of Cameron's Peak, it was nighttime, and all that could be seen of them were their eyes, the shining orbs teeming with the bodies of the sticklebacks.

The creatures now helmed the human vessels as their own.

With hooks in tow, it would soon be time for the group to go fishing once more.

BLOODSTREAM

V.M. ZITO

"**S**hit, kid," a man's voice said. "That drawing is *fucked up*."

The voice startled Jake, and he looked up fast without remembering to cover the sketchpad on his knees. He'd thought he was alone here in the aquarium's Shark Room—so focused on his sketches that he hadn't noticed the man enter and sit on the bleacher behind him. Down lower, a dozen bull sharks coasted in silence behind a wall of thick glass, circling the same fake reef for probably the millionth time in their lives.

The man was bald but not old, forty maybe, a hint of razor burn on his soft cheeks. His skin rippled with dark blue reflections from the tank. He grinned and inched closer, and Jake caught a queasy whiff of peppermint aftershave.

"Fucked up," the man said again. He nodded at the page in Jake's pad.

Embarrassed, Jake regarded his sketch. Penciled in rough graphite was a bull shark, perfectly drawn and monstrous, snatching a swimmer from the ocean surface. The victim's mouth gaped in horror, salt water pouring into his lungs as the shark's serrated teeth crunched his ribcage and dragged him to a gruesome death. Bubbles exploded, and clouds of thickly scribbled blood swirled around the bite.

"Thanks," Jake mumbled.

His earlobes burned. *Relax,* he told himself. The bald man had no idea what was *really* fucked-up about the drawing.

Only Jake knew that the swimmer he'd fantasized in mid-death—the muscled arms, creeping black sideburns, broad-stubbled chin—was his father.

Deep bell tones sounded from speakers overhead, soothing and aquatic, as if the room were underwater. The man rubbed his jaw, considering the sketch. A fat gold watch hugged his wrist.

"Looks real," the man concluded. "You in art school or somethin'?"

Jake shrugged. "Nah."

"How old are you?"

None of your business, Jake wanted to say. "Nineteen."

"Well, you can fuckin' draw," the man said. "Come here a lot?"

"I don't know...a couple days, yeah." He flipped the pad shut, careful not to let the man see any more pages. Not yesterday's sketches, or the day before that.

He'd been feeding his father to the sharks all week.

He turned back to the tank, hopeful the conversation had ended, but it hadn't. "Yeah," the man went on. "I'm here a lot. Saw you yesterday, too."

Jake shuddered. He hadn't noticed the man then, either.

A sign by the tank promised **Shark Feeding 11:30**. Jake felt a tug in his chest and wondered if he should leave. Instead he waited—just a little longer.

The bald man said nothing for a while, though Jake could hear him breathing. At last the top of the tank slid open, and a long metal feeding pole plunged into the water. Meat quivered on the hook. The bull sharks spun, agitated. The biggest of the bulls struck first, and attacked the pole with a furious thrashing of fins and tail. It tore the chunk of meat and gulped it down in one bite. Its massive throat wobbled like rubber.

"Fucked up," the man marveled. "You drew it right, kid."

Jake didn't answer. He wanted to be sketching, by himself, with nobody giving him shit. That's what made this place perfect. Not like home.

"Hey," the man said. His voice came softer now, closer to Jake's ear. The peppermint smell was revolting. "So you like fucked-up things, yeah?"

Jake's stomach rolled. He bent, tugged his book bag from the carpeted floor, and slid the pad inside.

Time to go.

He flinched when the man put a hand on his shoulder.

"Hey, kid, easy. I'm not trying to suck your dick, promise." The man smiled. He reached into the silk pocket of his shirt and pulled out a small business card. "Here."

Jake eyed the card. "What's this?"

The man extended his arm. "Take it."

Hesitating, he reached for the card, while thinking, *If this perv grabs me...*

He took the card and held it to the blue light, squinting.

It was a drawing—nothing fancy, just a creepy little doodle of a skinny fish with large, exaggerated teeth. A barracuda, maybe. Below that, in silver type, *Kempton Road.*

The man nodded as though he'd just proven a point. "See that? If you like fucked-up things, you *gotta* check that out."

Jake frowned, not understanding. "What is it?"

"A private aquarium. A special exhibit. Not like these family crapholes—mine's got no school trips, no babies in strollers screamin' and pissin', no boring shit like starfish. Invitation only: and that card's your invitation. But screw that, words aren't enough. You gotta see it. That's all I can say. You gotta *see* it." The man sat back and rested his elbows on the bleacher behind him. His eyes were green, intense. Just above his left ear, on the side of his head, a small tattoo stood out. Jake hadn't noticed it before.

The same skinny fish with the large teeth.

He almost handed the card back, then thought better of it. Instead, he placed it on the bleacher next to him. "No thanks," he said. "I don't really..."

The man smiled and cocked his head, as if he could hear a different answer inside Jake fighting to be spoken.

"Thanks anyway," Jake finished. He clutched his bag and stood, wincing. His ribs ached. They were still sore, almost broken three nights ago. Punched hard.

Words from that night replayed in his mind. *Pussy, yer a fuckin pussy.*

"Wait." The man pulled a duplicate card from his pocket. He leaned over and tucked it into Jake's bag. "Keep that. Come around midnight, and show that card. I'm tellin' you, if you think these sharks are badass, just wait'll you see the fishies we got—*so* fucked up. But hey, only if you want. Should be a good crowd, too."

Jake ignored him and shuffled along the bleachers toward the dim red **EXIT** sign. In the tank, the feeding session had ended. The pole had disappeared back above the surface and the sharks returned to their slow, mindless circling.

Jake had almost reached the exit when the man called to him. "Hey, kid."

Jake turned back. The man was grinning at him.

"That guy gettin' shark-attacked in your drawing. Somebody you know?"

Jake's face drained cold. Who *was* this guy? Some buddy of his dad's who was screwing with him?

Please not that. Please, he thought.

The man chuckled and waved a hand dismissively. "Hey, no worries—I get it. When I was your age, I had somebody like that, too. Shit works itself out, you'll see."

Flustered, Jake hoisted his bag over his shoulder and hurried into the hall outside the Shark Room.

The man's voice chased behind him. *"See you tonight... Kempton Road, look for the sign. You'll love it. Kids like you always do. Free admission. Just bring money for the gift shop."*

Jake bolted down the stairwell, two steps at a time, and burst through the exit door at the bottom. The sun outside was bright. He rested against a bicycle rack stuck with old bubblegum and covered in peeling paint.

His heart quivered like red meat on the feeding hook.

Kempton Road was a graveyard of crumbling brick warehouses and abandoned factories outside the city; a fallen civilization turning to dust below a highway overpass. Jake could hear cars speeding fifty feet above, but the distant rush of their motors only made the Kempton ruins seem lonelier, more forgotten.

He eyed the dark facades and alleyways slinking past his car. Most of the streetlights were smashed or unlit and only his high beams revealed blocks of grass growing through the cracked pavement. Scattered about were food wrappers plastered to curbs, an empty shopping cart, a burnt-out car on cinder blocks and old newspapers yellow with age. He saw nobody. But now and then a shrill scream from a side street made his skin prickle.

So far, the man had told the truth. This *was* fucked up.

The clock in his car read 12:18 in the morning. After the aquarium, he'd put in his shift at the Safeway, stocking shelves, then gone to a five-dollar movie at the community theater—*Iron Man*. He loved it. Sometimes when he was depressed, he sketched himself as a superhero, his body chiseled and strong on the pages of his pad.

Kind of a loser thing to do, but it did help him feel better—a little anyway.

Pussy, yer a fuckin pussy, he heard again in his head. *Can't believe yer my blood.*

His eyes glazed, and he stepped on the gas pedal.

At this hour, going home had its own set of risks. His father got drunkest after midnight. Often it was safer to crash at a friend's, then return in the morning when the house was calm—nothing but snores from the bedroom and a lingering odor of Budweiser.

The road traveled on and on, and he had no idea how far he was supposed to go.

Screw this, he thought. He was exhausted, and he'd only intended to drive past the place anyway, just for a look. He decided to turn around at the next corner.

His foot stomped on the brake pedal.

He'd found it.

Through his windshield, a sign beckoned over an iron-gated doorway, lit by the only working bulb on the block. The sign was dirty-white, no lettering at all—just a single unmistakable image burned into the wood.

The skinny fish with the teeth; same as on the card.

Six or seven expensive cars—Porsches, a Jag—were parked along the curb. He pulled behind them and turned off his headlights. But he kept the engine running.

From the outside, the building looked like just another empty factory. Neglected, spray-painted with graffiti, the windows boarded.

But inside?

Special exhibit, the man had said.

Too bad the windows were so high up. No way to peek.

He shook his head, exhaling. Okay, maybe he was a little curious, but he wasn't an idiot. No way was he going in, getting gang-raped up the ass by whomever.

Scraping metal made him jump.

The iron gate had opened.

He half-expected some monster to lunge from the doorway, but instead a short old man shuffled out, harmless like a grandfather, dressed in a doorman's long coat with big gold buttons and tassels on his stooped shoulders. He nodded welcomingly at Jake and made little circles with his hand. *Roll down your window.*

Jake hesitated, then pressed the button. The window cracked an inch.

"Howdy," the old man said. "Hurry and park. Show's in five minutes."

Without waiting for a reply, he turned and shuffled back through the gate, leaving it ajar.

Jake studied the doorway. His thumbs tapped the steering wheel. On the dashboard, the clock ticked off a minute, then two. His ribs hurt. These days, something always hurt. The bruises on his arms, the welts on his back.

Pussy, yer a fuckin pussy.

He was tired of always hurting.

He killed the engine and got out, the bald man's card in his hand.

Know what? he thought. *I'm ready for something fucked up.*

Behind the gate, a dented metal door opened into a lobby as unappealing as the building outside. The concrete floor was uneven and chipped, damp with water damage. To Jake's right, blue-crusted copper pipes ran the length of the wall and disappeared around a corner. The only furniture was an elegant oak podium straight ahead.

The old doorman stood there. "Welcome," he said. He had a raspy cigarette voice and yellowed teeth to match. "Glad you made it. Just in time."

On the podium sat a clear box with a slot in the top; green bills filled the interior. A small metal plate read **Suggested Donation $500.**

Jake blanched. "I...I don't have that."

The doorman waved him off. "Eh, it's only a suggestion. You're a guest of Mr. Phillips, right? Free admission. Just drop in your card."

Jake steadied his hand. The card fell through the slot onto a stack of hundreds.

"People really paid this?" he asked. The idea scared him somehow.

"Some do," the old man answered simply. "Follow me."

Behind the podium, a red velvet rope had been strung between two gold pedestals, blocking the entrance to an archway farther back. The doorman unhooked the rope, they passed through the arch, then down a long tunnel of unpainted drywall. The air reeked with mildew, and overhead, hanging fluorescent lights flickered and hummed. Jake followed behind the doorman. The back of the old man's scalp was splashed with liver spots and moles. And over his ear, a smudge—an aged tattoo, the lines blurred.

The skinny fish.

An industrial push-bar door waited for them at the end of the hall. From the other side, Jake heard voices, a conversation echoing in a large space. The doorman paused with his wrinkled fingers on the push-bar.

"Here we go. The show's starting."

He popped the door and held it open.

Jake stepped into the next room, his mouth dry as sandpaper. Not a room, actually but a vast factory floor, now emptied of equipment. Giant oil spots stained the cement floor where machines once stood, and the atmosphere still stunk of diesel and exhaust fumes. The ceiling was cavernous, high overhead, and he heard raucous birds squawking somewhere in the rafters, and the flutter of wings.

In the center of the room, there was a group of twenty men standing around a raised platform. The stage was bathed in a white glow by footlights along the base. Dust glittered in the beams. To the left and right loomed four spectacular video screens, the size of billboards, erected on tall steel girders. The screens were black. Thick electrical cords hung from the consoles, wound down the girders like ivy, then snaked across the stage.

Jake sucked in a sharp breath.

A man was strapped to a black frame on the platform—naked.

He looked middle-aged, fifty or so with matted, dirty hair. He might have been a vagrant. His limbs splayed wide, locked into metal clasps on the edges of the frame; gray hair tufted from his underarms and crotch. The video wires tangled around his skeletal body, each ending in a long silver needle that had been stabbed through his skin, then taped in place—two in his thighs, two beneath his biceps. The needles bulged like rigid veins beneath his flesh.

His eyelids drooped, and his head rolled to the side. He looked stoned.

Fear trickled like ice-water down Jake's back. *Go*, he told himself. *Run before anybody notices.* If only he could control his legs, stop them from shaking.

"*Kid!*"

Jake's focus jerked to the stage. The bald man from the aquarium was there now, next to the dazed man on the frame. He was waving Jake closer. The crowd around the platform turned, all distinguished men in fine dark shirts and slacks. They were watching him.

"Told you, didn't I?" the bald man called. "You gotta see it, right?" He mouthed two silent words—*fucked up*—like a secret message only for Jake, then winked and continued aloud. "C'mon, step up, get a look, fellas. Make some room."

The men jostled and a nook opened in the crowd. Jake's heart convulsed. His feet were full of pins-and-needles. He took a tentative step forward, then another. It became easier after that. He joined the rear of the group, and to his relief the men seemed to forget him immediately, turning their eyes back to the stage.

"Excellent. Thank you all for your patience," the bald man said. He clapped his hands once. "The show begins now."

He reached for a small electrical switch on the frame, teased it with his finger.

"Presenting..." He paused. Then uttered the next word in a whisper. "*Candiru.*"

His finger flipped the switch and the video screens crackled to life. Jake watched, too tense to breathe.

The four screens began to squirm with....horrible *things*, silver and slippery like eels, wriggling on a red background. They were swimming, he realized. Liquid flowed through a maze of narrow canals, dozens of eels in the current.

Not eels, skinny fish. He could see the long jaws snapping open and shut, the razor-sharp teeth he remembered from the drawings. He frowned, still not quite understanding.

The man on the frame groaned and shuddered, and the crowd murmured its approval, and then Jake *knew*.

The fish were *inside* the man.

The needles inserted into his arm and legs... were cameras, microscopic, filming the fish as they struggled and twisted through the man's blood vessels.

A cry of revulsion boiled up in Jake's throat but he stifled it.

"*Candiru*," the bald man repeated, making a triumphant gesture to the screens. "The parasite fish, the smallest and rarest of the subfamily, *Vandelliinae*. In Brazilian jungles, there's a warning—never piss into the Amazon River or the *candiru* will swim through your urine and enter your cock at the tip."

The bald man grimaced for effect and flicked the naked man's penis with his finger, as if flicking away a bug. The audience stirred with uncomfortable laughter.

"What you see are bloodeaters, an extreme subspecies, known to myself and a few others. They were collected from a lost branch of the Rio Negro, and kept alive over the years through the hospitality of many hosts. The bloodeaters enter the body through ingestion...so don't get them in your mouth." He grinned. "From there, they burrow through the stomach wall and chew their way into the bloodstream."

Onscreen the magnified fish nibbled at the man's arterial walls. Ragged corpuscles tore off in their teeth and two fish battled over the same mouthful.

Actually, Jake mused, watching the video wasn't so bad. Like a science film. You could almost ignore the man groaning onstage as he was devoured alive.

"The bloodeaters here are hatchlings," the bald man continued. "Babies, less than a millimeter, but they'll keep feeding and growing, and in a month they'll hit four inches. Too big for the host, sadly. And that's when our exhibit gets messy...lots of squishy noises, and popping, and lots of clean-up afterward. Keeps the janitor busy, though. But it's a great show, fellas. Trust me. Buy your advance ticket on the way out tonight."

The crowd laughed.

Jake kept his eyes glued to the monitors. He felt his heart beating in time to the pulse onscreen, adrenaline pumping through his own blood. The morning at the Shark Room seemed like ten years ago, like his childhood. Aquariums, superheroes, even his best drawings...that was kid-stuff. This here was real life. Horrible, but real.

On the frame the man's eyes shot open, wild and bloodshot. He gasped for air, his ribs heaving, like he'd just woken from a nightmare and found himself in another.

"Well, hello," the bald man said. He faced the audience. "We try to keep our exhibit sedated," he explained. "But sometimes he does perk up."

The trapped man began to wail—and didn't stop.

The awful sound echoed in the vast room, frightening the birds in the rafters into a flapping panic. Feathers floated down from the ceiling like ghosts as the man screamed and screamed.

He's nothing now, Jake thought. The skinny fish had all the power.

* * *

After the show, the doorman ushered Jake and the others off the factory floor and down a hallway different than the one they'd entered. The corridor turned twice to the left and ended in a small alcove. A sign on the wall read, **Gift Shop**.

A single wall shelf was screwed into steel brackets. On top sat a row of small glass jars, filled with a goo-like brown jelly. Jake picked one up. Printed on a label was the drawing of the skinny fish—the *candiru*—and below that, two words. **Home Kit**.

"Eggs, you can grow your own." The bald man spoke from behind him. This time Jake wasn't startled. He'd smelled the peppermint aftershave.

"Makes a great gift," the bald man said.

Jake turned the jar in his hand. "Yeah."

"A great gift," the man repeated. He winked. "For somebody you know."

"How much? There's no price."

"There's always a price. You'll learn that. You bring any money?"

Jake shrugged. "Probably not enough." He reached to put the jar back on the shelf, but the man caught his arm.

"Nah, take it," the man said. "On the house, for my fucked-up friend."

Jake stared at him for a long, quiet moment. Then he pocketed the jar.

The man nodded. "So...hope you liked the show. Glad you came?"

"Yeah."

"Good. Maybe I'll see you back at the aquarium some time."

"I don't know," Jake said. "Probably not."

The man laughed. "All right, I get that. Good luck, then." He turned and wandered over to another man examining a jar on the shelf. Jake pushed through an exit door in the rear of the alcove, his head buzzing. He emerged on Kempton Road, three doors down from the iron gate he'd first entered. The light bulb over the sign had been turned off; the entire block was dark now.

He wondered if his father would be awake when he got home.

Pussy, yer a fuckin pussy. Can't believe yer my blood, my fuckin son.

"Shut the fuck up, Dad," Jake snapped under his breath.

He climbed into his car and drove home.

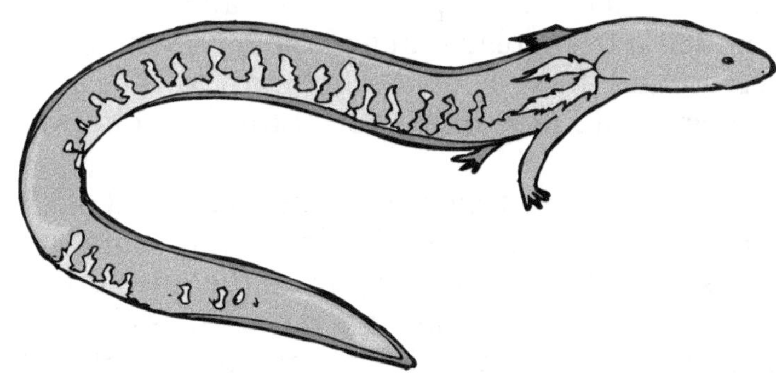

AIN'T NOTHIN' LIKE LIVE BAIT

DANE T. HATCHELL

It was getting close to noon and Otis Landry hadn't gotten a bite in over forty-five minutes. At least the mosquitoes decided they were either full from draining him of his blood, or that it was time for them to take a nap.

He had caught enough snapping turtles to make a nice size sauce for dinner, but he still had some bait left on the end of his line, and didn't want to waste it.

Otis grabbed another beer from his ice chest and delighted at the *pop-spraying* sound it made when he opened it. He was getting close to the end of his twelve pack and either the no beer, or the no bait, would dictate when he would head back in.

If anyone ever wondered what people do who win the State Lottery, to the tune of a few million dollars, Otis wouldn't be typical of the norm. Instead of living high on the hog with a new house and fancy cars, he chose to become a recluse and live way down at the end of the boot of Louisiana, near the small town of Empire.

He bought an old shack on a bayou far from the main center of the little town of some two thousand plus inhabitants. His main concern in life was doing what he loved best; turning beer into urine, and fishing.

The beer can's bottom was up and the last drop hit his tongue. He crushed the can in a flash and tossed it on the deck. A childhood memory popped into his mind when beer cans used to be made of steel and had no pop-tops. You had to pierce the top with a tool that left a triangular shaped hole on one side, turn the can 180 degrees, and make a smaller hole to allow for air to enter so that the beer could flow freely out of the can. Life was so much better now.

Otis lifted his pole to check the bait on the end of his line. The hook was still secure in the back of the little denim jumper, and there was some left leg remaining from the knee up and a whole left arm that could bait at least two more turtles by itself. He had been more successful while the infant was still alive. That little bugger pitched a fit, slapping the water like a bug in distress. Hell, turtles love to eat a fresh meal. The kid might as well said, "Eat me! Come and get it!" Those turtles swam on over like they were in an Olympic competition, stretching their necks out as if they would be first to reach the finish. Once they started feeding, it was easy to get the pole net under them and pull them into the boat.

He reached blindly into the ice chest and came back with an empty hand. The sun was starting to beam straight down on the top of his head and he knew he wouldn't last much longer without more beer. He lifted the bait out of the water and into the boat, then removed the little jumper with the bright colored embroidered flowers from what was left of the carcass.

As he paddled his narrow pirogue down the murky bayou, he searched the muddy banks until he found a sunning alligator. It looked like a smiling log and he figured it would stretch out from head to tail over four feet long. When he was within throwing distance, he tossed the remains of the infant to the living fossil, telling it that it owed him.

Otis remembered meeting a man years ago that grew up in South America where crocodiles were raised in farms. He said, "If you feed the croc fish, the meat tasted like fish. If you fed the croc chicken, the meat tasted like chicken. If you caught a croc in the wild and the meat had an indescribable taste, don't eat it."

Enemies of the Government were easily disposed of in such a way.

His trip back to his camp was quite picturesque. Large cypress trees with their mighty moss-covered arms reached to the sky, their bare roots growing directly into the water. According to legend, Spanish moss was the beard of the bully Gorez Goz. As he climbed after a young Indian girl, his beard became tangled in the tree branches. The girl escaped, but the moss remained as a testimony of his failed effort to this day.

Palmettos, ferns, and emerging blackberry stalks grew around water tupelo and red maples. All of which provided homes for indigenous birds and insects.

Otis tied his pirogue to his new modern boat dock, one of the few excesses that he spent some of his lottery winnings on. The newness did take away from the quaint ambiance of his fisherman's camp, but it was nothing like the eye sore of his forty by fifty steel building workshop he had built. Even though he chose hunter-green for the color for camouflage, it still looked like a nasty metal box amongst the cool dark bayou forest.

Otis took his burlap sack full of turtles out of the boat and carried them into his workshop. After punching in his lock code, the alarm light changed from red to green, and he entered through one of the standard doors.

The building was well lit with florescent lights hanging from the ceiling, giving off their yellowish glow and low pitch buzzing sound. The walls were organized and everything was in its place. There were a countless number of rods and reels, and hundreds if not a thousand of fresh and salt water baits, all labeled and ready to be used on a moment's notice. A welding machine/generator and a number of power tools were dedicated to one corner, his walk-in deep freeze and fish cleaning sink in the other.

A six foot wooden bench was blatantly out of place in the middle of the building, and a hanging steel cable was suspended parallel above it.

Otis placed the turtles on the side of his fish cleaning sink and started the water running. He pulled the sack open with one hand, and with the other used a two inch oak branch to prod the nearest turtle until it latched on to it with its powerful jaws. The turtle held tightly to the stick as if his life depended on it. And with its neck stretched to the limit, Otis chopped it off with his Bowie knife, then beat the stick against a garbage can until the head let loose.

"How you two gals doing?" he asked while prying the shell off the first turtle. "Y'all's about ready for some lunch?" Otis turned his head to the side, giving them a jagged grin.

"You're sick, you bastard, you're just fucking sick." A young woman with a creamy complexion and an athletic build stood naked, dressed only with a string of catfish around her hips and a necklace of brim around her neck.

"Sarah, don't," the other girl begged. "He'll hurt us."

"He's not going to let us go, Marie. He kidnapped us and now has us wearing fish for some sick fetish he has. He won't let us go until we're dead," Sarah said. Both women were handcuffed and chained to the steel cable above. They were free to move from side to side the length of the cable, which wasn't more than ten feet.

"Now, now, don't go jumping to conclusions," Otis said. He cleared his throat and spat out some phlegm. "I told you gals when I picked you up; cash, grass, or ass, no one rides for free. Once you work it off, I'll let you go."

"Hey, asshole, I told you I'm a neurologist. I had plastic; I could have gotten you the cash. You're so full of shit, you sick fuck. What about Marie? She was here two days before I was, when are you going to let her go?" Sarah fumed.

"So much education and yet such a foul mouth," Otis said as he fished another turtle out of the sack and cut through the neck. "I don't like women with foul mouths," he added with a deep frown.

"I don't like sick, mother-fucking asshole, pigshit-eating sadists!" Sarah screamed and broke into tears.

"Sarah, don't...please..." Marie's voice trailed off.

"Huh, I could have just left you on the side of the road and let the gators get you," Otis mumbled. He turned his head again and yelled back, "I've given you food and a five gallon bucket to squat in! Things could be a whole lot worse! Hell, Marie there can leave anytime she wants, just ask her."

Marie turned away from Sarah, crossed her arms and stared at the floor.

"Marie, is that true?" Sarah asked.

"When...when Otis picked me up...he made me an offer. He's paying me five hundred dollars a day to...to play like this," Marie said in a low voice.

"What? Are you serious? Are you just as fucked up as he is?" Sarah asked.

"He paid me three thousand dollars up front...he...he said that he would give me a thousand more if I could get you to...do things...with me," Marie said embarrassingly.

"I'm sitting here half naked wearing dead fish whose fins are cutting into me, stinking to high heaven, and you think I'd want to do something kinky for that sick son-of-a-bitch?" Sarah asked incredulously.

"He said he'd pay you, too," Marie said persuasively.

"My God, I can't believe any of this," Sarah sighed.

Otis finished with the last of the turtles and put the rest of the meat in a metal colander to drain. He wiped his hand on an old towel, opened a mini-fridge set in the corner, and took out a beer, "Anyone thirsty?"

"Water, I want some water," Sarah demanded.

"Well, I told you that I don't have water. I got beer. You want some beer?"

"Give me a damn beer then, you freak," Sarah said.

"Yeah, Otis, I'll take one, too," Marie's demeanor changed entirely.

Otis tossed them each a can, keeping an eye on Sarah. He wanted to be ready if she decided to throw it back at him. Marie opened the beer and drank it down without coming up for air. Sarah stared at her in disbelief and confusion.

"Otis, you got any smokes? Hell, you might as well get me out of these cuffs. She ain't into this, you need to put her ass back on the road," Marie said.

"Huh, well I guess you're right. We've gone about as far with this as we can." He carried a ring of keys on his belt. He pulled the keys off and flipped through them until he found the key to the cuffs and unlocked Marie.

"What? That's it? Just like that? What about me? When do I get to go?" Sarah asked.

"I got to take Marie back to New Orleans. I'll be back later tonight and we'll see about getting you to your car tomorrow," Otis said.

"Let me go now!" Sarah said.

"Look, you're in no position to tell me what to do," Otis said creepily.

"What makes you think you can get away with this?" Sarah asked in a challenging way.

"You mean the law? Haw! I bought the sheriff and the judge the first week I moved here. They'll never believe you, and the sheriff'll probably arrest you for drug trafficking or some other shit charge if you ever show your face back down here again."

Sarah took a slow sip of the beer, she was dehydrated and the malted beverage just tasted salty in her mouth.

"Of course, if you were willing to do a few favors for me...well...I could let you go today," Otis said slyly.

"You touch me and I'll kill you, you sick prick," Sarah said coldly.

Otis frowned and the sides of his neck turned beet red. "Let's go, Marie."

The two left the steel building. Otis reset the alarm behind him, and told Marie, "Turn around and I'll cut the fish line off, then you can go inside and shower." As she turned her back to him, he pulled a blackjack out of his back pocket and hit her on the side of the head.

* * *

Marie awoke to the stars and the moon hanging in a cloudless night sky above her, floating somewhere in the Gulf of Mexico. She was lying on her back, tied to a piece of plywood that had floats attached underneath. Her legs hung off the side, bobbing up and down in the water, feeling like they were on fire.

There was a spotlight from Otis' Bay boat focused directly on her. The stinging sensation from her legs was from the numerous slices he had cut into her skin using a box cutter. He made sure only the tip of the blade was exposed, and avoided hitting an artery. The water would prevent the shallow wounds from healing, and would provide an excellent attraction for the bull shark he was fishing for.

Marie became more aware of her surroundings as she gained consciousness, and started to panic and cry out immediately. Otis picked up the ancient telephone magneto off the deck; the wires led from the back of his boat, down the rope, to the floating plywood, to where they were attached to Marie's ankles.

"Marie, hush that hollering now," he called to her.

"Otis, what the hell are you doing to me? Get me off this damn thing..."

What came next out of Marie's mouth was a combination of incoherent babble and screams of pain. Her upper body jerked against the ropes and her legs flailed about uncontrollably.

Otis laughed to himself as he turned the crank and 'dialed her in', sending 110 volts down the wires to her ankles. "Ain't nuthin' like live bait."

Another beer from the ice chest and he was ready for his 'catch of the day'. Marie was sobbing in terror, repeating a prayer her mother taught her years ago.

It happened so quickly and unexpectedly that Otis almost missed it. His head was tilted back for a guzzle of beer when Marie's leg—from her left foot to her knee—disappeared, as a dark object went up and down in the water. Marie made a high pitch gasp and immediately fell silent, succumbing to shock.

Otis let the beer fall from his hand and onto the deck as he scrambled to retrieve his harpoon. He made sure the coil of rope and floats weren't tangled, and positioned himself in the rear of the boat, ready for action.

This time when the great bull shark came up it bit Marie right between her tits, getting more than he bargained for with a mouthful of plywood and plastic. Otis steadied his aim and plunged the harpoon into its back, near the head of the ferocious shark.

The shark didn't care too much for the harpoon, and it abandoned Marie, and headed straight for the bottom of the Gulf. Otis moved quickly to one side as the rope attached to the harpoon uncoiled and zipped into the water. The floats attached to the rope followed one by one, putting the brakes on the two hundred pound eating machine.

Otis decided he would celebrate by having another beer while the shark played itself out.

Poor Marie had seen her last fishing trip and her last day on Earth. Her body lay peacefully on her floating death bed. Otis thought about setting her on fire and giving her a proper Viking burial. But she was Cajun, and he was Irish, so he blamed that thought on the beer and a recent movie he watched.

He was finishing the last gulp in the can when he noticed the rope had gone limp on the deck of the boat. He looped the rope around an electric winch and slowly started to reel his catch in. The shark gave sporadic challenges, at which times Otis would wait and let the shark tire. And before long, the gray monster of the

Gulf with a face only a mother could love made it to the surface, then floated by the side of the boat.

Otis retrieved his revolver, took careful aim at one of the shark's two heads, and squeezed the trigger. The bullet slammed harmlessly into the water, missing the target. So, he closed one eye and was pleased to see only one head this time. The shot rang out and the bullet found its target. He powered up the winch and reeled the dead shark into the boat.

First he cut the fin off the shark and then the head and tail. He flipped it on its back and carved off the lower section and removed the internal organs. Then he cut the body into equal size steaks, tossing them in the ice chest.

He pulled in Marie's remains and chopped her up into smaller pieces. He mixed Marie's parts with the shark leftovers, and dumped the chum off the side. He wanted creatures of the deep to have a meal on him; he didn't want to have any evidence of Marie onboard when he returned to land.

* * *

"I told you I took her back to New Orleans last night," Otis said, handing Sarah a pair of cut-offs and a t-shirt. "I paid her the money I owed her and she waved goodbye. Hell, we're going to do it again in a month or so. I'm just a lonely man looking for some fun."

"Cocksucker...take me back to my car right now," Sarah said as he pulled the shorts up.

"Not before I take you fishing. We're going fishing today, and tomorrow I'll take you back to your car," he said.

"If you're going to let me go, then let me go now. I'm not going fishing, and there's nothing you can do to make me go with you," Sarah said and crossed her arms over her chest.

Otis' face stiffened. He looked at Sarah with piercing eyes, and pointed at the sawed-off shotgun hanging by door, "Oh, we're going fishing...we're going fishing right now."

The coldness in his voice grabbed her spine and chilled her to the core. She was a strong woman and wasn't accustomed to backing down to anyone for any reason. But this was different; she was alone with an insane man that was capable of doing anything to her. He was bigger than her and could easily overpower her if he wanted to.

And she wasn't sure that Otis ever sobered up. He either had a beer in his hand or was on his way to getting one. If she pissed him off too much, he might kill her. He might kill her and not even remember that he'd done it the next day. Or, he might get so shit-faced that he might let his guard down, and she could have a chance to escape.

The veins in Otis' neck started to bulge, and his face deepened a dark red.

"Fine, great, let's go fishing," she said, faking a smile. "Let's go catch some fucking fish so I can get out of this shit hole." She said it lightheartedly to ease the tension.

Otis relaxed a bit, "Now, I don't want it to be like that. I want you to have some fun. I want you to have an experience of a life time."

"Oh, I've already had an experience of a life time," she mumbled to herself. "Okay, yes, fishing, let's go fishing. Give me one of those fucking beers and let's go."

"Well, now you're talkin'." Otis reached into his cooler and tossed her a beer. He picked up the cooler by the handle and indicated for Sarah to leave first. The two made it out of the building and on to the dock. It had been two days since Sarah had seen the sun, and there were a few times when she had wondered if she would ever see it again.

It was hot outside but the breeze blowing in her face almost made her feel normal again.

Otis pointed with the muzzle of the shotgun he was carrying, signaling for her to get into the bass boat. The pirogue was too small for the type of fishing he had in mind.

As the boat left the dock, the sun reflected off something made of glass hidden behind the workshop, catching Sarah's eye.

She looked at him and asked, "Say Otis, where's my car again?"

"It's where you left it. I'll bring a spare and change your tire when I bring you back." He never looked up at her.

"Oh, that would be great," she said, her heart sinking. She was able to make out the rear of a vehicle hidden behind the workshop. She was pretty sure it was her car.

The two rode in silence down the winding bayou. Turtles bailed off logs and splashed into the water as they passed by. Sarah kept hoping and praying they would come across someone, anyone. She had decided she was going scream for help and make a swim for it if any opportunity presented itself.

Otis slowed and shut down the engine as they came to some cypress stumps near the bank. A fallen cypress tree laid three quarters submerged under the water near the stumps.

"Okay, we're here." He dropped anchor.

Sarah looked around the boat and realized there weren't any fishing rods onboard.

"Uh, what are we going to fish with?" she asked.

"Your fist," he said, grinning. "You're going to fish with your fist," he said matter of factly while opening a fresh beer.

"My…fist?"

"Yeah, you know, fisting…stumping…hogging, you're going to catch a great big catfish on your arm, using your fist as bait," Otis smiled. "Ain't nuthin' like live bait."

Sarah had no idea what he was talking about, but decided if she was going to make a move to escape, then this might be her last opportunity.

"Okay, what the fuck do I do," she asked.

"Well, it's not rocket surgery." Otis let out a belch that echoed off the still waters. "All's you got to do is get in the water and go over by that cypress tree by the bank. Feel around the tree and the bank a few feet under the water for a hole. When you find one, stick your fist in there and wiggle it about. If you do it right, a big ol' flat head catfish will swallow your arm. Let him take it, and then grab onto the inside of his gill and pull him out. I'll come over and give you a hand and we'll get him in the boat." He took another gulp of beer after his drying diatribe.

She thought that you had to be drunk, insane, or both, to do something like this for fun. Who the hell in their right mind would stick their arm in a hole not knowing what could be hiding in there? But this was it; this was the chance he was giving her to get out of the boat and away from him.

"Well, here goes," she said.

She eased one leg over the side and then followed with the other. Otis leaned to the opposite side to keep the boat from tipping too far over. The water was colder than she thought it would be and momentarily took her breath away; she was in up to her chest.

"That's it, go on over and start feeling for a hole," he told her.

Sarah had a plan. She needed to get the fallen cypress between her and Otis, and then make a break up the bank. The bank was steep with plenty of brush and trees, and once on land it would shield her from flying shotgun pellets if he managed a shot.

The trunk of the fallen tree roots were still partially growing into the bank. She would start there, and then swim underwater along side of the tree and get behind it. Then she would make her move when she thought she had a chance. It was risky, but it didn't matter, she knew Otis wasn't going to let her get out of this alive.

She walked past the stumps and started searching for holes by the bank. The water was only up to her waist here and she was glad when Otis told her to try around the fallen tree. When she was about to the halfway point up the tree from the bank, the water was back up to her chest. Otis was looking at her with one eye closed; she wasn't sure why.

"I think I found a hole!" she called out.

"Stick your arm in there and pull one out," Otis said in a 'what are you waiting for' voice.

"Just a minute...I...think...ahhhh!" Sarah disappeared under the water.

Otis stood up in the boat with his hands to his hips, waiting for her to pop back up with a big catfish flapping on her arm.

Sarah had held her breath and was swimming on the bottom of the bayou, using her right hand to feel alongside the cypress. She had been a competition swimmer in high school, and could still hold her breath for over three minutes underwater. Her hand came to the end of the tree, and she turned and swam on the backside, returning silently to the surface for air and to wait.

Otis kept waiting for her to come up kicking and splashing. But there was nothing, not even bubbles where she went under. He looked up and down the bayou as if he could find a clue as to what happened to her. He paddled over to midpoint of the tree and stuck the paddle down in the water to see if he could feel her trapped underneath. It wouldn't be the first time a catfish or gator got someone hung up under a tree.

He could feel nothing.

Sarah was now waist deep behind the fallen tree, she had moved to just a few feet from the bank, hoping to hear Otis get in the water to look for her. Then she would know there was no way for him to get her, and she could make her move.

But she similarly feared he would paddle the boat to her side, and decided she would make a slow crawl to the bank, then run for it—all or nothing.

She moved one foot forward, and when she moved the other, something latched on to it. She hit the water with a loud splash and went under. Otis heard the commotion from behind the tree, cranked up his trolling motor, and made it to the other side.

The waves were still spreading outward from the splash, but there was nothing there for him to see. Then a pair of arms popped out of the water and Sarah's head appeared long enough for her to take a breath, then back under she went.

"That bitch," Otis growled. "Trying to get away. Well, she ain't goin' nowhere." He shut down the motor and paddled to where she last came up.

The flathead catfish had pulled Sarah under and had her trapped in some branches. She managed to kick herself free, but it came back and pulled her down again. Her lungs were screaming for air, and in her panic, she finally twisted her foot out of the fish's mouth and headed back for the surface.

Otis was waiting by the side of the boat. As her head came up, he grabbed her by the hair and shoved it back down.

Sarah slapped at his arms, doing her frantic best to get him to let go, but he held fast.

He looked into her bulging eyes floating just inches below the water, and laughed.

So close to precious air; she could feel it with her hands, but it was denied her lips. And as she realized he had won, and her life would soon be over, the fear of death left her face. Her eyes turned an evil gaze towards Otis, her upper lip curled upward, and she wore the scowl of a beast ready to strike.

Even through the beer haze of Otis' reality, her death stare left him cold. He let go of her like she was an ember of fire and huddled in the side of the boat as far away from her as he could get. With shaking hands, he grabbed another beer from the cooler and drank it till it was empty.

He wiped his mouth with the back of his hand and took a deep breath. The bitch was dead; there was nothing to be scared of. He paddled over to her body and lifted her into the boat. Her head flopped to the side and her eyes stared up into the clear blue sky as she lay in the bottom of the boat; her face now looking as innocent as a child's.

* * *

It was just past ten in the morning the following day, and Otis was checking his crawfish traps for the third time that morning. A large sack of the small crustaceans sat in the middle of the boat, nearly half full. He was going to have close to two sacks total by the end of the run.

The boat glided gently on the water as he paddled towards the next empty bleach bottle bobbing on the surface. The bottle was attached to the trap sitting at the very bottom of the bayou.

He had made his own traps, as it wasn't hard to do. First he took a roll of chicken wire, folded it over in a two foot cylinder, cut it, and tied the sides together. He constructed a funnel out of the wire and attached that to one end. On the other, he cut a round piece and attached a hinge to make a door he could open and close. The crawfish could squeeze in the entrance to the funnel, but they couldn't exit from the same hole.

Those tasty little mudbugs were not particular in what they ate either. Anything live and small enough that they could snag with their pinchers was a preference. Usually though, there was an abundance of dead meat that nature provided available in the bayou. That was okay, too.

Chicken necks, turkey necks, fish heads, even cow pancreas called beef melt could be used for baiting the traps.

This morning, Otis used chopped up pieces of Sarah for bait.

He killed another beer can and chucked it to the front of the boat with the others. He reached his hand under the next bleach bottle floating in the water, grabbed on to the rope tied to it, and pulled up another mostly full trap of agitated, tail flapping, crawfish.

He positioned the end of the trap over the sack, opened the hinged end, and shook out another fine catch. This trap had one of Sarah's forearms tied inside for the tantalizing tidbit, and just about all the meat had been completely eaten off.

"Well, little gal, at least you were good for somethin'," he muttered to himself as he placed the trap in the boat, and finished the run.

The first thing to do when preparing for a crawfish boil is to wash the slime and gunk off the little critters and put them in fresh water for a couple of hours to flush out the bayou water. Some people sprinkled a little salt in the water, to get the crawfish to purge the last of the remains it was last eating. Otis didn't do that, he thought it made the tails turn rubbery.

He had one of those blue plastic kiddy pools that he bought from the store to purge the crawfish in. With a garden hose in one hand and a fresh beer in the other, he rinsed it out, dumped it, then filled it up halfway.

He grabbed one of the sacks with his free hand and it slipped from his grasp as he pulled. It weighed over fifty pounds and was too much for him to drag with one hand. He hated the inconvenience of setting his beer down. With three large gulps he finished it and returned to the task at hand.

He bent over and lifted the sack. His back strained from the weight and he felt a little dizzy from standing up so fast. The little sparklies and comets that painted his vision soon faded, and he dumped the sack of crawfish into the pool.

The little critters hit the water with a splash and they came alive in the water, churning it up into a frenzied boil. Otis had never seen anything like it before. They were flapping their tails forward, propelling themselves backwards as they always did, but he had never seen them act so aggressively.

Their large for their size front claws were held high in the air as if ready to challenge Otis in battle.

He thought of two things that would help the situation: a twenty pound bag of ice to cool them down, and a beer to cool him down. He made a quick trip to his freezer for the ice and stopped by his mini-fridge for another beer.

As he was exiting his workshop with the ice in hand, he was shocked to see the crawfish escaping over the side of the kiddy pool.

"What the hell is this?" he muttered.

The crawfish were as busy as a mound of fire ants, stacking on top of each other and making a ladder that led over the edge of the pool.

Otis dropped the ice to the ground, took a swig of beer, and started picking the crawfish off the ground with his free hand, then tossing them back into the pool.

At least, that was what he was trying to do. The little buggers latched on to his fingers and held tight as he tried to throw them back in.

"Ouch, you little bastards! Let go!"

His fingers were cut from the claws digging in as they were forcefully slung off. Some of the claws remained attached to his fingers, breaking off from the crawfish.

He tried to drink down his beer to free that hand up when sharp pains stabbed into him on both of his Achilles tendons. He was wearing flip flops and no socks, and a mass of crawfish were now all over his feet. The claws were snipping little bits of flesh faster and faster as he went to his knees, frantically trying to brush them off.

The other sack of crawfish fell on its side and the contents were pouring out in his direction.

He looked like a man on fire as he tried to slap the flames out. The little creatures were relentless in their attack, tearing at any exposed flesh. Otis felt like he'd been stung by a thousand wasps, and decided to make a break for it. He was going to jump off the deck and into the bayou.

He took two steps towards the water before the searing pain behind his ankles brought him face down on the ground. His Achilles tendons had been severed and he could no longer walk.

The crawfish swarmed his back, tearing through his shirt, methodically making tiny incisions along his spine.

He pulled himself up on his hands and knees. He moved his left arm forward to crawl. As it came back down, his palm slid from underneath him and he landed face down on the ground again. He tried to right himself, but he couldn't move his left arm. He could feel the claws of the crawfish tearing at his flesh, but he had no control of his muscles.

He put his weight on his right arm, but before he could get up, it too, went limp. The crawfish had broken through vertebrae and reached his spinal cord, and cut the muscle control to his upper body.

As if sensing success, the crawfish doubled their efforts, clawing at his spine as if guided by the hands of a surgeon. Otis tried to move his knees underneath him, but they didn't respond either. He was fucked, and he needed a beer in the worst sort of way.

The swarm of crawfish stopped their relentless attack as if someone threw a switch and said 'stop'. They slowly crawled off his prone body and disappeared from sight.

He could still move his head from side to side, and he closed one eye to focus on what was going on around him.

The crawfish all gathered on his right side, and with a combined effort, they slid between him and the ground, pushing him up. As he was lifted, more crawfish filled in the empty space, lifting his side higher and higher, until he tipped over onto his back.

He looked up to the sky at the hot midday sun, then down along his chest at the mass of crustaceans gathering at his feet.

One of the larger crawfish separated itself from the pack, and crawled up Otis' leg and came to a stop on his chest, right below his chin. The tiny creature waved both open claws to the sky, signaling victory.

"Little fucker," he spit with a dry mouth. He bent his head forward, snapping like a mad dog, trying to put the crawfish between his teeth.

The crawfish backed away, just inches from his yellowing teeth and putrid breath, as if taunting him.

Otis let out a scream as a team of crawfish gathered around his head and latched on to his ears, neck, and hair in an effort to keep his head still. The leader crawled on his chin and plunged a claw into his left eye, pulling it out of the socket.

He yelled ten times louder that time, and cursed up a storm.

The leader held the severed eye in front of him and shook its prize back and forth to agitate him more. Otis immediately felt a swarm of the little bastards tearing at his gym shorts, pulling them away from his genitals. Then he felt a horrific pinch beneath the head of his dick, and then multiple claws sawing through it. He felt every single pincher as it cut through each bit of meat. He closed his eyes tightly and screamed until his vocal cords felt like they were bleeding.

Finally, the pain stopped, and he felt a crawfish crawling back up his stomach and onto his chest. He opened his eyes and looked down to see the leader was back, this time holding his pecker-head between its claws.

Before he could utter another curse, pain shot through his left testicle as the crawfish tore into his sack. He screamed again with his mouth wide open, and the leader tossed his pecker-head into his mouth. It landed in the back of his throat, and he gagged, coughed, and choked until it worked its way between his lips and he spit it out.

The pain in his testicles stopped, and the leader returned to his chest with one of his man-balls held high in its claws. Otis thought it looked like a chicken gizzard.

The leader laid the humble gland on his chin, just below his lower lip.

He immediately shook his head until it slid off.

"That all you got, fucker?"

The leader lowered its claws and let them come to rest, crossing them in front of it. It just sat there, staring.

Otis stared back, trying to kill the leader with the look in his eyes alone.

Then the leader stood as high as its tiny legs allowed, and raised its claws once again as if it was going to attack.

Otis felt an underlying fear wash over him. And then, for just an instant as he stared down the leader, he saw Sarah's eyes looking back at him. That last look of hate she gave him as she drowned in the bayou was there to haunt him again.

He threw his head back and blinked a few times, and then looked down at the leader. But the leader was gone.

Then he felt the pinchers go to work on his arms, his legs, and then his stomach. Tiny little nips, each little bit of flesh torn off by the claws and into the hungry mouths of the crawfish.

Otis was a defeated man; he lay thinking what on Earth did he do to deserve to be eaten alive by a bunch of ditch bugs?

Then, a sound snapped him out of his delirium, a familiar, wonderful sound that gave him hope.

It was the sound of a beer can opening. He turned his head to see several crawfish lingering around a can of open beer that was spilling to the ground. They had pieces of his flesh in their claws, and would take a bite of meat and then lap at the pool of beer.

The leader raised a claw full of meat as Otis looked on; a big frothy beer mustache was smeared just above its mouth.

Before Otis passed out from blood loss, he could have sworn he heard Sarah's voice say, *"Ain't nuthin' like live bait."*

ABOUT THE WRITERS

Rebecca Besser lives in Ohio with her husband and little man. She's a graduate of the Institute of Children's Literature, a member of Write-On Writers and the Ohio Poetry Association (OPA). Her writing has appeared in the Coshocton Tribune, Irish Story Playhouse, Spaceports & Spidersilk, joyful!, Soft Whispers, Illuminata, Common Threads, and Golden Visions Magazine. She also has stories published in multiple anthologies by Living Dead Press, where she is currently an editor.

Visit her website to learn more about her: www.rebeccabesser.com

Tonia Brown's short stories have appeared in a variety of anthologies, such as Letters From The Dead, Eyewitness Zombie, and Hungry for Your Love. She is also the proud author of several books, including Lucky Stiff: Memoirs of an Undead Lover, and the erotic steampunk series Clockworks and Corsets. Tonia lives in the hills of North Carolina with her loving husband

You can learn more about her and her pen name, Regina Riley, at: www.thebackseatwriter.com

Anthony Giangregorio is the author and editor of more than 45 novels, almost all of them about zombies. His work has appeared in Dead Science by Coscomentertainment, Dead Worlds: Undead Stories Volumes 1-7, and Wolves of War by Library of the Living Dead Press. He also has stories in End of Days: An Apocalyptic Anthology Vol. 1 -3, the Book of the Dead series Vol. 1-5 by LDP, Zombie Zoology by Severed Press, and two anthologies with Pill Hill Press.

He is also the creator of the popular action/zombie series titled Deadwater. Check out his website at www.undeadpress.com.

Dane T. Hatchell lives in Baton Rouge Louisiana. In his youth he was a fan of old school horror movies, and a collector of magazines such as Creepy and Eerie. Published stories in various anthologies include: Dead Worlds 6, The Book of Horror, Night of the Wolf, and End of Days 3+4. You can contact Dane at Enadious@gmail.com. Special thanks to Sarah Graves for her contributions as my copy editor.

Kelly M. Hudson grew up in the wilds of Kentucky and currently resides in California. He has had numerous short stories published in many anthologies and has two novels available: The Turning, a zombie tale, from Living Dead Press, and Men Of Perdition, available for download on Amazon.com. If you wish to contact Kelly or find links to other stories he's had published, please visit www.kellymhudson.com for further details.

Matt Nord is an aspiring young writer from Central New York. At 34 years old, he is already a published fiction author specializing in the horror genre, with work under his belt including contributions to such books as, "Book of the Dead 4: Dead Rising," "The Book of Horror," and "The Book of Cannibals" from Living Dead Press, "Letters from the Dead" from Library of the Living Dead Press and recently, "Haunted: An Anthology of the Supernatural" from Pill Hill Press. You can view his blog at zombiecustodian.blogspot.com/

Jessy Marie Roberts lives in a "haunted" house in Western Nebraska with her husband and two dogs. She grew up in Morgan Hill, California. Jessy writes, edits and cooks, and most enjoys days where she can do all three.

Rob Rosen, author of the novels "Sparkle" and "Divas Las Vegas", has had short stories featured in more than 100 anthologies, most notably Living Dead Press's Christmas is Dead, Love is Dead, and The Book of Cannibals. Please visit him at his website, www.therobrosen.com

Marc Shemmans has had several short stories published in various magazines and anthologies. He also writes movie scripts and has just finished a screenplay based on a novel by Graham Masterton. He is close to finishing a second which is an apocalyptic tale based in the UK. Marc lives in Birmingham, England with his wife and thirteen year old son.

Nelia Thompson has been happily married for nine years and is a creative writer who lets her mind go wherever it takes her. She believes that life is too short not to have some fun along the way.

Alan Spencer has published two novels, entitled, "The Body Cartel" (Damnation Books) and "Inside the Perimeter: Scavengers of the Dead" (Living Dead Press). Look for his work in many of the Living Dead Press anthologies, including "Love is Dead," "The Book of Cannibals," and "Book of the Dead 2," to a name a few. This fall, his story "Mother's Solace" will appear in the anthology "Toe Tags 2."

V. M. Zito, and is currently spilling brains in his online zombie novel at www.HireTheReturnMan.com. He is also a contributor to the web horror series Scared Stiff.
He lives in Connecticut with his wife Krissy, daughter Maggie, and no fish.

PLAYING GOD: A ZOMBIE NOVEL
by Jeffery Dye

It was supposed to be a regeneration virus to help soldiers on the battle-field—regrowing limbs and healing wounds— but a simple act of carelessness unleashed it on an unsuspecting world.

For the virus was not perfected, and once exposed, the host quickly dies, only to rise again as one of the undead.

As countries are quickly overrun, scientists and military teams battle to contain the outbreak.

There is no other option.

If the infection continues to spread, soon the entire globe will be consumed. And perhaps that will be a just punishment for a mankind that dared to try to play God.

DEAD HOUSE: A ZOMBIE GHOST STORY
by Keith Adam Luethke

The old mansion on the edge of town, aptly named Dead House, has a history of blood, pain, and death, but what Victor Leeds knows of this past only scratches the surface of the true horrors within.

But when his girlfriend is attacked by a shadowy figure one rainy night, he soon finds himself caught up in a world where the dead walk and ghostly wraiths abound. And to make matters worse, a pair of serial killers are fulfilling carefully made plans, and when they are done, the small town of Stormville, New York will run red. The last ingredient to open the gates of Hell, and plunge this small upstate town into madness, is rain.

And in Stormville, it pours by the gallons.

The Lazarus Culture
by Pasquale J. Morrone

Secret Service Agent Christopher Kearns had no idea what he was up against. Assigned on a temporary basis to the Center for Disease Control, he only knew that somehow it was connected to the lives of those the agency pro-tected...namely, the President of the United States. If there were possible terrorist activities in the making, he could only guess it was at a red alert basis.

When Kearns meets and befriends Doctor Marlene Peterson of the Breezy Point Medical Center in Maryland, he soon finds that science fiction can indeed become a reality. In a solitary room walked a man with no vital signs: dead. The explanation he received came from Doctor Lee Fret, a man assigned to the case from the CDC. Something was attached to the brain stem. Something alive that was quickly spreading rapidly through Maryland and other states.

Kearns and his ragtag army of agents and medical personnel soon find them-selves in a world of meaningless slaughter and mayhem. The armies of the walking dead were far more than mere zombies. Some began to change into whatever it was they ate. The government had found a way to reanimate the dead by implanting a parasite found on the tongue of the Red Snapper to the human brain. It looked good on paper, but it was a project straight from Hell. The dead now walked, but it wasn't a mystery. It was The Lazarus Culture.

DEAD RAGE
by Anthony Giangregorio
Book 2 in the Rage virus series!

An unknown virus spreads across the globe, turning ordinary people into bloodthirsty, ravenous killers.

Only a small percentage of the population is immune and soon become prey to the infected.

Amongst the infected comes a man, stricken by the virus, yet still retaining his grasp on reality. His need to destroy the *normals* becomes an obsession and he raises an army of killers to seek out and kill all who aren't *changed* like himself. A few survivors gather together on the outskirts of Chicago and find themselves running for their lives as the specter of death looms over all.

The Dead Rage virus will find you, no matter where you hide.

CHRISTMAS IS DEAD: A ZOMBIE ANTHOLOGY
Edited by Anthony Giangregorio

Twas the night before Christmas and all through the house, not a creature was stirring, not even a. . . zombie?

That's right; this anthology explores what would happen at Christmas time if there was a full blown zombie outbreak. Reanimated turkeys, zombie Santas, and demon reindeers that turn people into flesh-eating ghouls are just some of the tales you will find in this merry undead book. So curl up under the Christmas tree with a cup of hot chocolate, and as the fireplace crackles with warmth, get ready to have your heart filled with holiday cheer. But of course, then it will be ripped from your heaving chest and fed upon by blood-thirsty elves with a craving for human flesh! For you see, Christmas is Dead!

And you will never look at the holiday season the same way again.

BLOOD RAGE
(The Prequel to DEAD RAGE)
by Anthony Giangregorio

The madness descended before anyone knew what was happening. Perfectly normal people suddenly became rage-fueled killers, tearing and slicing their way across the city. Within hours, Chicago was a battlefield, the dead strewn in the streets like trash.

Stacy, Chad and a few others are just a few of the immune, unaffected by the virus but not to the violence surrounding them. The *changed* are ravenous, sweeping across Chicago and perhaps the world, destroying any *normals* they come across. Fire, slaughter, and blood rule the land, and the few survivors are now an endangered species.

This is the story of the first days of the Dead Rage virus and the brave souls who struggle to live just one more day.

When the smoke clears, and the *changed* have maimed and killed all who stand in their way, only the strong will remain.

The rest will be left to rot in the sun.

THE BOOK OF CANNIBALS

Edited by Anthony Giangregorio

Human meat . . . the ultimate taboo.

Deep down, in the dark recesses of your mind, can you honestly say you never wondered how it might taste?

Honestly, never wondered if a chunk of thigh tasted like chicken or pork?

Or if a hunk of an arm was similar to steak? And what kind of wine would be served with it, red or white?

Would a human liver be no different than one from a cow, or a pig?

For all we know, human flesh is as tender as veal, better than the finest tenderloin. And that is what the stories in this book are about, eating each other. But be warned, after reading these tales of mastication, you may just become a vegetarian, or at the very least, think twice before taking your first bite of that juicy steak at your local restaurant.

THE TURNING: A STORY OF THE LIVING DEAD

by Kelly M. Hudson

The Dead Walk!

And no place on earth is safe from their ravening hunger. Civilization falls, leaving groups of struggling survivors to navigate a world that has descended into Hell.

Jeff Richards is one such survivor. He and his lover Jenny flee their home in the Bay Area and take a perilous journey through Northern California into Oregon, seeking shelter in rural areas to avoid both the living dead and that most treacherous animal of all: their fellow humans.

But can a man who has lost everything, including his humanity, ever be reborn? When the dead walk, will any of us survive?

Or will we all join the ranks of the undead to forever walk the earth.

VISIONS OF THE DEAD: A ZOMBIE STORY

by Anthony & Joseph Giangregorio

Jake Roberts felt like he was the luckiest man alive.

He had a great family, a beautiful girlfriend, who was soon to be his wife, and a job, that might not have been the best, but it paid the bills.

At least until the dead began to walk.

Now Jake is fighting to survive in a dead world while searching for his lost love, Melissa, knowing she's out there somewhere.

But the past isn't dead, and as he struggles for an uncertain future, the past threatens to consume him. With the present a constant battle between the living and the dead, Jake finds himself slipping in and out of the past, the visions of how it all happened haunting him. But Jake knows Melissa is out there somewhere and he'll find her or die trying.

In a world of the living dead, you can never escape your past.

DEAD MOURNING: A ZOMBIE HORROR STORY
by Anthony Giangregorio

Carl Jenkins was having a run of bad luck. Fresh out of jail, his probation tenuous, he'd lost every job he'd taken since being released. So now was his last chance, only one more job to prevent him from going back to prison. Assigned to work in a funeral home, he accidentally loses a shipment of embalming fluid. With nothing to lose, he substitutes it with a batch of chemicals from a nearby factory.

The results don't go as planned, though. While his screw-up goes unnoticed, his machinations revive the cadavers in the funeral home, unleashing an evil on the world that it has not seen before. Not wanting to become a snack for the rampaging dead, he flees the city, joining up with other survivors. An old, dilapidated zoo becomes their haven, while the dead wait outside the walls, hungry and patient.

But Carl is optimistic, after all, he's still alive, right? Perhaps his luck has changed and help will arrive to save them all?

Unfortunately, unknown to him and the other survivors, a serial killer has fallen into their group, trapped inside the zoo with them.

With the undead army clamoring outside the walls and a murderer within, it'll be a miracle if any of them live to see the next sunrise.

On second thought, maybe Carl would've been better off if he'd just gone back to jail.

ROAD KILL: A ZOMBIE TALE
by Anthony Giangregorio

In the summer of 2008, a rogue comet entered earth's orbit for 72 hours. During this time, a strange amber glow suffused the sky.

But something else happened; something in the comet's tail had an adverse affect on dead tissue and the result was the reanimation of every dead animal carcass on the planet.

A handful of survivors hole up in a diner in the backwoods of New Hampshire while the undead creatures of the night hunt for human prey.

There's a new blue plate special at DJ's Diner and Truck Stop, and it's you!

DEAD THINGS
by Anthony Giangregorio

Beneath the veil of reality we all know as truth, there is another world, one where creatures only seen in nightmares exist.

But what if these creatures do actually exist, and it is us that are only fleeting images, mere visions conjured up by some unknown being.

Werewolves, zombies, vampires, and other lost things that go bump in the night, inhabit the world of imagination and myth, but all will be found in this collection of tales. But in this world, fiction becomes fact, and what lurks in the shadows is real. Beware the next time you sense you are being watched or catch movement in the corner of your eye, for though it may be nothing, it might just be your doom.

THE DARK
by Anthony Giangregorio
DARKNESS FALLS

The darkness came without warning.

First New York, then the rest of United States, and then the world became enveloped in a perpetual night without end.

With no sunlight, eventually the planet will wither and die, bringing on a new Ice Age. But that isn't problem for the human race, for humanity will be dead long before that happens.

There is something in the dark, creatures only seen in nightmares, and they are on the prowl. Evolution has changed and man is no longer the dominant species. When we are children, we're told not to fear the dark, that what we believe to exist in the shadows is false.

Unfortunately, that is no longer true.

SOULEATER
by Anthony Giangregorio

Twenty years ago, Jason Lawson witnessed the brutal death of his father by something only seen in nightmares, something so horrible he'd blocked it from his mind.

Now twenty years later the creature is back, this time for his son.

Jason won't let that happen.

He'll travel to the demon's world, struggling every second to rescue his son from its clutches.

But what he doesn't know is that the portal will only be open for a finite time and if he doesn't return with his son before it closes, then he'll be trapped in the demon's dimension forever.

SEE HOW IT ALL BEGAN IN THE NEW DOUBLE-SIZED 460 PAGE SPECIAL EDITION!

DEADWATER: EXPANDED EDITION
by Anthony Giangregorio

Through a series of tragic mishaps, a small town's water supply is contaminated with a deadly bacterium that transforms the town's population into flesh eating ghouls.

Without warning, Henry Watson finds himself thrown into a living hell where the living dead walk and want nothing more than to feed on the living.

Now Henry's trying to escape the undead town before he becomes the next victim.

With the military on one side, shooting civilians on sight, and a horde of bloodthirsty zombies on the other, Henry must try to battle his way to freedom.

With a small group of survivors, including a beautiful secretary and a wise-cracking janitor to aid him, the ragtag group will do their best to stay alive and escape the city codenamed: **Deadwater.**

DEAD END: A ZOMBIE NOVEL

by Anthony Giangregorio

THE DEAD WALK!

Newspapers everywhere proclaim the dead have returned to feast on the living!

A small group of survivors hole up in a cellar, afraid to brave the masses of animated corpses, but when food runs out, they have no choice but to venture out into a world gone mad.

What they will discover, however, is that the fall of civilization has brought out the worst in their fellow man.

Cannibals, psychotic preachers and rapists are just some of the atrocities they must face.

In a world turned upside down, it is life that has hit a Dead End.

BOOK OF THE DEAD 2: NOT DEAD YET

A ZOMBIE ANTHOLOGY

Edited by Anthony Giangregorio

Out of the ashes of death and decay, comes the second volume filled with the walking dead.

In this tomb, there are only slow, shambling monstrosities that were once human.

No one knows why the dead walk; only that they do, and that they are hungry for human flesh.

But these aren't your neighbors, your co-workers, or your family.
Now they are the living dead, and they will tear your throat out at a moment's notice.

So be warned as you delve into the pages of this book; the dead will find you, no matter where you hide.

ANOTHER EXCITING ADVENTURE IN THE DEADWATER SERIES!

DEAD SALVATION

BOOK 9

by Anthony Giangregorio

HANGMAN'S NOOSE!

After one of the group is hurt, the need for transportation is solved by a roving cannie convoy. Attacking the camp, the companions save a man who invites them back to his home.

Cement City it's called and at first the group is welcomed with thanks for saving one of their own. But when a bar fight goes wrong, the companions find themselves awaiting the hangman's noose.

Their only salvation is a suicide mission into a raider camp to save captured townspeople.

Though the odds are long, it's a chance, and Henry knows in the land of the walking dead, sometimes a chance is all you can hope for.

In the world of the dead, life is a struggle, where the only victor is death.

INSIDE THE PERIMETER: SCAVENGERS OF THE DEAD
by Alan Spencer

In the middle of nowhere, the vestiges of an abandoned town are surrounded by inescapably high concrete barriers, permitting no trespass or escape. The town is dormant of human life, but rampant with the living dead, who choose not to eat flesh, but to instead continue their survival by cruder means.

Boyd Broman, a detective arrested and falsely imprisoned, has been transferred into the secret town. He is given an ultimatum: recapture Hayden Grubaugh, the cannibal serial killer, who has been banished to the town, in exchange for his freedom.

During Boyd's search, he discovers why the psychotic cannibal must really be captured and the sinister secrets the dead town holds.

With no chance of escape, Broman finds himself trapped among the ravenous, violent dead.

With the cannibal feeding on the animated cadavers and the undead searching for Boyd, he must fulfill his end of the deal before the rotting corpses turn him into an unwilling organ donor.

But Boyd wasn't told that no one gets out alive, that the town is a death sentence.

For there is no escape from *Inside the Perimeter*.

DEADFALL
by Anthony Giangregorio

It's Halloween in the small suburban town of Wakefield, Mass.

While parents take their children trick or treating and others throw costume parties, a swarm of meteorites enter the earth's atmosphere and crash to earth.

Inside are small parasitic worms, no larger than maggots.

The worms quickly infect the corpses at a local cemetery and so begins the rise of the undead.

The walking dead soon get the upper hand, with no one believing the truth. That the dead now walk.

Will a small group of survivors live through the zombie apocalypse?

Or will they, too, succumb to the Deadfall.

LOVE IS DEAD: A ZOMBIE ANTHOLOGY
Edited by Anthony Giangregorio
THE DEATH OF LOVE

Valentine's Day is a day when young love is fulfilled.

Where hopeful young men bring candy and flowers to their sweethearts, in hopes of a kiss...or perhaps more. But not in this anthology.

For you see, LOVE IS DEAD, and in this tome, the dead walk, wanting to feed on those same hearts that once pumped in chests, bursting with love.

So toss aside that heart-shaped box of candy and throw away those red roses, you won't need them any longer. Instead, strap on a handgun, or pick up a shotgun and defend yourself from the ravenous undead.

Because in a world where the dead walk, even love isn't safe.

ETERNAL NIGHT: A VAMPIRE ANTHOLOGY
Edited by Anthony Giangregorio

Blood, fangs, darkness and terror...these are the calling cards of the vampire mythos.

Inside this tome are stories that embrace vampire history but seek to introduce a new literary spin on this longstanding fictional monster. Follow a dark journey through cigarette-smoking creatures hunted by rogue angels, vampires that feed off of thoughts instead of blood, immortals presenting the fantastic in a local rock band, to a legendary monster on the far reaches of town.

Forget what you know about vampires; this anthology will destroy historical mythos and embrace incredible new twists on this celebrated, fictional character.

Welcome to a world of the undead, welcome to the world of Eternal Night.

BOOK OF THE DEAD
A ZOMBIE ANTHOLOGY VOL 1
ISBN 978-1-935458-25-8
Edited by Anthony Giangregorio

This is the most faithful, truest zombie anthology ever written, and we invite you along for the ride. Every single story in this book is filled with slack-jawed, eyes glazed, slow moving, shambling zombies set in a world where the dead have risen and only want to eat the flesh of the living. In these pages, the rules are sacrosanct. There is no deviation from what a zombie should be or how they came about. The Dead Walk.

There is no reason, though rumors and suppositions fill the radio and television stations. But the only thing that is fact is that the walking dead are here and they will not go away. So prepare yourself for the ultimate homage to the master of zombie legend. And remember... Aim for the head!

REVOLUTION OF THE DEAD
by Anthony Giangregorio
THE DEAD SHALL RISE AGAIN!

Five years ago, a deadly plague wiped out 97% of the world's population, America suffering tragically. Bodies were everywhere, far too many to bury or burn. But then, through a miracle of medical science, a way is found to reanimate the dead.

With the manpower of the United States depleted, and the remaining survivors not wanting to give up their internet and fast food restaurants, the undead are conscripted as slave labor.

Now they cut the grass, pick up the trash, and walk the dogs of the surviving humans.

But whether alive or dead, no race wants to be controlled, and sooner or later the dead will fight back, wanting the freedom they enjoyed in life.

The revolution has begun!

And when it's over, the dead will rule the land, and the remaining humans will become the slaves...or worse.

KINGDOM OF THE DEAD
by Anthony Giangregorio
THE DEAD HAVE RISEN!

In the dead city of Pittsburgh, two small enclaves struggle to survive, eking out an existence of hand to mouth.

But instead of working together, both groups battle for the last remaining fuel and supplies of a city filled with the living dead.

Six months after the initial outbreak, a lone helicopter arrives bearing two more survivors and a newborn baby. One enclave welcomes them, while the other schemes to steal their helicopter and escape the decaying city.

With no police, fire, or social services existing, the two will battle for dominance in the steel city of the walking dead. But when the dust settles, the question is: will the remaining humans be the winners, or the losers?

When the dead walk, the line between Heaven and Hell is so twisted and bent there is no line at all.

RISE OF THE DEAD
by Anthony Giangregorio
DEATH IS ONLY THE BEGINNING!

In less than forty-eight hours, more than half the globe was infected.
In another forty-eight, the rest would be enveloped.
The reason?
A science experiment gone horribly wrong which enabled the dead to walk, their flesh rotting on their bones even as they seek human prey.

Jeremy was an ordinary nineteen year old slacker. He partied too much and had done poorly in high school. After a night of drinking and drugs, he awoke to find the world a very different place from the one he'd left the night before.

The dead were walking and feeding on the living, and as Jeremy stepped out into a world gone mad, the dead spotting him alone and unarmed in the middle of the street, he had to wonder if he would live long enough to see his twentieth birthday.

THE CHRONICLES OF JACK PRIMUS
BOOK ONE
by Michael D. Griffiths

Beneath the world of normalcy we all live in lies another world, one where supernatural beings exist.

These creatures of the night hunt us; want to feed on our very souls, though only a few know of their existence.

One such man is Jack Primus, who accidentally pierces the veil between this world and the next. With no other choice if he wants to live, he finds himself on the run, hunted by beings called the Xemmoni, an ancient race that sees humans as nothing but cattle. They want his soul, to feed on his very essence, and they will kill all who stand in their way. But if they thought Jack would just lie down and accept his fate, they were sorely mistaken.   He didn't ask for this battle, but he knew he would fight them with everything at his disposal, for to lose is a fate worse than death.

He would win this war, and he would take down anyone who got in his way.

THE WAR AGAINST THEM: A ZOMBIE NOVEL
by Jose Alfredo Vazquez

Mankind wasn't prepared for the onslaught.

An ancient organism is reanimating the dead bodies of its victims, creating worldwide chaos and panic as the disease spreads to every corner of the globe. As governments struggle to contain the disease, courageous individuals across the planet learn what it truly means to make choices as they struggle to survive.

Geopolitics meet technology in a race to save mankind from the worst threat it has ever faced. Doctors, military and soldiers from all walks of life battle to find a cure. For the dead walk, and if not stopped, they will wipe out all life on Earth. Humanity is fighting a war they cannot win, for who can overcome Death itself? Man versus the walking dead with the winner ruling the planet. Welcome to *The War Against Them*.

DEADTOWN: A DEADWATER STORY
BOOK 8
by Anthony Giangregorio

The world is a very different place now. The dead walk the land and humans hide in small towns with walls of stone and debris for protection, constantly keeping the living dead at bay.

Social law is gone and right and wrong is defined by the size of your gun.

UNWELCOME VISITORS

Henry Watson and his band of warrior survivalists become guests in a fortified town in Michigan. But when the kidnapping of one of the companions goes bad and men die, the group finds themselves on the wrong side of the law, and a town out for blood.

Trapped in a hotel, surrounded on all sides, it will be up to Henry to save the day with a gamble that may not only take his life, but that of his friends as well.

In a dead world, when justice is not enough, there is always vengeance.

END OF DAYS: AN APOCALYPTIC ANTHOLOGY
VOLUMES 1-4
Edited by Anthony Giangregorio

Our world is a fragile place.

Meteors, famine, floods, nuclear war, solar flares, and hundreds of other calamities can plunge our small blue planet into turmoil in an instant.

What would you do if tomorrow the sun went super nova or the world was swallowed by water, submerging the world into the cold darkness of the ocean? This anthology explores some of those scenarios and plunges you into total annihilation.

But remember, it's only a book, and tomorrow will come as it always does. Or will it?